MW01096955

Frederik Pohl, Cyril M. Kornbluth

The World of Morons

e-artnow 2020

Frederik Pohl, Cyril M. Kornbluth

The World of Morons

Cyril M. Kornbluth's View of the Future: The Little Black Bag, The Marching Morons Search the Sky

Illustrator: Don Sibley

e-artnow, 2020
Contact: info@e-artnow.org

ISBN 978-80-273-0931-3

Contents

The Little Black Bag

Old Dr. Full felt the winter in his bones as he limped down the alley. It was the alley and the back door he had chosen rather than the sidewalk and the front door because of the brown paper bag under his arm. He knew perfectly well that the flat-faced, stringy-haired women of his street and their gap-toothed, sour-smelling husbands did not notice if he brought a bottle of cheap wine to his room. They all but lived on the stuff themselves, varied with whiskey when pay checks were boosted by overtime. But Dr. Full, unlike them, was ashamed. A complicated disaster occurred as he limped down the littered alley. One of the neighborhood dogs —a mean little black one he knew and hated, with its teeth always bared and always snarling with menace- hurled at his legs through a hole in the board fence that lined his path. Dr. Full flinched, then swung his leg in what was to have been a satisfying kick to the animal's gaunt ribs. But the winter in his bones weighed down the leg. His foot failed to clear a half-buried brick, and he sat down abruptly, cursing. When he smelled unbottled wine and realized his brown paper package had slipped from under his arm and smashed, his curses died on his lips. The snarling black dog was circling him at a yard's distance, tensely stalking, but he ignored it in the greater disaster.

With stiff fingers as he sat on the filth of the alley, Dr. Full unfolded the brown paper bag's top, which had been crimped over, grocer-wise. The early autumnal dusk had come; he could not see plainly what was left. He lifted out the jug-handled top of his half gallon, and some fragments, and then the bottom of the bottle. Dr. Full was far too occupied to exult as he noted that there was a good pint left. He had a problem, and emotions could be deferred until the fitting time.

The dog closed in, its snarl rising in pitch. He set down the bottom of the bottle and pelted the dog with the curved triangular glass fragments of its top. One of them connected, and the dog ducked back through the fence, howling. Dr. Full then placed a razor-like edge of the half-gallon bottle's foundation to his lips and drank from it as though it were a giant's cup. Twice he had to put it down to rest his arms, but in one minute he had swallowed the pint of wine.

He thought of rising to his feet and walking through the alley to his room, but a flood of well-being drowned the notion. It was, after all, inexpressibly pleasant to sit there and feel the frost-hardened mud of the alley turn soft, or seem to, and to feel the winter evaporating from his bones under a warmth which spread from his stomach through his limbs.

A three-year-old girl in a cut-down winter coat squeezed through the same hole in the board fence from which the black dog had sprung its ambush. Gravely she toddled up to Dr. Full and inspected him with her dirty forefinger in her mouth. Dr. Full's happiness had been providentially made complete; he had been supplied with an audience.

"Ah, my dear," he said hoarsely. And then: "Preposterous accusation. 'If that's what you call evidence,' I should have told them, 'you better stick to your doctoring.' I should have told them: 'I was here before your County Medical Society. And the License Commissioner never proved a thing on me. So, gennulmen, doesn't it stand to reason? I appeal to you as fellow memmers of a great profession —'"

The little girl, bored, moved away, picking up one of the triangular pieces of glass to play with as she left. Dr. Full forgot her immediately, and continued to himself earnestly: "But so help me, they *couldn't* prove a thing. Hasn't a man got any *rights?*" He brooded over the question, of whose answer he was so sure, but on which the Committee on Ethics of the County Medical Society had been equally certain. The winter was creeping into his bones again, and he had no money and no more wine.

Dr. Full pretended to himself that there was a bottle of whiskey somewhere in the fearful litter of his room. It was an old and cruel trick he played on himself when he simply had to be galvanized into getting up and going home. He might freeze there in the alley. In his room he would be bitten by bugs and would cough at the moldy reek from his sink, but he would not freeze and be cheated of the hundreds of bottles of wine that he still might drink, the thousands of hours of glowing content he still might feel. He thought about that bottle of whiskey-was it back of a mounded heap of medical journals? No; he had looked there last time. Was it under the sink, shoved well to the rear, behind the rusty drain? The cruel trick began to play itself out again. Yes, he told himself with mounting excitement, yes, it might be! Your memory isn't so good nowadays, he told himself with rueful good-fellowship. You know perfectly well you might have bought a bottle of whiskey and shoved it behind the sink drain for a moment just like this.

The amber bottle, the crisp snap of the sealing as he cut it, the pleasurable exertion of starting the screw cap on its threads, and then the refreshing tangs in his throat, the warmth in his stomach, the dark, dull happy oblivion of drunkenness-they became real to him. You *could* have, you know! You *could* have! he told himself. With the blessed conviction growing in his mind-It *could* have happened, you know! It *could* have! —he struggled to his right knee. As he did, he heard a yelp behind him, and curiously craned his neck around while resting. It was the little girl, who had cut her hand quite badly on her toy, the piece of glass. Dr. Full could see the rilling bright blood down her coat, pooling at her feet.

He almost felt inclined to defer the image of the amber bottle for her, but not seriously. He knew that it was there, shoved well to the rear under the sink, behind the rusty drain where he had hidden it. He would have a drink and then magnanimously return to help the child. Dr. Full got to his other knee and then his feet, and proceeded at a rapid totter down the littered alley toward his room, where he would hunt with calm optimism at first for the bottle that was not there, then with anxiety, and then with frantic violence. He would hurl books and dishes about before he was done looking for the amber bottle of whiskey, and finally would beat his swollen knuckles against the brick wall until old scars on them opened and his thick old blood oozed over his hands. Last of all, he would sit down somewhere on the floor, whimpering, and would plunge into the abyss of purgative nightmare that was his sleep.

* * * * *

After twenty generations of shilly-shallying and "we'll cross that bridge when we come to it," genus homo had bred himself into an impasse. Dogged biometricians had pointed out with irrefutable logic that mental subnormals were outbreeding mental normals and supernormals, and that the process was occurring on an exponential curve. Every fact that could be mustered in the argument proved the biometricians' case, and led inevitably to the conclusion that genus homo was going to wind up in a preposterous jam quite soon. If you think that had any effect on breeding practices, you do not know genus homo.

There was, of course, a sort of masking effect produced by that other exponential function, the accumulation of technological devices. A moron trained to punch an adding machine seems to be a more skillful computer than a medieval mathematician trained to count on his fingers. A moron trained to operate the twenty-first century equivalent of a linotype seems to be a better typographer than a Renaissance printer limited to a few fonts of movable type. This is also true of medical practice.

It was a complicated affair of many factors. The supernormals "improved the product" at greater speed than the subnormals degraded it, but in smaller quantity because elaborate train- ing of their children was practiced on a custom-made basis. The fetish of higher education had some weird avatars by the twentieth generation: "colleges" where not a member of the stu- dent body could read words of three syllables; "universities" where such degrees as "Bachelor of Typewriting," "Master of Shorthand" and "Doctor of Philosophy (Card Filing)" were conferred with the traditional pomp. The handful of supernormals used such devices in order that the vast majority might keep some semblance of a social order going.

Some day the supernormals would mercilessly cross the bridge; at the twentieth generation they were standing irresolutely at its approaches wondering what had hit them. And the ghosts of twenty generations of biometricians chuckled malignantly.

It is a certain Doctor of Medicine of this twentieth generation that we are concerned with. His name was Hemingway-John Hemingway, B.Sc., M.D. He was a general practitioner, and did not hold with running to specialists with every trifling ailment. He often said as much, in approximately these words: "Now, uh, what I mean is you got a good old G.P. See what I mean? Well, uh, now a good old G.P. don't claim he knows all about lungs and glands and them things, get me? But you got a G.P., you got, uh, you got a, well, you got a ...*all-around man!* That's what you got when you got a G.P —you got a all-around man."

But from this, do not imagine that Dr. Hemingway was a poor doctor. He could remove tonsils or appendixes, assist at practically any confinement and deliver a living, uninjured infant, correctly diagnose hundreds of ailments, and prescribe and administer the correct medication or treatment for each. There was, in fact, only one thing he could not do in the medical line, and that was, violate the ancient canons of medical ethics. And Dr. Hemingway knew better than to try.

Dr. Hemingway and a few friends were chatting one evening when the event occurred that precipitates him into our story. He had been through a hard day at the clinic, and he wished his physicist friend Walter Gillis, B.Sc., M.Sc., Ph.D., would shut up so he could tell everybody about it. But Gillis kept rambling on, in his stilted fashion: "You got to hand it to old Mike; he don't have what we call the scientific method, but you got to hand it to him. There this poor little dope is, puttering around with some glassware and I come up and I ask him, kidding of course, 'How's about a time-travel machine, Mike?'"

Dr. Gillis was not aware of it, but "Mike" had an I.Q. six times his own, and was-to be blunt-his keeper. "Mike" rode herd on the pseudo-physicists in the pseudo-laboratory, in the guise of a bottle-washer. It was a social waste-but as has been mentioned before, the super-normals were still standing at the approaches to a bridge. Their irresolution led to many such preposterous situations. And it happens that "Mike," having grown frantically bored with his task, was malevolent enough to-but let Dr. Gillis tell it:

"So he gives me these here tube numbers and says, 'Series circuit. Now stop bothering me. Build your time machine, sit down at it and turn on the switch. That's all I ask, Dr. Gillis-that's all I ask.'"

"Say," marveled a brittle and lovely blonde guest, "you remember real good, don't you, doc?" She gave him a melting smile.

"Heck," said Gillis modestly, "I always remember good. It's what you call an inherent facility. And besides I told it quick to my secretary, so she wrote it down. I don't read so good, but I sure remember good, all right. Now, where was I?"

Everybody thought hard, and there were various suggestions:

"Something about bottles, doc?"

"You was starting a fight. You said 'time somebody was traveling.'"

"Yeah-you called somebody a swish. Who did you call a swish?"

"Not swish —*switch.*"

Dr. Gillis's noble brow grooved with thought, and he declared: "Switch is right. It was about time travel. What we call travel through time. So I took the tube numbers he gave me and I put them into the circuit-builder; I set it for 'series' and there it is-my time-traveling machine. It travels things through time real good." He displayed a box.

"What's in the box?" asked the lovely blonde.

Dr. Hemingway told her: "Time travel. It travels things through time."

"Look," said Gillis, the physicist. He took Dr. Hemingway's little black bag and put it on the box. He turned on the switch and the little black bag vanished.

"Say," said Dr. Hemingway, "that was, uh, swell. Now bring it back."

"Huh?"

"Bring back my little black bag."

"Well," said Dr. Gillis, "they don't come back. I tried it backwards and they don't come back. I guess maybe that dummy Mike give me a bum steer."

There was wholesale condemnation of "Mike" but Dr. Hemingway took no part in it. He was nagged by a vague feeling that there was something he would have to do. He reasoned: "I am a doctor and a doctor has got to have a little black bag. I ain't got a little black bag-so ain't I a doctor no more?" He decided that this was absurd. He *knew* he was a doctor. So it must be the bag's fault for not being there. It was no good, and he would get another one tomorrow from that dummy Al, at the clinic. Al could find things good, but he was a dummy-never liked to talk sociable to you.

So the next day Dr. Hemingway remembered to get another little black bag from his keeper-another little black bag with which he could perform tonsillectomies, appendectomies and the most difficult confinements, and with which he could diagnose and cure his kind until the day when the supernormals could bring themselves to cross that bridge. Al was kinda nasty about the missing little black bag, but Dr. Hemingway didn't exactly remember what had happened, so no tracer was sent out, so —

* * * * *

Old Dr. Full awoke from the horrors of the night to the horrors of the day. His gummy eyelashes pulled apart convulsively. He was propped against a corner of his room, and something was making a little drumming noise. He felt very cold and cramped. As his eyes focused on his lower body, he croaked out a laugh. The drumming noise was being made by his left heel, agitated by fine tremors against the bare floor. It was going to be the D.T.'s again, he decided dispassionately. He wiped his mouth with his bloody knuckles, and the fine tremor coarsened; the snare-drum beat became louder and slower. He was getting a break this fine morning, he decided sardonically. You didn't get the horrors until you had been tightened like a violin string, just to the breaking point. He had a reprieve, if a reprieve into his old body with the blazing, endless headache just back of the eyes and the screaming stiffness in the joints were anything to be thankful for.

There was something or other about a kid, he thought vaguely. He was going to doctor some kid. His eyes rested on a little black bag in the center of the room, and he forgot about the kid. "I could have sworn," said Dr. Full, "I hocked that two years ago!" He hitched over and reached the bag, and then realized it was some stranger's kit, arriving here he did not know how. He tentatively touched the lock and it snapped open and lay flat, rows and rows of instruments and medications tucked into loops in its four walls. It seemed vastly larger open than closed. He didn't see how it could possibly fold up into that compact size again, but decided it was some stunt of the instrument makers. Since his time-that made it worth more at the hock shop, he thought with satisfaction.

Just for old times' sake, he let his eyes and fingers rove over the instruments before he snapped the bag shut and headed for Uncle's. More than a few were a little hard to recognize-exactly, that is. You could see the things with blades for cutting, the forceps for holding and pulling, the retractors for holding fast, the needles and gut for suturing, the hypos —a fleeting thought crossed his mind that he could peddle the hypos separately to drug addicts.

Let's go, he decided, and tried to fold up the case. It didn't fold until he happened to touch the lock, and then it folded all at once into a little black bag. Sure have forged ahead, he thought, almost able to forget that what he was primarily interested in was its pawn value.

With a definite objective, it was not too hard for him to get to his feet. He decided to go down the front steps, out the front door and down the sidewalk. But first —

He snapped the bag open again on his kitchen table, and pored through the medication tubes. "Anything to sock the autonomic nervous system good and hard," he mumbled. The tubes were numbered, and there was a plastic card which seemed to list them. The left margin of the card was a run-down of the systems-vascular, muscular, nervous. He followed the last entry across to the right. There were columns for "stimulant," "depressant," and so on. Under "nervous system" and "depressant" he found the number 17, and shakily located the little glass tube which bore it. It was full of pretty blue pills and he took one.

It was like being struck by a thunderbolt.

Dr. Full had so long lacked any sense of well-being except the brief glow of alcohol that he had forgotten its very nature. He was panic-stricken for a long moment at the sensation that spread through him slowly, finally tingling in his fingertips. He straightened up, his pains gone and his leg tremor stilled.

That was great, he thought. He'd be able to *run* to the hock shop, pawn the little black bag and get some booze. He started down the stairs. Not even the street, bright with mid-morning sun, into which he emerged made him quail. The little black bag in his left hand had a satisfying, authoritative weight. He was walking erect, he noted, and not in the somewhat furtive crouch that had grown on him in recent years. A little self-respect, he told himself, that's what I need. Just because a man's down doesn't mean —

"Docta, please-a come wit'!" somebody yelled at him, tugging his arm. "Da litt-la girl, she's-a burn' up!" It was one of the slum's innumerable flat-faced, stringy-haired women, in a slovenly wrapper.

"Ah, I happen to be retired from practice —" he began hoarsely, but she would not be put off.

"In by here, Docta!" she urged, tugging him to a doorway. "You come look-a da litt-la girl. I got two dolla, you come look!" That put a different complexion on the matter. He allowed himself to be towed through the doorway into a mussy, cabbage-smelling flat. He knew the woman now, or rather knew who she must be —a new arrival who had moved in the other night. These people moved at night, in motorcades of battered cars supplied by friends and relations, with furniture lashed to the tops, swearing and drinking until the small hours. It explained why she had stopped him: she did not yet know he was old Dr. Full, a drunken reprobate whom nobody would trust. The little black bag had been his guarantee, outweighing his whiskery face and stained black suit.

He was looking down on a three-year-old girl who had, he rather suspected, just been placed in the mathematical center of a freshly changed double bed. God knew what sour and dirty mattress she usually slept on. He seemed to recognize her as he noted a crusted bandage on her right hand. Two dollars, he thought — An ugly flush had spread up her pipe-stem arm. He poked a finger into the socket of her elbow, and felt little spheres like marbles under the skin and ligaments roll apart. The child began to squall thinly; beside him, the woman gasped and began to weep herself.

"Out," he gestured briskly at her, and she thudded away, still sobbing.

Two dollars, he thought — Give her some mumbo jumbo, take the money and tell her to go to a clinic. Strep, I guess, from that stinking alley. It's a wonder any of them grow up. He put down the little black bag and forgetfully fumbled for his key, then remembered and touched the lock. It flew open, and he selected a bandage shears, with a blunt wafer for the lower jaw. He fitted the lower jaw under the bandage, trying not to hurt the kid by its pressure on the infection, and began to cut. It was amazing how easily and swiftly the shining shears snipped through the crusty rag around the wound. He hardly seemed to be driving the shears with fingers at all. It almost seemed as though the shears were driving his fingers instead as they scissored a clean, light line through the bandage.

Certainly have forged ahead since my time, he thought-sharper than a microtome knife. He replaced the shears in their loop on the extraordinarily big board that the little black bag turned into when it unfolded, and leaned over the wound. He whistled at the ugly gash, and the violent infection which had taken immediate root in the sickly child's thin body. Now what can you do with a thing like that? He pawed over the contents of the little black bag, nervously. If he lanced it and let some of the pus out, the old woman would think he'd done something for her and he'd get the two dollars. But at the clinic they'd want to know who did it and if they got sore enough they might send a cop around. Maybe there was something in the kit —

He ran down the left edge of the card to "lymphatic" and read across to the column under "infection." It didn't sound right at all to him; he checked again, but it still said that. In the square to which the line and column led were the symbols: "IV-g-3cc." He couldn't find any bottles marked with Roman numerals, and then noticed that that was how the hypodermic needles were designated. He lifted number IV from its loop, noting that it was fitted with a needle already and even seemed to be charged. What a way to carry those things around! So-three cc. of whatever was in hypo number IV ought to do something or other about infections settled in the lymphatic system-which, God knows, this one was. What did the lower-case "g" mean, though? He studied the glass hypo and saw letters engraved on what looked like a rotating disk at the top of the barrel. They ran from "a" to "i," and there was an index line engraved on the barrel on the opposite side from the calibrations.

Shrugging, old Dr. Full turned the disk until "g" coincided with the index line, and lifted the hypo to eye level. As he pressed in the plunger he did not see the tiny thread of fluid squirt from the tip of the needle. There was a sort of dark mist for a moment about the tip. A closer inspection showed that the needle was not even pierced at the tip. It had the usual slanting cut across the bias of the shaft, but the cut did not expose an oval hole. Baffled, he tried pressing the plunger again. Again *something* appeared around the tip and vanished. "We'll settle this," said the doctor. He slipped the needle into the skin of his forearm. He thought at first that he had missed-that the point had glided over the top of his skin instead of catching and slipping under it. But he saw a tiny blood-spot and realized that somehow he just hadn't felt the puncture. Whatever was in the barrel, he decided, couldn't do him any harm if it lived up to its billing-and if it could come out through a needle that had no hole. He gave himself three cc. and twitched the needle out. There was the swelling-painless, but otherwise typical.

Dr. Full decided it was his eyes or something, and gave three cc. of "g" from hypodermic IV to the feverish child. There was no interruption to her wailing as the needle went in and the swelling rose. But a long instant later, she gave a final gasp and was silent.

Well, he told himself, cold with horror, you did it that time. You killed her with that stuff. Then the child sat up and said: "Where's my mommy?"

Incredulously, the doctor seized her arm and palpated the elbow. The gland infection was zero, and the temperature seemed normal. The blood-congested tissues surrounding the wound were subsiding as he watched. The child's pulse was stronger and no faster than a child's should be. In the sudden silence of the room he could hear the little girl's mother sobbing in her kitchen, outside. And he also heard a girl's insinuating voice:

"She gonna be O.K., doc?"

He turned and saw a gaunt-faced, dirty-blonde sloven of perhaps eighteen leaning in the doorway and eyeing him with amused contempt. She continued: "I heard about you, *Doc-tor* Full. So don't go try and put the bite on the old lady. You couldn't doctor up a sick cat."

"Indeed?" he rumbled. This young person was going to get a lesson she richly deserved. "Perhaps you would care to look at my patient?"

"Where's my mommy?" insisted the little girl, and the blonde's jaw fell. She went to the bed and cautiously asked: "You O.K. now, Teresa? You all fixed up?"

"Where's my mommy?" demanded Teresa. Then, accusingly, she gestured with her wounded hand at the doctor. "You *poke* me!" she complained, and giggled pointlessly.

"Well —" said the blonde girl, "I guess I got to hand it to you, doc. These loud-mouth women around here said you didn't know your ... I mean, didn't know how to cure people. They said you ain't a real doctor."

"I *have* retired from practice," he said. "But I happened to be taking this case to a colleague as a favor, your good mother noticed me, and —" a deprecating smile. He touched the lock of the case and it folded up into the little black bag again.

"You stole it," the girl said flatly.

He sputtered.

"Nobody'd trust you with a thing like that. It must be worth plenty. You stole that case. I was going to stop you when I come in and saw you working over Teresa, but it looked like you wasn't doing her any harm. But when you give me that line about taking that case to a colleague I know you stole it. You gimme a cut or I go to the cops. A thing like that must be worth twenty-thirty dollars."

The mother came timidly in, her eyes red. But she let out a whoop of joy when she saw the little girl sitting up and babbling to herself, embraced her madly, fell on her knees for a quick prayer, hopped up to kiss the doctor's hand, and then dragged him into the kitchen, all the while rattling in her native language while the blonde girl let her eyes go cold with disgust. Dr. Full allowed himself to be towed into the kitchen, but flatly declined a cup of coffee and a plate of anise cakes and St. John's Bread.

"Try him on some wine, ma," said the girl sardonically.

"Hyass! Hyass!" breathed the woman delightedly. "You like-a wine, docta?" She had a carafe of purplish liquid before him in an instant, and the blonde girl snickered as the doctor's hand twitched out at it. He drew his hand back, while there grew in his head the old image of how it would smell and then taste and then warm his stomach and limbs. He made the kind of calculation at which he was practiced; the delighted woman would not notice as he downed two tumblers, and he could overawe her through two tumblers more with his tale of Teresa's narrow brush with the Destroying Angel, and then-why, then it would not matter. He would be drunk.

But for the first time in years, there was a sort of counter-image: a blend of the rage he felt at the blonde girl to whom he was so transparent, and of pride at the cure he had just effected. Much to his own surprise, he drew back his hand from the carafe and said, luxuriating in the words: "No, thank you. I don't believe I'd care for any so early in the day." He covertly watched the blonde girl's face, and was gratified at her surprise. Then the mother was shyly handing him two bills and saying: "Is no much-a money, docta-but you come again, see Teresa?"

"I shall be glad to follow the case through," he said. "But now excuse me —I really must be running along." He grasped the little black bag firmly and got up; he wanted very much to get away from the wine and the older girl.

"Wait up, doc," said she. "I'm going your way." She followed him out and down the street. He ignored her until he felt her hand on the black bag. Then old Dr. Full stopped and tried to reason with her:

"Look, my dear. Perhaps you're right. I might have stolen it. To be perfectly frank, I don't remember how I got it. But you're young and you can earn your own money —

"Fifty-fifty," she said, "or I go to the cops. And if I get another word outta you, it's sixty-forty. And you know who gets the short end, don't you, doc?"

Defeated, he marched to the pawnshop, her impudent hand still on the handle with his, and her heels beating out a tattoo against his stately tread.

In the pawnshop, they both got a shock.

"It ain't stendard," said Uncle, unimpressed by the ingenious lock. "I ain't nevva seen one like it. Some cheap Jap stuff, maybe? Try down the street. This I nevva could sell."

Down the street they got an offer of one dollar. The same complaint was made: "I ain't a collecta, mista —I buy stuff that got resale value. Who could I sell this to, a Chinaman who don't know medical instruments? Every one of them looks funny. You sure you didn't make these yourself?" They didn't take the one-dollar offer.

The girl was baffled and angry; the doctor was baffled too, but triumphant. He had two dollars, and the girl had a half-interest in something nobody wanted. But, he suddenly marveled, the thing had been all right to cure the kid, hadn't it?

"Well," he asked her, "do you give up? As you see, the kit is practically valueless."

She was thinking hard. "Don't fly off the handle, doc. I don't get this but something's going on all right …would those guys know good stuff if they saw it?"

"They would. They make a living from it. Wherever this kit came from —"

She seized on that, with a devilish faculty she seemed to have of eliciting answers without asking questions. "I thought so. You don't know either, huh? Well, maybe I can find out for you. C'mon in here. I ain't letting go of that thing. There's money in it-some way, I don't know how, there's money in it." He followed her into a cafeteria and to an almost-empty corner.

She was oblivious to stares and snickers from the other customers as she opened the little black bag-it almost covered a cafeteria table-and ferreted through it. She picked out a retractor from a loop, scrutinized it, contemptuously threw it down, picked out a speculum, threw it down, picked out the lower half of an O.B. forceps, turned it over, close to her sharp young eyes-and saw what the doctor's dim old ones could not have seen.

All old Dr. Full knew was that she was peering at the neck of the forceps and then turned white. Very carefully, she placed the half of the forceps back in its loop of cloth and then replaced the retractor and the speculum. "Well?" he asked. "What did you see?"

"'Made in U.S.A.'" she quoted hoarsely. "'Patent Applied for July 2450.'"

He wanted to tell her she must have misread the inscription, that it must be a practical joke, that —

But he knew she had read correctly. Those bandage shears: they *had* driven his fingers, rather than his fingers driving them. The hypo needle that had no hole. The pretty blue pill that had struck him like a thunderbolt.

"You know what I'm going to do?" asked the girl, with sudden animation. "I'm going to go to charm school. You'll like that, won't ya, doc? Because we're sure going to be seeing a lot of each other."

Old Dr. Full didn't answer. His hands had been playing idly with that plastic card from the kit on which had been printed the rows and columns that had guided him twice before. The card had a slight convexity; you could snap the convexity back and forth from one side to the other. He noted, in a daze, that with each snap a different text appeared on the cards. *Snap.* "The knife with the blue dot in the handle is for tumors only. Diagnose tumors with your Instrument Seven, the Swelling Tester. Place the Swelling Tester —" *Snap.* "An overdose of the pink pills in Bottle 3 can be fixed with one white pill from Bottle —" *Snap.* "Hold the suture needle by the end without the hole in it. Touch it to one end of the wound you want to close and let go. After it has made the knot, touch it —" *Snap.* "Place the top half of the O.B. Forceps near the opening. Let go. After it has entered and conformed to the shape of—" *Snap.*

* * * * *

The slot man saw "Flannery 1 —Medical" in the upper left corner of the hunk of copy. He automatically scribbled "trim to .75" on it and skimmed it across the horseshoe-shaped copy desk to Piper, who had been handling Edna Flannery's quack-exposé series. She was a nice youngster, he thought, but like all youngsters she over-wrote. Hence, the "trim."

Piper dealt back a city hall story to the slot, pinned down Flannery's feature with one hand and began to tap his pencil across it, one tap to a word, at the same steady beat as a teletype carriage traveling across the roller. He wasn't exactly reading it this first time. He was just looking at the letters and words to find out whether, as letters and words, they conformed to *Herald* style. The steady tap of his pencil ceased at intervals as it drew a black line ending with a stylized letter "d" through the word "breast" and scribbled in "chest" instead, or knocked down the capital "E" in "East" to lower case with a diagonal, or closed up a split word-in whose middle Flannery had bumped the space bar of her typewriter-with two curved lines like parentheses rotated through ninety degrees. The thick black pencil zipped a ring around the "30" which, like all youngsters, she put at the end of her stories. He turned back to the first page for the second reading. This time the pencil drew lines with the stylized "d's" at the end of them through adjectives and whole phrases, printed big "L's" to mark paragraphs, hooked some of Flannery's own paragraphs together with swooping recurved lines.

At the bottom of "Flannery Add 2 —Medical" the pencil slowed down and stopped. The slot man, sensitive to the rhythm of his beloved copy desk, looked up almost at once. He saw Piper squinting at the story, at a loss. Without wasting words, the copy reader skimmed it back across the Masonite horseshoe to the chief, caught a police story in return and buckled down, his pencil tapping. The slot man read as far as the fourth add, barked at Howard, on the rim: "Sit in for me," and stumped through the clattering city room toward the alcove where the managing editor presided over his own bedlam.

The copy chief waited his turn while the make-up editor, the pressroom foreman and the chief photographer had words with the M.E. When his turn came, he dropped Flannery's copy on his desk and said: "She says this one isn't a quack."

The M.E. read:

"Flannery 1 —Medical, by Edna Flannery, *Herald* Staff Writer.

"The sordid tale of medical quackery which the *Herald* has exposed in this series of articles undergoes a change of pace today which the reporter found a welcome surprise. Her quest for the facts in the case of today's subject started just the same way that her exposure of one dozen shyster M.D.'s and faith-healing phonies did. But she can report for a change that Dr. Bayard Full is, despite unorthodox practices which have drawn the suspicion of the rightly hypersensitive medical associations, a true healer living up to the highest ideals of his profession.

"Dr. Full's name was given to the *Herald*'s reporter by the ethical committee of a county medical association, which reported that he had been expelled from the association on July 18, 1941 for allegedly 'milking' several patients suffering from trivial complaints. According to sworn statements in the committee's files, Dr. Full had told them they suffered from cancer, and that he had a treatment which would prolong their lives. After his expulsion from the association, Dr. Full dropped out of their sight-until he opened a midtown 'sanitarium' in a brownstone front which had for years served as a rooming house.

"The *Herald*'s reporter went to that sanitarium, on East 89th Street, with the full expectation of having numerous imaginary ailments diagnosed and of being promised a sure cure for a flat sum of money. She expected to find unkempt quarters, dirty instruments and the mumbo-jumbo paraphernalia of the shyster M.D. which she had seen a dozen times before.

"She was wrong.

"Dr. Full's sanitarium is spotlessly clean, from its tastefully furnished entrance hall to its shining, white treatment rooms. The attractive, blonde receptionist who greeted the reporter was soft-spoken and correct, asking only the reporter's name, address and the general nature of her complaint. This was given, as usual, as 'nagging backache.' The receptionist asked the *Herald*'s reporter to be seated, and a short while later conducted her to a second-floor treatment room and introduced her to Dr. Full.

"Dr. Full's alleged past, as described by the medical society spokesman, is hard to reconcile with his present appearance. He is a clear-eyed, white-haired man in his sixties, to judge by his appearance —a little above middle height and apparently in good physical condition. His voice was firm and friendly, untainted by the ingratiating whine of the shyster M.D. which the reporter has come to know too well.

"The receptionist did not leave the room as he began his examination after a few questions as to the nature and location of the pain. As the reporter lay face down on a treatment table the doctor pressed some instrument to the small of her back. In about one minute he made this astounding statement: 'Young woman, there is no reason for you to have any pain where you say you do. I understand they're saying nowadays that emotional upsets cause pains like that. You'd better go to a psychologist or psychiatrist if the pain keeps up. There is no physical cause for it, so I can do nothing for you.'

"His frankness took the reporter's breath away. Had he guessed she was, so to speak, a spy in his camp? She tried again: 'Well, doctor, perhaps you'd give me a physical checkup. I feel run-down all the time, besides the pains. Maybe I need a tonic.' This is never-failing bait to shyster M.D.'s —an invitation for them to find all sorts of mysterious conditions wrong with a patient, each of which 'requires' an expensive treatment. As explained in the first article of this series, of course, the reporter underwent a thorough physical checkup before she embarked on her quack-hunt, and was found to be in one hundred percent perfect condition, with the exception of a 'scarred' area at the bottom tip of her left lung resulting from a childhood attack of tuberculosis and a tendency toward 'hyperthyroidism' —overactivity of the thyroid gland which makes it difficult to put on weight and sometimes causes a slight shortness of breath.

"Dr. Full consented to perform the examination, and took a number of shining, spotlessly clean instruments from loops in a large board literally covered with instruments-most of them unfamiliar to the reporter. The instrument with which he approached first was a tube with a curved dial in its surface and two wires that ended on flat disks growing from its ends. He placed one of the disks on the back of the reporter's right hand and the other on the back of her left. 'Reading the meter,' he called out some number which the attentive receptionist took down on a ruled form. The same procedure was repeated several times, thoroughly covering the reporter's anatomy and thoroughly convincing her that the doctor was a complete quack. The reporter had never seen any such diagnostic procedure practiced during the weeks she put in preparing for this series.

"The doctor then took the ruled sheet from the receptionist, conferred with her in low tones and said: 'You have a slightly overactive thyroid, young woman. And there's something wrong with your left lung-not seriously, but I'd like to take a closer look.'

"He selected an instrument from the board which, the reporter knew, is called a 'speculum' —a scissorlike device which spreads apart body openings such as the orifice of the ear, the nostril and so on, so that a doctor can look in during an examination. The instrument was, however, too large to be an aural or nasal speculum but too small to be anything else. As the *Herald*'s reporter was about to ask further questions, the attending receptionist told her: 'It's customary for us to blindfold our patients during lung examinations-do you mind?' The reporter, bewildered, allowed her to tie a spotlessly clean bandage over her eyes, and waited nervously for what would come next.

"She still cannot say exactly what happened while she was blindfolded-but X rays confirm her suspicions. She felt a cold sensation at her ribs on the left side —a cold that seemed to enter inside her body. Then there was a snapping feeling, and the cold sensation was gone. She heard Dr. Full say in a matter-of-fact voice: 'You have an old tubercular scar down there. It isn't doing any particular harm, but an active person like you needs all the oxygen she can get. Lie still and I'll fix it for you.'

"Then there was a repetition of the cold sensation, lasting for a longer time. 'Another batch of alveoli and some more vascular glue,' the *Herald*'s reporter heard Dr. Full say, and the receptionist's crisp response to the order. Then the strange sensation departed and the eye-bandage was removed. The reporter saw no scar on her ribs, and yet the doctor assured her: 'That did it. We took out the fibrosis-and a good fibrosis it was, too; it walled off the infection so you're still alive to tell the tale. Then we planted a few clumps of alveoli-they're the little gadgets that get the oxygen from the air you breathe into your blood. I won't monkey with your thyroxin supply. You've got used to being the kind of person you are, and if you suddenly found yourself easygoing and all the rest of it, chances are you'd only be upset. About the backache: just check with the county medical society for the name of a good psychologist or psychiatrist. And look out for quacks; the woods are full of them.'

"The doctor's self-assurance took the reporter's breath away. She asked what the charge would be, and was told to pay the receptionist fifty dollars. As usual, the reporter delayed paying until she got a receipt signed by the doctor himself, detailing the services for which it paid. Unlike most, the doctor cheerfully wrote: 'For removal of fibrosis from left lung and restoration of alveoli,' and signed it.

"The reporter's first move when she left the sanitarium was to head for the chest specialist who had examined her in preparation for this series. A comparison of X rays taken on the day of the 'operation' and those taken previously would, the *Herald*'s reporter then thought, expose Dr. Full as a prince of shyster M.D.'s and quacks.

"The chest specialist made time on his crowded schedule for the reporter, in whose series he has shown a lively interest from the planning stage on. He laughed uproariously in his staid Park Avenue examining room as she described the weird procedure to which she had been subjected.

But he did not laugh when he took a chest X ray of the reporter, developed it, dried it, and compared it with the ones he had taken earlier. The chest specialist took six more X rays that afternoon, but finally admitted that they all told the same story. The *Herald*'s reporter has it on his authority that the scar she had eighteen days ago from her tuberculosis is now gone and has been replaced by healthy lung-tissue. He declares that this is a happening unparalleled in medical history. He does not go along with the reporter in her firm conviction that Dr. Full is responsible for the change.

"The *Herald*'s reporter, however, sees no two ways about it. She concludes that Dr. Bayard Full-whatever his alleged past may have been-is now an unorthodox but highly successful practitioner of medicine, to whose hands the reporter would trust herself in any emergency.

"Not so is the case of 'Rev.' Annie Dimsworth —a female harpy who, under the guise of 'faith' preys on the ignorant and suffering who come to her sordid 'healing parlor' for help and remain to feed 'Rev.' Annie's bank account, which now totals up to $53,238.64. Tomorrow's article will show, with photostats of bank statements and sworn testimony that —"

The managing editor turned down "Flannery Last Add-Medical" and tapped his front teeth with a pencil, trying to think straight. He finally told the copy chief: "Kill the story. Run the teaser as a box." He tore off the last paragraph-the "teaser" about "Rev." Annie-and handed it to the desk man, who stumped back to his Masonite horseshoe.

The make-up editor was back, dancing with impatience as he tried to catch the M.E.'s eye. The interphone buzzed with the red light which indicated that the editor and publisher wanted to talk to him. The M.E. thought briefly of a special series on this Dr. Full, decided nobody would believe it and that he probably was a phony anyway. He spiked the story on the "dead" hook and answered his interphone.

* * * * *

Dr. Full had become almost fond of Angie. As his practice had grown to engross the neighborhood illnesses, and then to a corner suite in an uptown taxpayer building, and finally to the sanitarium, she seemed to have grown with it. Oh, he thought, we have our little disputes —

The girl, for instance, was too much interested in money. She had wanted to specialize in cosmetic surgery-removing wrinkles from wealthy old women and whatnot. She didn't realize, at first, that a thing like this was in their trust, that they were the stewards and not the owners of the little black bag and its fabulous contents.

He had tried, ever so cautiously, to analyze them, but without success. All the instruments were slightly radioactive, for instance, but not quite so. They would make a Geiger-Müller counter indicate, but they would not collapse the leaves of an electroscope. He didn't pretend to be up on the latest developments, but as he understood it, that was just plain *wrong*. Under the highest magnification there were lines on the instruments' superfinished surfaces: incredibly fine lines, engraved in random hatchments which made no particular sense. Their magnetic properties were preposterous. Sometimes the instruments were strongly attracted to magnets, sometimes less so, and sometimes not at all.

Dr. Full had taken X rays in fear and trembling lest he disrupt whatever delicate machinery worked in them. He was *sure* they were not solid, that the handles and perhaps the blades must be mere shells filled with busy little watchworks-but the X rays showed nothing of the sort. Oh, yes-and they were always sterile, and they wouldn't rust. Dust *fell* off them if you shook them: now, that was something he understood. They ionized the dust, or were ionized themselves, or something of the sort. At any rate, he had read of something similar that had to do with phonograph records.

She wouldn't know about that, he proudly thought. She kept the books well enough, and perhaps she gave him a useful prod now and then when he was inclined to settle down. The move from the neighborhood slum to the uptown quarters had been her idea, and so had the sanitarium. Good, good, it enlarged his sphere of usefulness. Let the child have her mink coats and her convertible, as they seemed to be calling roadsters nowadays. He himself was too busy and too old. He had so much to make up for.

Dr. Full thought happily of his Master Plan. She would not like it much, but she would have to see the logic of it. This marvelous thing that had happened to them must be handed on. She was herself no doctor; even though the instruments practically ran themselves, there was more to doctoring than skill. There were the ancient canons of the healing art. And so, having seen the logic of it, Angie would yield; she would assent to his turning over the little black bag to all humanity.

He would probably present it to the College of Surgeons, with as little fuss as possible-well, perhaps a *small* ceremony, and he would like a souvenir of the occasion, a cup or a framed testimonial. It would be a relief to have the thing out of his hands, in a way; let the giants of the healing art decide who was to have its benefits. No, Angie would understand. She was a goodhearted girl.

It was nice that she had been showing so much interest in the surgical side lately-asking about the instruments, reading the instruction card for hours, even practicing on guinea pigs. If something of his love for humanity had been communicated to her, old Dr. Full sentimentally thought, his life would not have been in vain. Surely she would realize that a greater good would be served by surrendering the instruments to wiser hands than theirs, and by throwing aside the cloak of secrecy necessary to work on their small scale.

Dr. Full was in the treatment room that had been the brownstone's front parlor; through the window he saw Angle's yellow convertible roll to a stop before the stoop. He liked the way she looked as she climbed the stairs; neat, not flashy, he thought. A sensible girl like her, she'd understand. There was somebody with her —a fat woman, puffing up the steps, overdressed and petulant. Now, what could she want?

Angie let herself in and went into the treatment room, followed by the fat woman. "Doctor," said the blonde girl gravely, "may I present Mrs. Coleman?" Charm school had not taught her everything, but Mrs. Coleman, evidently *nouveau riche*, thought the doctor, did not notice the blunder.

"Miss Aquella told me *so* much about you, doctor, and your remarkable system!" she gushed.

Before he could answer, Angie smoothly interposed: "Would you excuse us for just a moment, Mrs. Coleman?"

She took the doctor's arm and led him into the reception hall. "Listen," she said swiftly, "I know this goes against your grain, but I couldn't pass it up. I met this old thing in the exercise class at Elizabeth Barton's. Nobody else'll talk to her there. She's a widow. I guess her husband was a black marketeer or something, and she has a pile of dough. I gave her a line about how you had a system of massaging wrinkles out. My idea is, you blindfold her, cut her neck open with the Cutaneous Series knife, shoot some Firmol into the muscles, spoon out some of that blubber with an Adipose Series curette and spray it all with Skintite. When you take the blindfold off she's got rid of a wrinkle and doesn't know what happened. She'll pay five hundred dollars. Now, don't say 'no,' doc. Just this once, let's do it my way, can't you? I've been working on this deal all along too, haven't I?"

"Oh," said the doctor, "very well." He was going to have to tell her about the Master Plan before long anyway. He would let her have it her way this time.

Back in the treatment room, Mrs. Coleman had been thinking things over. She told the doctor sternly as he entered: "Of course, your system is permanent, isn't it?"

"It is, madam," he said shortly. "Would you please lie down there? Miss Aquella, get a sterile three-inch bandage for Mrs. Coleman's eyes." He turned his back on the fat woman to avoid conversation, and pretended to be adjusting the lights. Angie blindfolded the woman, and the doctor selected the instruments he would need. He handed the blonde girl a pair of retractors, and told her: "Just slip the corners of the blades in as I cut —" She gave him an alarmed look, and gestured at the reclining woman. He lowered his voice: "Very well. Slip in the corners and rock them along the incision. I'll tell you when to pull them out."

Dr. Full held the Cutaneous Series knife to his eyes as he adjusted the little slide for three centimeters depth. He sighed a little as he recalled that its last use had been in the extirpation of an "inoperable" tumor of the throat.

"Very well," he said, bending over the woman. He tried a tentative pass through her tissues. The blade dipped in and flowed through them, like a finger through quicksilver, with no wound left in the wake. Only the retractors could hold the edges of the incision apart.

Mrs. Coleman stirred and jabbered: "Doctor, that felt so peculiar! Are you sure you're rubbing the right way?"

"Quite sure, madam," said the doctor wearily. "Would you please try not to talk during the massage?"

He nodded at Angie, who stood ready with the retractors. The blade sank in to its three centimeters, miraculously cutting only the dead horny tissues of the epidermis and the live tissue of the dermis, pushing aside mysteriously all major and minor blood vessels and muscular tissue, declining to affect any system or organ except the one it was-tuned to, could you say? The doctor didn't know the answer, but he felt tired and bitter at this prostitution. Angie slipped in the retractor blades and rocked them as he withdrew the knife, then pulled to separate the lips of the incision. It bloodlessly exposed an unhealthy string of muscle, sagging in a dead-looking loop from blue-grey ligaments. The doctor took a hypo, number IX, pre-set to "g" and raised it to his eye level. The mist came and went. There probably was no possibility of an embolus with one of these gadgets, but why take chances? He shot one cc. of "g" —identified as "Firmol" by the card-into the muscle. He and Angie watched as it tightened up against the pharynx.

He took the Adipose Series curette, a small one, and spooned out yellowish tissue, dropping it into the incinerator box, and then nodded to Angie. She eased out the retractors and the gaping incision slipped together into unbroken skin, sagging now. The doctor had the atomizer-dialed to "Skintite" —ready. He sprayed, and the skin shrank up into the new firm throat line.

As he replaced the instruments, Angie removed Mrs. Coleman's bandage and gayly announced: "We're finished! And there's a mirror in the reception hall —"

Mrs. Coleman didn't need to be invited twice. With incredulous fingers she felt her chin, and then dashed for the hall. The doctor grimaced as he heard her yelp of delight, and Angie turned to him with a tight smile. "I'll get the money and get her out," she said. "You won't have to be bothered with her any more."

He was grateful for that much.

She followed Mrs. Coleman into the reception hall, and the doctor dreamed over the case of instruments. A ceremony, certainly-he was *entitled* to one. Not everybody, he thought, would turn such a sure source of money over to the good of humanity. But you reached an age when money mattered less, and when you thought of these things you had done that *might* be open to misunderstanding if, just if, there chanced to be any of that, well, that judgment business. The doctor wasn't a religious man, but you certainly found yourself thinking hard about some things when your time drew near —

Angie was back, with a bit of paper in her hands. "Five hundred dollars," she said matter-of-factly. "And you realize, don't you, that we could go over her an inch at a time-at five hundred dollars an inch?"

"I've been meaning to talk to you about that," he said.

There was bright fear in her eyes, he thought-but why?

"Angie, you've been a good girl and an understanding girl, but we can't keep this up forever, you know."

"Let's talk about it some other time," she said flatly. "I'm tired now."

"No —I really feel we've gone far enough on our own. The instruments —"

"Don't say it, doc!" she hissed. "Don't say it, or you'll be sorry!" In her face there was a look that reminded him of the hollow-eyed, gaunt-faced, dirty-blonde creature she had been. From under the charm-school finish there burned the guttersnipe whose infancy had been spent on a sour and filthy mattress, whose childhood had been play in the littered alley and whose adolescence had been the sweatshops and the aimless gatherings at night under the glaring street lamps.

He shook his head to dispel the puzzling notion. "It's this way," he patiently began. "I told you about the family that invented the O.B. forceps and kept them a secret for so many generations, how they could have given them to the world but didn't?"

"They knew what they were doing," said the guttersnipe flatly.

"Well, that's neither here nor there," said the doctor, irritated. "My mind is made up about it. I'm going to turn the instruments over to the College of Surgeons. We have enough money to be comfortable. You can even have the house. I've been thinking of going to a warmer climate, myself." He felt peeved with her for making the unpleasant scene. He was unprepared for what happened next.

Angie snatched the little black bag and dashed for the door, with panic in her eyes. He scrambled after her, catching her arm, twisting it in a sudden rage. She clawed at his face with her free hand, babbling curses. Somehow, somebody's finger touched the little black bag, and it opened grotesquely into the enormous board, covered with shining instruments, large and small. Half a dozen of them joggled loose and fell to the floor.

"*Now* see what you've done!" roared the doctor, unreasonably. Her hand was still viselike on the handle, but she was standing still, trembling with choked-up rage. The doctor bent stiffly to pick up the fallen instruments. Unreasonable girl! he thought bitterly. Making a scene —

Pain drove in between his shoulderblades and he fell face-down. The light ebbed. "Unreasonable girl!" he tried to croak. And then: "They'll know I tried, anyway —

Angie looked down on his prone body, with the handle of the Number Six Cautery Series knife protruding from it. " —will cut through all tissues. Use for amputations before you spread on the Re-Gro. Extreme caution should be used in the vicinity of vital organs and major blood vessels or nerve trunks —"

"I didn't mean to do that," said Angie, dully, cold with horror. Now the detective would come, the implacable detective who would reconstruct the crime from the dust in the room. She would run and turn and twist, but the detective would find her out and she would be tried in a courtroom before a judge and jury; the lawyer would make speeches, but the jury would convict her anyway, and the headlines would scream: "Blonde Killer Guilty!" and she'd maybe get the chair, walking down a plain corridor where a beam of sunlight struck through the dusty air, with an iron door at the end of it. Her mink, her convertible, her dresses, the handsome man she was going to meet and marry —

The mist of cinematic clichés cleared, and she knew what she would do next. Quite steadily, she picked the incinerator box from its loop in the board —a metal cube with a different-textured spot on one side. " —to dispose of fibroses or other unwanted matter, simply touch the disk —" You dropped something in and touched the disk. There was a sort of soundless whistle, very powerful and unpleasant if you were too close, and a sort of lightless flash. When you opened the box again, the contents were gone. Angie took another of the Cautery Series knives and went grimly to work. Good thing there wasn't any blood to speak of — She finished the awful task in three hours.

She slept heavily that night, totally exhausted by the wringing emotional demands of the slaying and the subsequent horror. But in the morning, it was as though the doctor had never been there. She ate breakfast, dressed with unusual care-and then undid the unusual care. Nothing out of the ordinary, she told herself. Don't do one thing different from the way you would have done it before. After a day or two, you can phone the cops. Say he walked out spoiling for a drunk, and you're worried. But don't rush it, baby —*don't rush it.*

Mrs. Coleman was due at 10:00 A.M. Angie had counted on being able to talk the doctor into at least one more five-hundred-dollar session. She'd have to do it herself now-but she'd have to start sooner or later.

The woman arrived early. Angie explained smoothly: "The doctor asked me to take care of the massage today. Now that he has the tissue-firming process beginning, it only requires somebody trained in his methods —" As she spoke, her eyes swiveled to the instrument case-open! She cursed herself for the single flaw as the woman followed her gaze and recoiled.

"What are those things!" she demanded. "Are you going to cut me with them? I *thought* there was something fishy —"

"Please, Mrs. Coleman," said Angie, "please, *dear* Mrs. Coleman-you don't understand about the ... the massage instruments!"

"Massage instruments, my foot!" squabbled the woman shrilly. "That doctor *operated* on me. Why, he might have killed me!"

Angie wordlessly took one of the smaller Cutaneous Series knives and passed it through her forearm. The blade flowed like a finger through quicksilver, leaving no wound in its wake. *That* should convince the old cow!

It didn't convince her, but it did startle her. "What did you do with it? The blade folds up into the handle-that's it!"

"Now look closely, Mrs. Coleman," said Angie, thinking desperately of the five hundred dollars. "Look very closely and you'll see that the, uh, the sub-skin massager simply slips beneath the tissues without doing any harm, tightening and firming the muscles themselves instead of having to work through layers of skin and adipose tissue. It's the secret of the doctor's method. Now, how can outside massage have the effect that we got last night?"

Mrs. Coleman was beginning to calm down. "It *did* work, all right," she admitted, stroking the new line of her neck. "But your arm's one thing and my neck's another! Let me see you do that with your neck!"

Angie smiled —

* * * * *

Al returned to the clinic after an excellent lunch that had almost reconciled him to three more months he would have to spend on duty. And then, he thought, and then a blessed year at the blessedly super-normal South Pole working on his specialty-which happened to be telekinesis exercises for ages three to six. Meanwhile, of course, the world had to go on and of course he had to shoulder his share in the running of it.

Before settling down to desk work he gave a routine glance at the bag board. What he saw made him stiffen with shocked surprise. A red light was on next to one of the numbers-the first since he couldn't think when. He read off the number and murmured "O.K., 674,101. That fixes *you*." He put the number on a card sorter and in a moment the record was in his hand. Oh, yes-Hemingway's bag. The big dummy didn't remember how or where he had lost it; none of them ever did. There were hundreds of them floating around.

Al's policy in such cases was to leave the bag turned on. The things practically ran themselves, it was practically impossible to do harm with them, so whoever found a lost one might as well be allowed to use it. You turn it off, you have a social loss-you leave it on, it may do some good. As he understood it, and not very well at that, the stuff wasn't "used up." A temporalist had tried to explain it to him with little success that the prototypes in the transmitter had been transducted through a series of point-events of transfinite cardinality. Al had innocently asked whether that meant prototypes had been stretched, so to speak, through all time, and the temporalist had thought he was joking and left in a huff.

"Like to see him do this," thought Al darkly, as he telekinized himself to the combox, after a cautious look to see that there were no medics around. To the box he said: "Police chief," and then to the police chief: "There's been a homicide committed with Medical Instrument Kit 674,101. It was lost some months ago by one of my people, Dr. John Hemingway. He didn't have a clear account of the circumstances."

The police chief groaned and said: "I'll call him in and question him." He was to be astonished by the answers, and was to learn that the homicide was well out of his jurisdiction.

Al stood for a moment at the bag board by the glowing red light that had been sparked into life by a departing vital force giving, as its last act, the warning that Kit 674,101 was in homicidal hands. With a sigh, Al pulled the plug and the light went out.

* * * * *

"Yah," jeered the woman. "You'd fool around with my neck, but you wouldn't risk your own with that thing!"

Angie smiled with serene confidence a smile that was to shock hardened morgue attendants. She set the Cutaneous Series knife to three centimeters before drawing it across her neck. Smiling, knowing the blade would cut only the dead horny tissue of the epidermis and the live tissue of the dermis, mysteriously push aside all major and minor blood vessels and muscular tissue —

Smiling, the knife plunging in and its microtomesharp metal shearing through major and minor blood vessels and muscular tissue and pharynx, Angie cut her throat.

In the few minutes it took the police, summoned by the shrieking Mrs. Coleman, to arrive, the instruments had become crusted with rust, and the flasks which had held vascular glue and clumps of pink, rubbery alveoli and spare grey cells and coils of receptor nerves held only black slime, and from them when opened gushed the foul gases of decomposition.

The Marching Morons

> In the country of the blind, the one-eyed man, of
> course, is king. But how about a live wire, a smart
> businessman, in a civilization of 100% pure chumps?

Some things had not changed. A potter's wheel was still a potter's wheel and clay was still clay. Efim Hawkins had built his shop near Goose Lake, which had a narrow band of good fat clay and a narrow beach of white sand. He fired three bottle-nosed kilns with willow charcoal from the wood lot. The wood lot was also useful for long walks while the kilns were cooling; if he let himself stay within sight of them, he would open them prematurely, impatient to see how some new shape or glaze had come through the fire, and —ping! —the new shape or glaze would be good for nothing but the shard pile back of his slip tanks.

A business conference was in full swing in his shop, a modest cube of brick, tile-roofed, as the Chicago-Los Angeles "rocket" thundered overhead-very noisy, very swept-back, very fiery jets, shaped as sleekly swift-looking as an airborne barracuda.

The buyer from Marshall Fields was turning over a black-glazed one liter carafe, nodding approval with his massive, handsome head. "This is real pretty," he told Hawkins and his own secretary, Gomez-Laplace. "This has got lots of what ya call real est'etic principles. Yeah, it is real pretty."

"How much?" the secretary asked the potter.

"Seven-fifty each in dozen lots," said Hawkins. "I ran up fifteen dozen last month."

"They are real est'etic," repeated the buyer from Fields. "I will take them all."

"I don't think we can do that, doctor," said the secretary. "They'd cost us $1,350. That would leave only $532 in our quarter's budget. And we still have to run down to East Liverpool to pick up some cheap dinner sets."

"Dinner sets?" asked the buyer, his big face full of wonder.

"Dinner sets. The department's been out of them for two months now. Mr. Garvy-Seabright got pretty nasty about it yesterday. Remember?"

"Garvy-Seabright, that meat-headed bluenose," the buyer said contemptuously. "He don't know nothin' about est'etics. Why for don't he lemme run my own department?" His eye fell on a stray copy of *Whambozambo Comix* and he sat down with it. An occasional deep chuckle or grunt of surprise escaped him as he turned the pages.

Uninterrupted, the potter and the buyer's secretary quickly closed a deal for two dozen of the liter carafes. "I wish we could take more," said the secretary, "but you heard what I told him. We've had to turn away customers for ordinary dinnerware because he shot the last quarter's budget on some Mexican piggy banks some equally enthusiastic importer stuck him with. The fifth floor is packed solid with them."

"I'll bet they look mighty est'etic."

"They're painted with purple cacti."

* * * * *

The potter shuddered and caressed the glaze of the sample carafe.

The buyer looked up and rumbled, "Ain't you dummies through yakkin' yet? What good's a seckertary for if'n he don't take the burden of *de*-tail off'n my back, harh?"

"We're all through, doctor. Are you ready to go?"

The buyer grunted peevishly, dropped *Whambozambo Comix* on the floor and led the way out of the building and down the log corduroy road to the highway. His car was waiting on the concrete. It was, like all contemporary cars, too low-slung to get over the logs. He climbed down into the car and started the motor with a tremendous sparkle and roar.

"Gomez-Laplace," called out the potter under cover of the noise, "did anything come of the radiation program they were working on the last time I was on duty at the Pole?"

"The same old fallacy," said the secretary gloomily. "It stopped us on mutation, it stopped us on culling, it stopped us on segregation, and now it's stopped us on hypnosis."

"Well, I'm scheduled back to the grind in nine days. Time for another firing right now. I've got a new luster to try...."

"I'll miss you. I shall be 'vacationing' —running the drafting room of the New Century Engineering Corporation in Denver. They're going to put up a two hundred-story office building, and naturally somebody's got to be on hand."

"Naturally," said Hawkins with a sour smile.

There was an ear-piercingly sweet blast as the buyer leaned on the horn button. Also, a yard-tall jet of what looked like flame spurted up from the car's radiator cap; the car's power plant was a gas turbine, and had no radiator.

"I'm coming, doctor," said the secretary dispiritedly. He climbed down into the car and it whooshed off with much flame and noise.

The potter, depressed, wandered back up the corduroy road and contemplated his cooling kilns. The rustling wind in the boughs was obscuring the creak and mutter of the shrinking refractory brick. Hawkins wondered about the number two kiln —a reduction fire on a load of lusterware mugs. Had the clay chinking excluded the air? Had it been a properly smoky blaze? Would it do any harm if he just took one close —?

* * * * *

Common sense took Hawkins by the scruff of the neck and yanked him over to the tool shed. He got out his pick and resolutely set off on a prospecting jaunt to a hummocky field that might yield some oxides. He was especially low on coppers.

The long walk left him sweating hard, with his lust for a peek into the kiln quiet in his breast. He swung his pick almost at random into one of the hummocks; it clanged on a stone which he excavated. A largely obliterated inscription said:

Ersity of Chic
Ogical Labo
Eloved Memory of
Killed in Act

The potter swore mildly. He had hoped the field would turn out to be a cemetery, preferably a once-fashionable cemetery full of once-massive bronze caskets moldered into oxides of tin and copper.

* * * * *

Well, hell, maybe there was some around anyway.

He headed lackadaisically for the second largest hillock and sliced into it with his pick. There was a stone to undercut and topple into a trench, and then the potter was very glad he'd stuck at it. His nostrils were filled with the bitter smell and the dirt was tinged with the exciting blue of copper salts. The pick went *clang*!

Hawkins, puffing, pried up a stainless steel plate that was quite badly stained and was also marked with incised letters. It seemed to have pulled loose from rotting bronze; there were rivets on the back that brought up flakes of green patina. The potter wiped off the surface dirt with his sleeve, turned it to catch the sunlight obliquely and read:

"Honest John Barlow

"Honest John," famed in university annals, represents a challenge which medical science has not yet answered: revival of a human being accidentally thrown into a state of suspended animation.

In 1988 Mr. Barlow, a leading Evanston real estate dealer, visited his dentist for treatment of an impacted wisdom tooth. His dentist requested and received permission to use the experimental anesthetic Cycloparadimethanol-B-7, developed at the University.

After administration of the anesthetic, the dentist resorted to his drill. By freakish mischance, a short circuit in his machine delivered 220 volts of 60-cycle current into the patient. (In a damage suit instituted by Mrs. Barlow against the dentist, the University and the makers of the drill, a jury found for the defendants.) Mr. Barlow never got up from the dentist's chair and was assumed to have died of poisoning, electrocution or both.

Morticians preparing him for embalming discovered, however, that their subject was-though certainly not living-just as certainly not dead. The University was notified and a series of exhaustive tests was begun, including attempts to duplicate the trance state on volunteers. After a bad run of seven cases which ended fatally, the attempts were abandoned.

Honest John was long an exhibit at the University museum, and livened many a football game as mascot of the University's Blue Crushers. The bounds of taste were overstepped, however, when a pledge to Sigma Delta Chi was ordered in '03 to "kidnap" Honest John from his loosely guarded glass museum case and introduce him into the Rachel Swanson Memorial Girls' Gymnasium shower room.

On May 22nd, 2003, the University Board of Regents issued the following order: "By unanimous vote, it is directed that the remains of Honest John Barlow be removed from the University museum and conveyed to the University's Lieutenant James Scott III Memorial Biological Laboratories and there be securely locked in a specially prepared vault. It is further directed that all possible measures for the preservation of these remains be taken by the Laboratory administration and that access to these remains be denied to all persons except qualified scholars authorized in writing by the Board. The Board reluctantly takes this action in view of recent notices and photographs in the nation's press which, to say the least, reflect but small credit upon the University."

* * * * *

It was far from his field, but Hawkins understood what had happened-an early and accidental blundering onto the bare bones of the Levantman shock anesthesia, which had since been replaced by other methods. To bring subjects out of Levantman shock, you let them have a squirt of simple saline in the trigeminal nerve. Interesting. And now about that bronze —

He heaved the pick into the rotting green salts, expecting no resistence and almost fractured his wrist. *Something* down there was *solid*. He began to flake off the oxides.

A half hour of work brought him down to phosphor bronze, a huge casting of the almost incorruptible metal. It had weakened structurally over the centuries; he could fit the point of his pick under a corroded boss and pry off great creaking and grumbling striae of the stuff.

Hawkins wished he had an archeologist with him, but didn't dream of returning to his shop and calling one to take over the find. He was an all-around man: by choice and in his free time, an artist in clay and glaze; by necessity, an automotive, electronics and atomic engineer who could also swing a project in traffic control, individual and group psychology, architecture or tool design. He didn't yell for a specialist every time something out of his line came up; there were so few with so much to do....

He trenched around his find, discovering that it was a great brick-shaped bronze mass with an excitingly hollow sound. A long strip of moldering metal from one of the long vertical faces pulled away, exposing red rust that went *whoosh* and was sucked into the interior of the mass.

It had been de-aired, thought Hawkins, and there must have been an inner jacket of glass which had crystalized through the centuries and quietly crumbled at the first clang of his pick. He didn't know what a vacuum would do to a subject of Levantman shock, but he had hopes, nor did he quite understand what a real estate dealer was, but it might have something to do with pottery. And *anything* might have a bearing on Topic Number One.

* * * * *

He flung his pick out of the trench, climbed out and set off at a dog-trot for his shop. A little rummaging turned up a hypo and there was a plasticontainer of salt in the kitchen.

Back at his dig, he chipped for another half hour to expose the juncture of lid and body. The hinges were hopeless; he smashed them off.

Hawkins extended the telescopic handle of the pick for the best leverage, fitted its point into a deep pit, set its built-in fulcrum, and heaved. Five more heaves and he could see, inside the vault, what looked like a dusty marble statue. Ten more and he could see that it was the naked body of Honest John Barlow, Evanston real estate dealer, uncorrupted by time.

The potter found the apex of the trigeminal nerve with his needle's point and gave him 60 cc.

In an hour Barlow's chest began to pump.

In another hour, he rasped, "Did it work?"

"*Did* it!" muttered Hawkins.

Barlow opened his eyes and stirred, looked down, turned his hands before his eyes —

"I'll sue!" he screamed. "My clothes! My fingernails!" A horrid suspicion came over his face and he clapped his hands to his hairless scalp. "My hair!" he wailed. "I'll sue you for every penny you've got! That release won't mean a damned thing in court —I didn't sign away my hair and clothes and fingernails!"

"They'll grow back," said Hawkins casually. "Also your epidermis. Those parts of you weren't alive, you know, so they weren't preserved like the rest of you. I'm afraid the clothes are gone, though."

"What is this-the University hospital?" demanded Barlow. "I want a phone. No, you phone. Tell my wife I'm all right and tell Sam Immerman-he's my lawyer-to get over here right away. Greenleaf 7-4022. Ow!" He had tried to sit up, and a portion of his pink skin rubbed against the inner surface of the casket, which was powdered by the ancient crystalized glass. "What the hell did you guys do, boil me alive? Oh, you're going to pay for this!"

"You're all right," said Hawkins, wishing now he had a reference book to clear up several obscure terms. "Your epidermis will start growing immediately. You're not in the hospital. Look here."

* * * * *

He handed Barlow the stainless steel plate that had labeled the casket. After a suspicious glance, the man started to read. Finishing, he laid the plate carefully on the edge of the vault and was silent for a spell.

"Poor Verna," he said at last. "It doesn't say whether she was stuck with the court costs. Do you happen to know —"

"No," said the potter. "All I know is what was on the plate, and how to revive you. The dentist accidentally gave you a dose of what we call Levantman shock anesthesia. We haven't used it for centuries; it was powerful, but too dangerous."

"Centuries ..." brooded the man. "Centuries ...I'll bet Sam swindled her out of her eyeteeth. Poor Verna. How long ago was it? What year is this?"

Hawkins shrugged. "We call it 7-B-936. That's no help to you. It takes a long time for these metals to oxidize."

"Like that movie," Barlow muttered. "Who would have thought it? Poor Verna!" He blubbered and sniffled, reminding Hawkins powerfully of the fact that he had been found under a flat rock.

Almost angrily, the potter demanded, "How many children did you have?"

"None yet," sniffed Barlow. "My first wife didn't want them. But Verna wants one-wanted one-but we're going to wait until-we *were* going to wait until —"

"Of course," said the potter, feeling a savage desire to tell him off, blast him to hell and gone for his work. But he choked it down. There was The Problem to think of; there was always The Problem to think of, and this poor blubberer might unexpectedly supply a clue. Hawkins would have to pass him on.

* * * * *

"Come along," Hawkins said. "My time is short."

Barlow looked up, outraged. "How can you be so unfeeling? I'm a human being like —"

The Los Angeles-Chicago "rocket" thundered overhead and Barlow broke off in mid-complaint. "Beautiful!" he breathed, following it with his eyes. "Beautiful!"

He climbed out of the vault, too interested to be pained by its roughness against his infantile skin. "After all," he said briskly, "this should have its sunny side. I never was much for reading, but this is just like one of those stories. And I ought to make some money out of it, shouldn't I?" He gave Hawkins a shrewd glance.

"You want money?" asked the potter. "Here." He handed over a fistful of change and bills. "You'd better put my shoes on. It'll be about a quarter-mile. Oh, and you're-uh, modest? —yes, that was the word. Here." Hawkins gave him his pants, but Barlow was excitedly counting the money.

"Eighty-five, eighty-six —and it's dollars, too! I thought it'd be credits or whatever they call them. 'E Pluribus Unum' and 'Liberty' —just different faces. Say, is there a catch to this? Are these real, genuine, honest twenty-two-cent dollars like we had or just wallpaper?"

"They're quite all right, I assure you," said the potter. "I wish you'd come along. I'm in a hurry."

* * * * *

The man babbled as they stumped toward the shop. "Where are we going-The Council of Scientists, the World Coordinator or something like that?"

"Who? Oh, no. We call them 'President' and 'Congress.' No, that wouldn't do any good at all. I'm just taking you to see some people."

"I ought to make plenty out of this. *Plenty!* I could write books. Get some smart young fellow to put it into words for me and I'll bet I could turn out a best-seller. What's the setup on things like that?"

"It's about like that. Smart young fellows. But there aren't any best-sellers any more. People don't read much nowadays. We'll find something equally profitable for you to do."

Back in the shop, Hawkins gave Barlow a suit of clothes, deposited him in the waiting room and called Central in Chicago. "Take him away," he pleaded. "I have time for one more firing and he blathers and blathers. I haven't told him anything. Perhaps we should just turn him loose and let him find his own level, but there's a chance —"

"The Problem," agreed Central. "Yes, there's a chance."

The potter delighted Barlow by making him a cup of coffee with a cube that not only dissolved in cold water but heated the water to boiling point. Killing time, Hawkins chatted about the "rocket" Barlow had admired, and had to haul himself up short; he had almost told the real estate man what its top speed really was-almost, indeed, revealed that it was not a rocket.

He regretted, too, that he had so casually handed Barlow a couple of hundred dollars. The man seemed obsessed with fear that they were worthless since Hawkins refused to take a note or I.O.U. or even a definite promise of repayment. But Hawkins couldn't go into details, and was very glad when a stranger arrived from Central.

"Tinny-Peete, from Algeciras," the stranger told him swiftly as the two of them met at the door. "Psychist for Poprob. Polasigned special overtake Barlow."

"Thank Heaven," said Hawkins. "Barlow," he told the man from the past, "this is Tinny-Peete. He's going to take care of you and help you make lots of money."

The psychist stayed for a cup of the coffee whose preparation had delighted Barlow, and then conducted the real estate man down the corduroy road to his car, leaving the potter to speculate on whether he could at last crack his kilns.

Hawkins, abruptly dismissing Barlow and the Problem, happily picked the chinking from around the door of the number two kiln, prying it open a trifle. A blast of heat and the heady, smoky scent of the reduction fire delighted him. He peered and saw a corner of a shelf glowing cherry-red, becoming obscured by wavering black areas as it lost heat through the opened door. He slipped a charred wood paddle under a mug on the shelf and pulled it out as a sample, the hairs on the back of his hand curling and scorching. The mug crackled and pinged and Hawkins sighed happily.

The bismuth resinate luster had fired to perfection, a haunting film of silvery-black metal with strange bluish lights in it as it turned before the eyes, and the Problem of Population seemed very far away to Hawkins then.

* * * * *

Barlow and Tinny-Peete arrived at the concrete highway where the psychist's car was parked in a safety bay.

"What —a —*boat!*" gasped the man from the past.

"Boat? No, that's my car."

Barlow surveyed it with awe. Swept-back lines, deep-drawn compound curves, kilograms of chrome. He ran his hands futilely over the door-or was it the door? —in a futile search for a handle, and asked respectfully, "How fast does it go?"

The psychist gave him a keen look and said slowly, "Two hundred and fifty. You can tell by the speedometer."

"Wow! My old Chevvy could hit a hundred on a straightaway, but you're out of my class, mister!"

Tinny-Peete somehow got a huge, low door open and Barlow descended three steps into immense cushions, floundering over to the right. He was too fascinated to pay serious attention to his flayed dermis. The dashboard was a lovely wilderness of dials, plugs, indicators, lights, scales and switches.

The psychist climbed down into the driver's seat and did something with his feet. The motor started like lighting a blowtorch as big as a silo. Wallowing around in the cushions, Barlow saw through a rear-view mirror a tremendous exhaust filled with brilliant white sparkles.

"Do you like it?" yelled the psychist.

"It's terrific!" Barlow yelled back. "It's —"

He was shut up as the car pulled out from the bay into the road with a great *voo-ooo-ooom!* A gale roared past Barlow's head, though the windows seemed to be closed; the impression of speed was terrific. He located the speedometer on the dashboard and saw it climb past 90, 100, 150, 200.

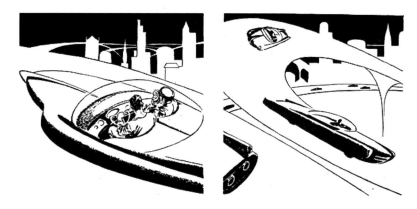

"Fast enough for me," yelled the psychist, noting that Barlow's face fell in response. "Radio?"

He passed over a surprisingly light object like a football helmet, with no trailing wires, and pointed to a row of buttons. Barlow put on the helmet, glad to have the roar of air stilled, and pushed a pushbutton. It lit up satisfyingly and Barlow settled back even farther for a sample of the brave new world's super-modern taste in ingenious entertainment.

"Take It and Stick It!" a voice roared in his ears.

* * * * *

He snatched off the helmet and gave the psychist an injured look. Tinny-Peete grinned and turned a dial associated with the pushbutton layout. The man from the past donned the helmet again and found the voice had lowered to normal.

"The show of shows! The super-show! The super-duper show! The quiz of quizzes! *Take it and stick it!*"

There were shrieks of laughter in the background.

"Here we got the contes-tants all ready to go. You know how we work it. I hand a contes-tant a triangle-shaped cut-out and like that down the line. Now we got these here boards, they got cut-out places the same shape as the triangles and things, only they're all different shapes, and the first contes-tant that sticks the cutouts into the board, he wins.

"Now I'm gonna innaview the first contes-tant. Right here, honey. What's your name?"

"Name? Uh —"

"Hoddaya like that, folks? She don't remember her name! Hah? *Would you buy that for a quarter?*" The question was spoken with arch significance, and the audience shrieked, howled and whistled its appreciation.

It was dull listening when you didn't know the punch lines and catch lines. Barlow pushed another button, with his free hand ready at the volume control.

"—latest from Washington. It's about Senator Hull-Mendoza. He is still attacking the Bureau of Fisheries. The North California Syndicalist says he got affidavits that John Kingsley-Schultz is a bluenose from way back. He didn't publistat the affydavits, but he says they say that Kingsley-Schultz was saw at bluenose meetings in Oregon State College and later at Florida University. Kingsley-Schultz says he gotta confess he did major in fly-casting at Oregon and got his Ph.D. in game-fish at Florida.

"And here is a quote from Kingsley-Schultz: 'Hull-Mendoza don't know what he's talking about. He should drop dead.' Unquote. Hull-Mendoza says he won't publistat the affydavits to pertect his sources. He says they was sworn by three former employes of the Bureau which was fired for in-com-petence and in-com-pat-ibility by Kingsley-Schultz.

"Elsewhere they was the usual run of traffic accidents. A three-way pileup of cars on Route 66 going outta Chicago took twelve lives. The Chicago-Los Angeles morning rocket crashed and exploded in the Mo-have —Mo-javvy —what-ever-you-call-it Desert. All the 94 people aboard got killed. A Civil Aeronautics Authority investigator on the scene says that the pilot was buzzing herds of sheep and didn't pull out in time.

"Hey! Here's a hot one from New York! A Diesel tug run wild in the harbor while the crew was below and shoved in the port bow of the luck-shury liner *S. S. Placentia*. It says the ship filled and sank taking the lives of an es-ti-mated 180 passengers and 50 crew members. Six divers was sent down to study the wreckage, but they died, too, when their suits turned out to be fulla little holes.

"And here is a bulletin I just got from Denver. It seems —"

* * * * *

Barlow took off the headset uncomprehendingly. "He seemed so callous," he yelled at the driver. "I was listening to a newscast —"

Tinny-Peete shook his head and pointed at his ears. The roar of air was deafening. Barlow frowned baffledly and stared out of the window.

A glowing sign said:

Moogs!
Would you buy it
For a quarter?

He didn't know what Moogs was or were; the illustration showed an incredibly proportioned girl, 99.9 per cent naked, writhing passionately in animated full color.

The roadside jingle was still with him, but with a new feature. Radar or something spotted the car and alerted the lines of the jingle. Each in turn sped along a roadside track, even with the car, so it could be read before the next line was alerted.

If there's a girl
You want to get
Deflocculize
Unromantic sweat.
"A*R*M*P*I*T*T*O"

Another animated job, in two panels, the familiar "Before and After." The first said, "Just Any Cigar?" and was illustrated with a two-person domestic tragedy of a wife holding her nose while her coarse and red-faced husband puffed a slimy-looking rope. The second panel glowed, "Or a Vuelta Abajo?" and was illustrated with —

Barlow blushed and looked at his feet until they had passed the sign.

"Coming into Chicago!" bawled Tinny-Peete.

Other cars were showing up, all of them dreamboats.

Watching them, Barlow began to wonder if he knew what a kilometer was, exactly. They seemed to be traveling so slowly, if you ignored the roaring air past your ears and didn't let the speedy lines of the dreamboats fool you. He would have sworn they were really crawling along at twenty-five, with occasional spurts up to thirty. How much was a kilometer, anyway?

The city loomed ahead, and it was just what it ought to be: towering skyscrapers, overhead ramps, landing platforms for helicopters —

He clutched at the cushions. Those two 'copters. They were going to-they were going to-they —

He didn't see what happened because their apparent collision courses took them behind a giant building.

* * * * *

Screamingly sweet blasts of sound surrounded them as they stopped for a red light. "What the hell is going on here?" said Barlow in a shrill, frightened voice, because the braking time was just about zero, he wasn't hurled against the dashboard. "Who's kidding who?"

"Why, what's the matter?" demanded the driver.

The light changed to green and he started the pickup. Barlow stiffened as he realized that the rush of air past his ears began just a brief, unreal split-second before the car was actually moving. He grabbed for the door handle on his side.

The city grew on them slowly: scattered buildings, denser buildings, taller buildings, and a red light ahead. The car rolled to a stop in zero braking time, the rush of air cut off an instant after it stopped, and Barlow was out of the car and running frenziedly down a sidewalk one instant after that.

They'll track me down, he thought, panting. *It's a secret police thing. They'll get you-mind-reading machines, television eyes everywhere, afraid you'll tell their slaves about freedom and stuff. They don't let anybody cross them, like that story I once read.*

Winded, he slowed to a walk and congratulated himself that he had guts enough not to turn around. That was what they always watched for. Walking, he was just another business-suited back among hundreds. He would be safe, he would be safe —

A hand tumbled from a large, coarse, handsome face thrust close to his: "Wassamatta bumpinninna people likeya owna sidewalk gotta miner slamya inna mushya bassar!" It was neither the mad potter nor the mad driver.

"Excuse me," said Barlow. "What did you say?"

"Oh, yeah?" yelled the stranger dangerously, and waited for an answer.

Barlow, with the feeling that he had somehow been suckered into the short end of an intricate land-title deal, heard himself reply belligerently, "Yeah!"

The stranger let go of his shoulder and snarled, "Oh, yeah?"

"Yeah!" said Barlow, yanking his jacket back into shape.

"Aaah!" snarled the stranger, with more contempt and disgust than ferocity. He added an obscenity current in Barlow's time, a standard but physiologically impossible directive, and strutted off hulking his shoulders and balling his fists.

* * * * *

Barlow walked on, trembling. Evidently he had handled it well enough. He stopped at a red light while the long, low dreamboats roared before him and pedestrians in the sidewalk flow with him threaded their ways through the stream of cars. Brakes screamed, fenders clanged and dented, hoarse cries flew back and forth between drivers and walkers. He leaped backward frantically as one car swerved over an arc of sidewalk to miss another.

The signal changed to green, the cars kept on coming for about thirty seconds and then dwindled to an occasional light-runner. Barlow crossed warily and leaned against a vending machine, blowing big breaths.

Look natural, he told himself. *Do something normal. Buy something from the machine.*

He fumbled out some change, got a newspaper for a dime, a handkerchief for a quarter and a candy bar for another quarter.

The faint chocolate smell made him ravenous suddenly. He clawed at the glassy wrapper printed "CRIGGLIES" quite futilely for a few seconds, and then it divided neatly by itself. The bar made three good bites, and he bought two more and gobbled them down.

Thirsty, he drew a carbonated orange drink in another one of the glassy wrappers from the machine for another dime. When he fumbled with it, it divided neatly and spilled all over his knees. Barlow decided he had been there long enough and walked on.

The shop windows were-shop windows. People still wore and bought clothes, still smoked and bought tobacco, still ate and bought food. And they still went to the movies, he saw with pleased surprise as he passed and then returned to a glittering place whose sign said it was THE BIJOU.

The place seemed to be showing a quintuple feature, *Babies Are Terrible*, *Don't Have Children*, and *The Canali Kid*.

It was irresistible; he paid a dollar and went in.

He caught the tail-end of *The Canali Kid* in three-dimensional, full-color, full-scent production. It appeared to be an interplanetary saga winding up with a chase scene and a reconciliation between estranged hero and heroine. *Babies Are Terrible* and *Don't Have Children* were fantastic arguments against parenthood-the grotesquely exaggerated dangers of painfully graphic childbirth, vicious children, old parents beaten and starved by their sadistic offspring. The audience, Barlow astoundedly noted, was placidly champing sweets and showing no particular signs of revulsion.

The *Coming Attractions* drove him into the lobby. The fanfares were shattering, the blazing colors blinding, and the added scents stomach-heaving.

* * * * *

When his eyes again became accustomed to the moderate lighting of the lobby, he groped his way to a bench and opened the newspaper he had bought. It turned out to be *The Racing Sheet*, which afflicted him with a crushing sense of loss. The familiar boxed index in the lower left hand corner of the front page showed almost unbearably that Churchill Downs and Empire City were still in business —

Blinking back tears, he turned to the Past Performances at Churchill. They weren't using abbreviations any more, and the pages because of that were single-column instead of double. But it was all the same-or was it?

He squinted at the first race, a three-quarter-mile maiden claimer for thirteen hundred dollars. Incredibly, the track record was two minutes, ten and three-fifths seconds. Any beetle in his time could have knocked off the three-quarter in one-fifteen. It was the same for the other distances, much worse for route events.

What the hell had happened to everything?

He studied the form of a five-year-old brown mare in the second and couldn't make head or tail of it. She'd won and lost and placed and showed and lost and placed without rhyme or reason. She looked like a front-runner for a couple of races and then she looked like a no-good pig and then she looked like a mudder but the next time it rained she wasn't and then she was a stayer and then she was a pig again. In a good five-thousand-dollar allowances event, too!

Barlow looked at the other entries and it slowly dawned on him that they were all like the five-year-old brown mare. Not a single damned horse running had the slightest trace of class.

Somebody sat down beside him and said, "That's the story."

* * * * *

Barlow whirled to his feet and saw it was Tinny-Peete, his driver.

"I was in doubts about telling you," said the psychist, "but I see you have some growing suspicions of the truth. Please don't get excited. It's all right, I tell you."

"So you've got me," said Barlow.

"*Got* you?"

"Don't pretend. I can put two and two together. You're the secret police. You and the rest of the aristocrats live in luxury on the sweat of these oppressed slaves. You're afraid of me because you have to keep them ignorant."

There was a bellow of bright laughter from the psychist that got them blank looks from other patrons of the lobby. The laughter didn't sound at all sinister.

"Let's get out of here," said Tinny-Peete, still chuckling. "You couldn't possibly have it more wrong." He engaged Barlow's arm and led him to the street. "The actual truth is that the millions of workers live in luxury on the sweat of the handful of aristocrats. I shall probably die before my time of overwork unless —" He gave Barlow a speculative look. "You may be able to help us."

"I know that gag," sneered Barlow. "I made money in my time and to make money you have to get people on your side. Go ahead and shoot me if you want, but you're not going to make a fool out of me."

"You nasty little ingrate!" snapped the psychist, with a kaleidoscopic change of mood. "This damned mess is all your fault and the fault of people like you! Now come along and no more of your nonsense."

He yanked Barlow into an office building lobby and an elevator that, disconcertingly, went *whoosh* loudly as it rose. The real estate man's knees were wobbly as the psychist pushed him from the elevator, down a corridor and into an office.

A hawk-faced man rose from a plain chair as the door closed behind them. After an angry look at Barlow, he asked the psychist, "Was I called from the Pole to inspect this-this —?"

"Unget updandered. I've dee-probed etfind quasichance exhim Poprobattackline," said the psychist soothingly.

"Doubt," grunted the hawk-faced man.

"Try," suggested Tinny-Peete.

"Very well. Mr. Barlow, I understand you and your lamented had no children."

"What of it?"

"This of it. You were a blind, selfish stupid ass to tolerate economic and social conditions which penalized child-bearing by the prudent and foresighted. You made us what we are to-day, and I want you to know that we are far from satisfied. Damn-fool rockets! Damn-fool automobiles! Damn-fool cities with overhead ramps!"

"As far as I can see," said Barlow, "you're running down the best features of time. Are you crazy?"

"The rockets aren't rockets. They're turbo-jets —good turbo-jets, but the fancy shell around them makes for a bad drag. The automobiles have a top speed of one hundred kilometers per hour —a kilometer is, if I recall my paleolinguistics, three-fifths of a mile-and the speedometers are all rigged accordingly so the drivers will think they're going two hundred and fifty. The cities are ridiculous, expensive, unsanitary, wasteful conglomerations of people who'd be better off and more productive if they were spread over the countryside.

"We need the rockets and trick speedometers and cities because, while you and your kind were being prudent and foresighted and not having children, the migrant workers, slum dwellers and tenant farmers were shiftlessly and short-sightedly having children-breeding, breeding. My God, how they bred!"

* * * * *

"Wait a minute," objected Barlow. "There were lots of people in our crowd who had two or three children."

"The attrition of accidents, illness, wars and such took care of that. Your intelligence was bred out. It is gone. Children that should have been born never were. The just-average, they'll-get-along majority took over the population. The average IQ now is 45."

"But that's far in the future —"

"So are you," grunted the hawk-faced man sourly.

"But who are *you* people?"

"Just people-real people. Some generations ago, the geneticists realized at last that nobody was going to pay any attention to what they said, so they abandoned words for deeds. Specifically, they formed and recruited for a closed corporation intended to maintain and improve the breed. We are their descendants, about three million of us. There are five billion of the others, so we are their slaves.

"During the past couple of years I've designed a skyscraper, kept Billings Memorial Hospital here in Chicago running, headed off war with Mexico and directed traffic at LaGuardia Field in New York."

"I don't understand! Why don't you let them go to hell in their own way?"

The man grimaced. "We tried it once for three months. We holed up at the South Pole and waited. They didn't notice it. Some drafting-room people were missing, some chief nurses didn't show up, minor government people on the non-policy level couldn't be located. It didn't seem to matter.

"In a week there was hunger. In two weeks there were famine and plague, in three weeks war and anarchy. We called off the experiment; it took us most of the next generation to get things squared away again."

"But why *didn't* you let them kill each other off?"

"Five billion corpses mean about five hundred million tons of rotting flesh."

Barlow had another idea. "Why don't you sterilize them?"

"Two and one-half billion operations is a lot of operations. Because they breed continuously, the job would never be done."

"I see. Like the marching Chinese!"

"Who the devil are they?"

"It was a —uh-paradox of my time. Somebody figured out that if all the Chinese in the world were to line up four abreast, I think it was, and start marching past a given point, they'd never stop because of the babies that would be born and grow up before they passed the point."

"That's right. Only instead of 'a given point,' make it 'the largest conceivable number of operating rooms that we could build and staff.' There could never be enough."

"Say!" said Barlow. "Those movies about babies-was that your propaganda?"

"It was. It doesn't seem to mean a thing to them. We have abandoned the idea of attempting propaganda contrary to a biological drive."

"So if you work *with* a biological drive —?"

"I know of none which is consistent with inhibition of fertility."

* * * * *

Barlow's face went poker-blank, the result of years of careful discipline. "You don't, huh? You're the great brains and you can't think of any?"

"Why, no," said the psychist innocently. "Can you?"

"That depends. I sold ten thousand acres of Siberian tundra-through a dummy firm, of course-after the partition of Russia. The buyers thought they were getting improved building lots on the outskirts of Kiev. I'd say that was a lot tougher than this job."

"How so?" asked the hawk-faced man.

"Those were normal, suspicious customers and these are morons, born suckers. You just figure out a con they'll fall for; they won't know enough to do any smart checking."

The psychist and the hawk-faced man had also had training; they kept themselves from looking with sudden hope at each other.

"You seem to have something in mind," said the psychist.

Barlow's poker face went blanker still. "Maybe I have. I haven't heard any offer yet."

"There's the satisfaction of knowing that you've prevented Earth's resources from being so plundered," the hawk-faced man pointed out, "that the race will soon become extinct."

"I don't know that," Barlow said bluntly. "All I have is your word."

"If you really have a method, I don't think any price would be too great," the psychist offered.

"Money," said Barlow.

"All you want."

"More than you want," the hawk-faced man corrected.

"Prestige," added Barlow. "Plenty of publicity. My picture and my name in the papers and over TV every day, statues to me, parks and cities and streets and other things named after me. A whole chapter in the history books."

The psychist made a facial sign to the hawk-faced man that meant, "Oh, brother!"

The hawk-faced man signaled back, "Steady, boy!"

"It's not too much to ask," the psychist agreed.

Barlow, sensing a seller's market, said, "Power!"

"Power?" the hawk-faced man repeated puzzledly. "Your own hydro station or nuclear pile?"

"I mean a world dictatorship with me as dictator!"

"Well, now —" said the psychist, but the hawk-faced man interrupted, "It would take a special emergency act of Congress but the situation warrants it. I think that can be guaranteed."

"Could you give us some indication of your plan?" the psychist asked.

"Ever hear of lemmings?"

"No."

"They are-were, I guess, since you haven't heard of them-little animals in Norway, and every few years they'd swarm to the coast and swim out to sea until they drowned. I figure on putting some lemming urge into the population."

"How?"

"I'll save that till I get the right signatures on the deal."

* * * * *

The hawk-faced man said, "I'd like to work with you on it, Barlow. My name's Ryan-Ngana." He put out his hand.

Barlow looked closely at the hand, then at the man's face. "Ryan what?"

"Ngana."

"That sounds like an African name."

"It is. My mother's father was a Watusi."

Barlow didn't take the hand. "I thought you looked pretty dark. I don't want to hurt your feelings, but I don't think I'd be at my best working with you. There must be somebody else just as well qualified, I'm sure."

The psychist made a facial sign to Ryan-Ngana that meant, "Steady *yourself*, boy!"

"Very well," Ryan-Ngana told Barlow. "We'll see what arrangement can be made."

"It's not that I'm prejudiced, you understand. Some of my best friends —"

"Mr. Barlow, don't give it another thought. Anybody who could pick on the lemming analogy is going to be useful to us."

And so he would, thought Ryan-Ngana, alone in the office after Tinny-Peete had taken Barlow up to the helicopter stage. So he would. Poprob had exhausted every rational attempt and the new Poprobattacklines would have to be irrational or sub-rational. This creature from the past with his lemming legends and his improved building lots would be a fountain of precious vicious self-interest.

Ryan-Ngana sighed and stretched. He had to go and run the San Francisco subway. Summoned early from the Pole to study Barlow, he'd left unfinished a nice little theorem. Between interruptions, he was slowly constructing an n-dimensional geometry whose foundations and superstructure owed no debt whatsoever to intuition.

* * * * *

Upstairs, waiting for a helicopter, Barlow was explaining to Tinny-Peete that he had nothing against Negroes, and Tinny-Peete wished he had some of Ryan-Ngana's imperturbability and humor for the ordeal.

The helicopter took them to International Airport where, Tinny-Peete explained, Barlow would leave for the Pole.

The man from the past wasn't sure he'd like a dreary waste of ice and cold.

"It's all right," said the psychist. "A civilized layout. Warm, pleasant. You'll be able to work more efficiently there. All the facts at your fingertips, a good secretary —"

"I'll need a pretty big staff," said Barlow, who had learned from thousands of deals never to take the first offer.

"I meant a private, confidential one," said Tinny-Peete readily, "but you can have as many as you want. You'll naturally have top-primary-top priority if you really have a workable plan."

"Let's not forget this dictatorship angle," said Barlow.

He didn't know that the psychist would just as readily have promised him deification to get him happily on the "rocket" for the Pole. Tinny-Peete had no wish to be torn limb from limb; he knew very well that it would end that way if the population learned from this anachronism that there was a small elite which considered itself head, shoulders, trunk and groin above the rest. The fact that this assumption was perfectly true and the fact that the elite was condemned by its superiority to a life of the most grinding toil would not be considered; the difference would.

The psychist finally put Barlow aboard the "rocket" with some thirty people-real people-headed for the Pole.

* * * * *

Barlow was airsick all the way because of a post-hypnotic suggestion Tinny-Peete had planted in him. One idea was to make him as averse as possible to a return trip, and another idea was to spare the other passengers from his aggressive, talkative company.

Barlow during the first day at the pole was reminded of his first day in the Army. It was the same now-where-the-hell-are-we-going-to-put-*you*? business until he took a firm line with them. Then instead of acting like supply sergeants they acted like hotel clerks.

It was a wonderful, wonderfully calculated buildup, and one that he failed to suspect. After all, in his time a visitor from the past would have been lionized.

At day's end he reclined in a snug underground billet with the 60-mile gales roaring yards overhead, and tried to put two and two together.

It was like old times, he thought-like a coup in real estate where you had the competition by the throat, like a 50-per cent rent boost when you knew damned well there was no place for the tenants to move, like smiling when you read over the breakfast orange juice that the city council had decided to build a school on the ground you had acquired by a deal with the city council. And it was simple. He would just sell tundra building lots to eagerly suicidal lemmings, and that was absolutely all there was to solving the Problem that had these double-domes spinning.

They'd have to work out most of the details, naturally, but what the hell, that was what subordinates were for. He'd need specialists in advertising, engineering, communications-did they know anything about hypnotism? That might be helpful. If not, there'd have to be a lot of bribery done, but he'd make sure-damned sure-there were unlimited funds.

Just selling building lots to lemmings....

He wished, as he fell asleep, that poor Verna could have been in on this. It was his biggest, most stupendous deal. Verna-that sharp shyster Sam Immerman must have swindled her....

* * * * *

It began the next day with people coming to visit him. He knew the approach. They merely wanted to be helpful to their illustrious visitor from the past and would he help fill them in about his era, which unfortunately was somewhat obscure historically, and what did he think could be done about the Problem? He told them he was too old to be roped any more, and they wouldn't get any information out of him until he got a letter of intent from at least the Polar President, and a session of the Polar Congress empowered to make him dictator.

He got the letter and the session. He presented his program, was asked whether his conscience didn't revolt at its callousness, explained succinctly that a deal was a deal and anybody who wasn't smart enough to protect himself didn't deserve protection —"Caveat emptor," he threw in for scholarship, and had to translate it to "Let the buyer beware." He didn't, he stated, give a damn about either the morons or their intelligent slaves; he'd told them his price and that was all he was interested in.

Would they meet it or wouldn't they?

The Polar President offered to resign in his favor, with certain temporary emergency powers that the Polar Congress would vote him if he thought them necessary. Barlow demanded the title of World Dictator, complete control of world finances, salary to be decided by himself, and the publicity campaign and historical writeup to begin at once.

"As for the emergency powers," he added, "they are neither to be temporary nor limited."

Somebody wanted the floor to discuss the matter, with the declared hope that perhaps Barlow would modify his demands.

"You've got the proposition," Barlow said. "I'm not knocking off even ten per cent."

"But what if the Congress refuses, sir?" the President asked.

"Then you can stay up here at the Pole and try to work it out yourselves. I'll get what I want from the morons. A shrewd operator like me doesn't have to compromise; I haven't got a single competitor in this whole cockeyed moronic era."

Congress waived debate and voted by show of hands. Barlow won unanimously.

"You don't know how close you came to losing me," he said in his first official address to the joint Houses. "I'm not the boy to haggle; either I get what I ask or I go elsewhere. The first thing I want is to see designs for a new palace for me-nothing *un*ostentatious, either-and your best painters and sculptors to start working on my portraits and statues. Meanwhile, I'll get my staff together."

He dismissed the Polar President and the Polar Congress, telling them that he'd let them know when the next meeting would be.

A week later, the program started with North America the first target.

Mrs. Garvy was resting after dinner before the ordeal of turning on the dishwasher. The TV, of course, was on and it said: "Oooh!" —long, shuddery and ecstatic, the cue for the *Parfum Assault Criminale* spot commercial. "Girls," said the announcer hoarsely, "do you want your man? It's easy to get him-easy as a trip to Venus."

"Huh?" said Mrs. Garvy.

"Wassamatter?" snorted her husband, starting out of a doze.

"Ja hear that?"

"Wha'?"

"He said 'easy like a trip to Venus.'"

"So?"

"Well, I thought ya couldn't get to Venus. I thought they just had that one rocket thing that crashed on the Moon."

"Aah, women don't keep up with the news," said Garvy righteously, subsiding again.

"Oh," said his wife uncertainly.

And the next day, on *Henry's Other Mistress*, there was a new character who had just breezed in: Buzz Rentshaw, Master Rocket Pilot of the Venus run. On *Henry's Other Mistress*, "the broadcast drama about you and your neighbors, *folksy* people, *ordinary* people, *real* people"! Mrs. Garvy listened with amazement over a cooling cup of coffee as Buzz made hay of her hazy convictions.

Mona: Darling, it's so good to see you again!

Buzz: You don't know how I've missed you on that dreary Venus run.

Sound: *Venetian blind run down, key turned in door lock.*

Mona: Was it *very* dull, dearest?

Buzz: Let's not talk about my humdrum job, darling. Let's talk about us.

Sound: *Creaking bed.*

Well, the program was back to normal at last. That evening Mrs. Garvy tried to ask again whether her husband was sure about those rockets, but he was dozing right through *Take It and Stick It*, so she watched the screen and forgot the puzzle.

She was still rocking with laughter at the gag line, "Would you buy it for a quarter?" when the commercial went on for the detergent powder she always faithfully loaded her dishwasher with on the first of every month.

* * * * *

The announcer displayed mountains of suds from a tiny piece of the stuff and coyly added: "Of course, Cleano don't lay around for you to pick up like the soap root on Venus, but it's pretty cheap and it's almost pretty near just as good. So for us plain folks who ain't lucky enough to live up there on Venus, Cleano is the real cleaning stuff!"

Then the chorus went into their "Cleano-is-the-stuff" jingle, but Mrs. Garvy didn't hear it. She was a stubborn woman, but it occurred to her that she was very sick indeed. She didn't want to worry her husband. The next day she quietly made an appointment with her family freud.

In the waiting room she picked up a fresh new copy of *Readers Pablum* and put it down with a faint palpitation. The lead article, according to the table of contents on the cover, was titled "The Most Memorable Venusian I Ever Met."

"The freud will see you now," said the nurse, and Mrs. Garvy tottered into his office.

His traditional glasses and whiskers were reassuring. She choked out the ritual: "Freud, forgive me, for I have neuroses."

He chanted the antiphonal: "Tut, my dear girl, what seems to be the trouble?"

"I got like a hole in the head," she quavered. "I seem to forget all kinds of things. Things like everybody seems to know and I don't."

"Well, that happens to everybody occasionally, my dear. I suggest a vacation on Venus."

The freud stared, open-mouthed, at the empty chair. His nurse came in and demanded, "Hey, you see how she scrammed? What was the matter with *her*?"

He took off his glasses and whiskers meditatively. "You can search me. I told her she should maybe try a vacation on Venus." A momentary bafflement came into his face and he dug through his desk drawers until he found a copy of the four-color, profusely illustrated journal of his profession. It had come that morning and he had lip-read it, though looking mostly at the pictures. He leafed through to the article *Advantages of the Planet Venus in Rest Cures*.

"It's right there," he said.

The nurse looked. "It sure is," she agreed. "Why shouldn't it be?"

"The trouble with these here neurotics," decided the freud, "is that they all the time got to fight reality. Show in the next twitch."

He put on his glasses and whiskers again and forgot Mrs. Garvy and her strange behavior.

"Freud, forgive me, for I have neuroses."

"Tut, my dear girl, what seems to be the trouble?"

* * * * *

Like many cures of mental disorders, Mrs. Garvy's was achieved largely by self-treatment. She disciplined herself sternly out of the crazy notion that there had been only one rocket ship and that one a failure. She could join without wincing, eventually, in any conversation on the desirability of Venus as a place to retire, on its fabulous floral profusion. Finally she went to Venus.

All her friends were trying to book passage with the Evening Star Travel and Real Estate Corporation, but naturally the demand was crushing. She considered herself lucky to get a seat at last for the two-week summer cruise. The space ship took off from a place called Los Alamos, New Mexico. It looked just like all the spaceships on television and in the picture magazines, but was more comfortable than you would expect.

Mrs. Garvy was delighted with the fifty or so fellow-passengers assembled before takeoff. They were from all over the country and she had a distinct impression that they were on the brainy side. The captain, a tall, hawk-faced, impressive fellow named Ryan-Something or other, welcomed them aboard and trusted that their trip would be a memorable one. He regretted that there would be nothing to see because, "due to the meteorite season," the ports would be dogged down. It was disappointing, yet reassuring that the line was taking no chances.

There was the expected momentary discomfort at takeoff and then two monotonous days of droning travel through space to be whiled away in the lounge at cards or craps. The landing was a routine bump and the voyagers were issued tablets to swallow to immunize them against any minor ailments. When the tablets took effect, the lock was opened and Venus was theirs.

It looked much like a tropical island on Earth, except for a blanket of cloud overhead. But it had a heady, other-worldly quality that was intoxicating and glamorous.

The ten days of the vacation were suffused with a hazy magic. The soap root, as advertised, was free and sudsy. The fruits, mostly tropical varieties transplanted from Earth, were delightful. The simple shelters provided by the travel company were more than adequate for the balmy days and nights.

It was with sincere regret that the voyagers filed again into the ship, and swallowed more tablets doled out to counteract and sterilize any Venus illnesses they might unwittingly communicate to Earth.

* * * * *

Vacationing was one thing. Power politics was another.

At the Pole, a small man was in a soundproof room, his face deathly pale and his body limp in a straight chair.

In the American Senate Chamber, Senator Hull-Mendoza (Synd., N. Cal.) was saying: "Mr. President and gentlemen, I would be remiss in my duty as a legislature if'n I didn't bring to the attention of the au-gust body I see here a perilous situation which is fraught with peril. As is well known to members of this au-gust body, the perfection of space flight has brought with it a situation I can only describe as fraught with peril. Mr. President and gentlemen, now that swift American rockets now traverse the trackless void of space between this planet and our nearest planetarial neighbor in space-and, gentlemen, I refer to Venus, the star of dawn, the brightest jewel in fair Vulcan's diadome-now, I say, I want to inquire what steps are being taken to colonize Venus with a vanguard of patriotic citizens like those minutemen of yore.

"Mr. President and gentlemen! There are in this world nations, envious nations —I do not name Mexico-who by fair means or foul may seek to wrest from Columbia's grasp the torch of freedom of space; nations whose low living standards and innate depravity give them an unfair advantage over the citizens of our fair republic.

"This is my program: I suggest that a city of more than 100,000 population be selected by lot. The citizens of the fortunate city are to be awarded choice lands on Venus free and clear, to have and to hold and convey to their descendants. And the national government shall provide free transportation to Venus for these citizens. And this program shall continue, city by city, until there has been deposited on Venus a sufficient vanguard of citizens to protect our manifest rights in that planet.

"Objections will be raised, for carping critics we have always with us. They will say there isn't enough steel. They will call it a cheap giveaway. I say there *is* enough steel for *one* city's population to be transferred to Venus, and that is all that is needed. For when the time comes for the second city to be transferred, the first, emptied city can be wrecked for the needed steel! And is it a giveaway? Yes! It is the most glorious giveaway in the history of mankind! Mr. President and gentlemen, there is no time to waste-Venus must be American!"

* * * * *

Black-Kupperman, at the Pole, opened his eyes and said feebly, "The style was a little uneven. Do you think anybody'll notice?"

"You did fine, boy; just fine," Barlow reassured him.

Hull-Mendoza's bill became law.

Drafting machines at the South Pole were busy around the clock and the Pittsburgh steel mills spewed millions of plates into the Los Alamos spaceport of the Evening Star Travel and Real Estate Corporation. It was going to be Los Angeles, for logistic reasons, and the three most accomplished psycho-kineticists went to Washington and mingled in the crowd at the drawing to make certain that the Los Angeles capsule slithered into the fingers of the blindfolded Senator.

Los Angeles loved the idea and a forest of spaceships began to blossom in the desert. They weren't very good space ships, but they didn't have to be.

A team at the Pole worked at Barlow's direction on a mail setup. There would have to be letters to and from Venus to keep the slightest taint of suspicion from arising. Luckily Barlow remembered that the problem had been solved once before-by Hitler. Relatives of persons incinerated in the furnaces of Lublin or Majdanek continued to get cheery postal cards.

The Los Angeles flight went off on schedule, under tremendous press, newsreel and television coverage. The world cheered the gallant Angelenos who were setting off on their patriotic voyage to the land of milk and honey. The forest of spaceships thundered up, and up, and out of sight without untoward incident. Billions envied the Angelenos, cramped and on short rations though they were.

Wreckers from San Francisco, whose capsule came up second, moved immediately into the city of the angels for the scrap steel their own flight would require. Senator Hull-Mendoza's constituents could do no less.

The president of Mexico, hypnotically alarmed at this extension of *yanqui imperialismo* beyond the stratosphere, launched his own Venus-colony program.

Across the water it was England versus Ireland, France versus Germany, China versus Russia, India versus Indonesia. Ancient hatreds grew into the flames that were rocket ships assailing the air by hundreds daily.

> Dear Ed, how are you? Sam and I are fine and hope you are fine. Is it nice up there like they say with food and close grone on trees? I drove by Springfield yesterday and it sure looked funny all the buildings down but of coarse it is worth it we have to keep the greasers in their place. Do you have any truble with them on Venus? Drop me a line some time. Your loving sister, Alma.
>
>> Dear Alma, I am fine and hope you are fine. It is a fine place here fine climate and easy living. The doctor told me today that I seem to be ten years younger. He thinks there is something in the air here keeps people young. We do not have much trouble with the greasers here they keep to theirselves it is just a question of us outnumbering them and staking out the best places for the Americans. In South Bay I know a nice little island that I have been saving for you and Sam with lots of blanket trees and ham bushes. Hoping to see you and Sam soon, your loving brother, Ed.

Sam and Alma were on their way shortly.

Poprob got a dividend in every nation after the emigration had passed the halfway mark. The lonesome stay-at-homes were unable to bear the melancholy of a low population density; their conditioning had been to swarms of their kin. After that point it was possible to foist off the crudest stripped-down accommodations on would-be emigrants; they didn't care.

Black-Kupperman did a final job on President Hull-Mendoza, the last job that genius of hypnotics would ever do on any moron, important or otherwise.

Hull-Mendoza, panic-stricken by his presidency over an emptying nation, joined his constituents. The *Independence*, aboard which traveled the national government of America, was the most elaborate of all the spaceships-bigger, more comfortable, with a lounge that was handsome, though cramped, and cloakrooms for Senators and Representatives. It went, however, to the same place as the others and Black-Kupperman killed himself, leaving a note that stated he "couldn't live with my conscience."

The day after the American President departed, Barlow flew into a rage. Across his specially built desk were supposed to flow all Poprob high-level documents and this thing-this outrageous thing-called Poprob*term* apparently had got into the executive stage before he had even had a glimpse of it!

He buzzed for Rogge-Smith, his statistician. Rogge-Smith seemed to be at the bottom of it. Poprobterm seemed to be about first and second and third derivatives, whatever they were. Barlow had a deep distrust of anything more complex than what he called an "average."

While Rogge-Smith was still at the door, Barlow snapped, "What's the meaning of this? Why haven't I been consulted? How far have you people got and why have you been working on something I haven't authorized?"

"Didn't want to bother you, Chief," said Rogge-Smith. "It was really a technical matter, kind of a final cleanup. Want to come and see the work?"

Mollified, Barlow followed his statistician down the corridor.

"You still shouldn't have gone ahead without my okay," he grumbled. "Where the hell would you people have been without me?"

"That's right, Chief. We couldn't have swung it ourselves; our minds just don't work that way. And all that stuff you knew from Hitler-it wouldn't have occurred to us. Like poor Black-Kupperman."

They were in a fair-sized machine shop at the end of a slight upward incline. It was cold. Rogge-Smith pushed a button that started a motor, and a flood of arctic light poured in as the roof parted slowly. It showed a small spaceship with the door open.

* * * * *

Barlow gaped as Rogge-Smith took him by the elbow and his other boys appeared: Swenson-Swenson, the engineer; Tsutsugimushi-Duncan, his propellants man; Kalb-French, advertising.

"In you go, Chief," said Tsutsugimushi-Duncan. "This is Poprobterm."

"But I'm the world Dictator!"

"You bet, Chief. You'll be in history, all right-but this is necessary, I'm afraid."

The door was closed. Acceleration slammed Barlow cruelly to the metal floor. Something broke and warm, wet stuff, salty-tasting, ran from his mouth to his chin. Arctic sunlight through a port suddenly became a fierce lancet stabbing at his eyes; he was out of the atmosphere.

Lying twisted and broken under the acceleration, Barlow realized that some things had not changed, that Jack Ketch was never asked to dinner however many shillings you paid him to do your dirty work, that murder will out, that crime pays only temporarily.

The last thing he learned was that death is the end of pain.

Search the Sky

CHAPTER I.

Decay.

Ross stood on the traders' ramp, overlooking the Yards, and the word kept bobbing to the top of his mind.

Decay.

About all of Halsey's Planet there was the imperceptible reek of decay. The clean, big, bustling, efficient spaceport only made the sensation stronger. From where he stood on the height of the Ramp, he could see the Yards, the spires of Halsey City ten kilometers away-and the tumble-down gray acres of Ghost Town between.

Ross wrinkled his nose. He wasn't a man given to brooding, but the scent of decay had saturated his nostrils that morning. He had tossed and turned all the night, wrestling with a decision. And he had got up early, so early that the only thing that made sense was to walk to work.

And that meant walking through Ghost Town. He hadn't done that in a long time, not since childhood. Ghost Town was a wonderful place to play. "Tag," "Follow My Fuehrer," "Senators and President" —all the ancient games took on new life when you could dodge and turn among crumbling ruins, dart down unmarked lanes, gallop through sagging shacks where you might stir out a screeching, unexpected recluse.

But it was clear that-in the fifteen years between childhood games and a troubled man's walk to work-Ghost Town had grown.

Everybody knew that! Ask the right specialists, and they'd tell you how much and how fast. An acre a year, a street a month, a block a week, the specialists would twinkle at you, convinced that the acre, street, block was under control, since they could measure it.

Ask the right specialists and they would tell you why it was happening. One answer per specialist, with an ironclad guarantee that there would be no overlapping of replies. "A purely psychological phenomenon, Mr. Ross. A vibration of the pendulum toward greater municipal compactness, a huddling, a mature recognition of the facts of interdependence, basically a step forward...."

"A purely biological phenomenon, Mr. Ross. Falling birth rate due to biochemical deficiency of trace elements processed out of our planetary diet. Fortunately the situation has been recognized in time and my bill before the Chamber will provide...."

"A purely technological problem, Mr. Ross. Maintenance of a sprawling city is inevitably less efficient than that of a compact unit. Inevitably there has been a drift back to the central areas and the convenience of air-conditioned walkways, winterized plazas...."

Yes. It was a purely psychological-biological-technological-educational-demographic problem, and it was basically a step forward.

Ross wondered how many Ghost Towns lay corpselike on the surface of Halsey's Planet. Decay, he thought. Decay.

But it had nothing to do with his problem, the problem that had kept him awake all the night, the problem that blighted the view before him now.

The trading bell clanged. The day's work began.

For Ross it might be his last day's work at the Yards.

* * * * *

He walked slowly from the ramp to the offices of the Oldham Trading Corporation. "Morning, Ross boy," his breezy young boss greeted him. Charles Oldham IV's father had always taken a paternal attitude toward his help, and Charles Oldham IV was not going to change anything that Daddy had done. He shook Ross's hand at the door of the suite and apologized because they hadn't been able to find a new secretary for him yet. They'd been looking for two weeks, but the three applicants they had been able to dredge up had all been hopeless. "It's the damn Chamber," said Charles Oldham IV, winsomely gesturing with his hands to show how helpless men of affairs were against the blundering interference of Government. "Damn labor shortage is nothing but a damn artificial scarcity crisis. Daddy saw it; he knew it was coming."

Ross almost told him he was quitting, but held back. Maybe it was because he didn't want to spoil Oldham's day with bad news, right on top of the opening bell. Or maybe it was because, in spite of a sleepless night, he still wasn't quite sure.

The morning's work helped him to become sure. It was the same monotonous grind.

Three freighters had arrived at dawn from Halsey's third moon, but none of them was any affair of his. There was an export shipment of jewelry and watches to be attended to, but the ship was not to take off for another week. It scarcely classified as urgent. Ross worked on the manifests for a couple of hours, stared through his window for an hour, and then it was time for lunch.

Little Marconi hailed him as he passed through the traders' lounge.

Of all the juniors on the Exchange, Marconi was the one Ross found easiest to take. He was lean and dark where Ross was solid and fair; worse, he stood four ranks above Ross in seniority. But, since Ross worked for Oldham, and Marconi worked for Haarland's, the difference could be waived in social intercourse.

Ross suspected that, to Marconi as to him, trading was only a job—a dull one, and not a crusade. And he knew that Marconi's reading was not confined to bills of lading. "Lunch?" asked Marconi. "Sure," Ross said. And he knew he'd probably spill his secret to the little man from Haarland's.

The skyroom was crowded-comparatively. All eight of the usual tables were taken; they pushed on into the roped-off area by the windows and found a table overlooking the Yards. Marconi blew dust off his chair. "Been a long time since this was used," he grumbled. "Drink?" He raised his eyebrows when Ross nodded. It made a break; Marconi was the one usually who had a drink with lunch, Ross never touched it.

When the drinks came, each of them said to the other in perfect synchronism: "I've got something to tell you."

They looked startled-then laughed. "Go ahead," said Ross.

The little man didn't even argue. Rapturously he drew a photo out of his pocket.

God, thought Ross wearily, Lurline again! He studied the picture with a show of interest. "New snap?" he asked brightly. "Lovely girl——" Then he noticed the inscription: *To my fiance, with crates of love.* "Well!" he said, "Fiance, is it? Congratulations, Marconi!"

Marconi was almost drooling on the photo. "Next month," he said happily. "A big, big wedding. For keeps, Ross-for keeps. With children!"

Ross made an expression of polite surprise. "You don't say!" he said.

"It's all down in black and white! She agrees to have two children in the first five years-no permissive clause, a straight guarantee. Fifteen hundred annual allowance per child. And, Ross, do you know what? Her lawyer told her right in front of me that she ought to ask for three thousand, and she told him, 'No, Mr. Turek. I happen to be in love.' How do you like that, Ross?"

"A girl in a million," Ross said feebly. His private thoughts were that Marconi had been gaffed and netted like a sugar perch. Lurline was of the Old Landowners, who didn't own anything much but land these days, and Marconi was an undersized nobody who happened to make a very good living. Sure she happened to be in love. Smartest thing she could be. Of course, promising to have children sounded pretty special; but the papers were full of those things every day. Marconi could reliably be counted on to hang himself. He'd promise her breakfast in bed every third week end, or the maid that he couldn't possibly find on the labor market, and the courts would throw all the promises on both sides out of the contract as a matter of simple equity. But the marriage would stick, all right.

Marconi had himself a final moist, fatuous sigh and returned the photo to his pocket. "And now," he asked brightly, craning his neck for the waiter, "what's your news?"

Ross sipped his drink, staring out at the nuzzling freighters in their hemispherical slips. He said abruptly, "I might be on one of those next week. Fallon's got a purser's berth open."

Marconi forgot the waiter and gaped. "Quitting?"

"I've got to do something!" Ross exploded. His own voice scared him; there was a knife blade of hysteria in the sound of it. He gripped the edge of the table and forced himself to be calm and deliberate.

Marconi said tardily, "Easy, Ross."

"Easy! You've said it, Marconi: 'Easy.' Everything's so damned easy and so damned boring that I'm just about ready to blow! I've got to do something," he repeated. "I'm getting nowhere! I push papers around and then I push them back again. You know what happens next. You get soft and paunchy. You find yourself going by the book instead of by your head. You're covered, if you go by the book-no matter what happens. And you might just as well be dead!"

"Now, Ross — —"

"Now, hell!" Ross flared. "Marconi, I swear I think there's something wrong with me! Look, take Ghost Town for instance. Ever wonder why nobody lives there, except a couple of crazy old hermits?"

"Why, it's Ghost Town," Marconi explained. "It's deserted."

"And why is it deserted? What happened to the people who used to live there?"

Marconi shook his head. "You need a vacation, son," he said sympathetically. "That was a long time ago. Hundreds of years, maybe."

"But where did the people go?" Ross persisted desperately. "All of the city was inhabited hundreds of years ago-the city was twice as big as it is now. How come?"

Marconi shrugged. "Dunno."

Ross collapsed. "Don't know. You don't know, I don't know, nobody knows. Only thing is, I care! I'm curious. Marconi, I get-well, moody. Depressed. I get to worrying about crazy things. Ghost Town, for one. And why can't they find a secretary for me? And am I really different from everybody else or do I just think so-and doesn't that mean that I'm insane?"

He laughed. Marconi said warmly, "Ross, you aren't the only one; don't ever think you are. I went through it myself. Found the answer, too. You wait, Ross."

He paused. Ross said suspiciously, "Yeah?"

Marconi tapped the breast pocket with the photo of Lurline. "She'll come along," he said.

Ross managed not to sneer in his face. "No," he said wearily. "Look, I don't advertise it, but I was married once. I was eighteen, it lasted for a year and I'm the one who walked out. Flat-fee settlement; it took me five years to pay off the loan, but I never regretted it."

Marconi began gravely, "Sexual incompatibility — —"

Ross cut him off with an impatient gesture. "In that department," he said, "it so happens she was a genius. But — —"

"But?"

Ross shrugged. "I must have been crazy," he said shortly. "I kept thinking that she was half-dead, dying on the vine like the rest of Halsey's Planet. And I must still be crazy, because I still think so."

The little man involuntarily felt his breast pocket. He said gently, "Maybe you've been working too hard."

"Too hard!" Ross laughed, a curious blend of true humor and self-disgust. "Well," he admitted, "I need a change, anyhow. I might as well be on a longliner. At least I'd have my spree to look back on."

"No!" Marconi said, so violently that Ross slopped the drink he was lifting to his mouth.

Ross looked hard at the little man-hard and speculatively. "No, then," he said. "It was just a figure of speech, of course. But tell me something, won't you, Marconi?"

"Tell you what?"

"Tell me why such a violent reaction to the word 'longliner.' I want to know."

"Hell, Ross," the little man grumbled, "you know what a longliner is. Gutter-scrapings for crews; nothing for a man like you."

"I want to know more," Ross insisted. "When I ask you what a longliner is, what the crew do with themselves for two or three centuries, you change the subject. You always change the subject! Maybe you know something I don't know. I want to know what it is, and this time the subject doesn't get changed. You don't get off the hook until I find out." He took a sip of his drink and leaned back. "Tell me about longliners," he said. "I've never seen one coming in; it's been fifteen years or so since that bucket from Sirius IV, hasn't it? But you were on the job then."

Marconi was no longer a man in love or one of the few people whom Ross considered to be wholly alive-like him. He was a hard-eyed little stranger with a stubborn mouth and an ingratiating veneer. In short he was again a trader, and a good one.

"I'll tell you anything I know," Marconi declared positively, and insincerely. "Tend to that fellow first though, will you?" He pointed to a uniformed Yards messenger whose eye had just alighted on Ross. The man threaded his way, stumbling, through the tables and laid a sealed envelope down in the puddle left by Ross's drink.

"Sorry, sir," he said crisply, wiped off the envelope with his handkerchief and, for lagniappe, wiped the puddle off the table into Ross's lap.

Speechless, Ross signed for the envelope on a red-tabbed slip marked Urgent * Priority * Rush. The messenger saluted, almost putting his own eye out, and left, crashing into tables and chairs.

"Half-dead," Ross muttered, following him with his eyes. "How the devil do they stay alive at all?"

Marconi said, unsmiling, "You're taking this kick pretty seriously, Ross. I admit he's a little clumsy, but — —"

"But nothing," said Ross. "Don't try to tell me you don't know something's wrong, Marconi! He's a bumbling incompetent, and half his generation is just like him." He looked bitterly at the envelope and dropped it on the table again. "More manifests," he said. "I swear I'll start throwing tableware if I have to check another bill of lading. Brighten my day, Marconi; tell me about the longliners. You're not off the hook yet, you know."

Marconi signaled for another drink. "All right," he said. "Marconi tells all about longliners. They're ships. They go from the planet of one star to the planet of another star. It takes a long time, because stars are many light-years apart and rocket ships cannot travel as fast as light. Einstein said so-whoever he was. Do we start with the Sirius IV ship? I was around when it came in, all right. Fifteen years ago, and Halsey's Planet is still enjoying the benefits of it. And so is Leverett and Sons Trading Corporation. They did fine on flowers from seeds that bucket brought, they did fine on sugar perch from eggs that bucket brought. I've never had it myself. Raw fish for dessert! But some people swear by it-at five shields a portion. They can have it."

"The hook, Marconi," Ross reminded grimly.

Trader Marconi laughed amiably. "Sorry. Well, what else? Pictures and music, but I'm not much on them. I do read, though, and as a reader I say, God bless that bucket from Sirius IV. We never had a novelist like Morris Halliday on this planet-or an essayist like Jay Waring. Let's see, there have been eight Halliday novels off the microfilms so far, and I think Leverett still has a couple in the vaults. Leverett must be — —"

"Marconi. I don't want to hear about Leverett and Sons. Or Morris Halliday, or Waring. I want to hear about longliners."

"I'm trying to tell you," Marconi said sullenly, the mask down.

"No, you're not. You're telling me that the longline ships go from one stellar system to another with merchandise. I know that."

"Then what do you want?"

"Don't be difficult, Marconi. I want to know the facts. All about longliners. The big hush-hush. The candid explanations that explain nothing-except that a starship is a starship. I know that they're closed-system, multigeneration jobs; a group of people get in on Sirius IV and their great-great-great-great-grandchildren come giggling and stumbling out on Halsey's Planet. I know that every couple of generations your firm-and mine, for that matter-builds one with profits that would be taxed off anyway and slings it out, stocked with seeds and film and sound tape and patent designs and manufacturing specifications for every new gimmick on the market, in the hope that it'll be back long after we're dead with a similar cargo to enrich your firm's and my firm's then-current owners. Sounds silly-but, as I say, it's tax money anyhow. I know that your firm and mine staff the ships with half a dozen bums of each sex, who are loaded aboard with a dandy case of delirium tremens, contracted from spending their bounty money the only way they know how. And that's just about all I know. Take it from there, Marconi. And be specific."

The little man shrugged irritably. "That gag's beginning to wear thin, Ross," he complained. "What do you want me to tell you-the number of welds in Bulkhead 47 of 'Starship 74'? What's the difference? As you said, a starship is a starship is a longliner. Without them the inhabited solar systems would have no means of contact or commerce. What else is there to say?"

Ross looked suddenly lost. "I —don't know," he said. "Don't you know, Marconi?"

Marconi hesitated, and for a moment Ross was sure he did know-knew something, at any rate, something that might be an answer to the doubts and nagging inconsistencies that were bothering him. But then Marconi shrugged and looked at his watch and ordered another drink.

But there was something wrong. Ross felt himself in the position of a diagnostician whose patient willfully refuses to tell where it hurts. The planet was sick-but wouldn't admit it. Sick? Dying! Maybe he was on the wrong track entirely. Maybe the starships had nothing to do with it. Maybe there was nothing that Marconi knew that would fit a piece into the puzzle and make the answer come out all clear-but Ghost Town continued to grow acre by acre, year by year. And Oldham still hadn't found him a secretary capable of writing her own name.

"According to the historians, everything fits nicely into place," Ross said, dubiously. "They say we came here ourselves in longliners once, Marconi. Our ancestors under some man named Halsey colonized this place, fourteen hundred years ago. According to the longliners that come in from other stars, their ancestors colonized wherever they came from in starships from a place called Earth. Where is this Earth, Marconi?"

Marconi said succinctly, "Look in the star charts. It's there."

"Yes, but — —"

"But, hell," Marconi said in annoyance. "What in the world has got into you, Ross? Earth is a planet like any other planet. The starship Halsey colonized in was a starship like any other starship-only bigger. I guess, that is —I wasn't there. After all, what are the longliners but colonists? They happen to be going to planets that are already inhabited, that's all. So a starship is nothing new or even very interesting, and this is beginning to bore me, and you ought to read your urgent-priority-rush message."

Ross felt repentant-knowing that that was just how Trader Marconi wanted him to feel. He said slowly, "I'm sorry if I'm being a nuisance, Marconi. You know how it is when you feel stale and restless. I know all the stories-but it's so damned hard to believe them. The famous colonizing ships. They must have been absolutely gigantic to take any reasonable number of people on a closed-circuit, multigeneration ride. We can't build them that big now!"

"No reason to."

"But we couldn't if we had to. Imagine shooting those things all over the Galaxy. How many inhabited planets in the charts-five hundred? A thousand? Think of the technology, Marconi. What became of it?"

"We don't need that sort of technology any more," Marconi explained. "That job is done. Now we concentrate on more important things. Learning to live with each other. Developing our own planet. Increasing our understanding of social factors and demographic — —"

Ross was laughing at last. "Well, Marconi," he said at last, "that takes care of that! We sure have figured out how to handle the social factors, all right. Every year there are fewer of them to handle. Pretty soon we'll all be dead, and then the problem can be marked 'solved.'"

Marconi laughed too-eagerly, as if he'd been waiting for the chance. He said, "Now that that's settled, are you going to open your message? Are you at least going to have some lunch?"

The Yards messenger stumbled up to their table again, this time with an envelope for Marconi. He looked sharply at Ross's unopened envelope and said nothing, pointedly. Ross guiltily picked it up and tore it open. You could act like a sulky child in front of a friend, but strangers didn't understand.

The message was from his office. Radar reports high velocity spacecraft on autocontrols. First approximation trajectory indicates interstellar origin. Probable eta yards 1500. No radio messages received. Don't have to tell you to get on this immediately and give it your best. Oldham.

Ross looked at Marconi, whose expression was perturbed. "Bet I know what your message says," he offered with an uneasy quaver in his voice.

Marconi said: "I'll bet you do. Oldham's radar setup on Sunward always has been better than Haarland's. Better location. Man, you are in trouble! Let's get out there and hope nobody's missed you so far."

They grabbed sandwiches from the snack bar on the way out and munched them while the Yards jeep took them to the ready line. Skirting the freighters in their pits, slipping past the enormous overhaul sheds, they saw excited debates going on. Twice they were passed by Yards vehicles heading toward the landing area. Halfway to the line they heard the recall sirens warning everybody and everything out of the ten seared acres surrounded by homing and Ground-Controlled Approach radars. That was where the big ones were landed.

The ready line was jammed when they got there. Ships from one or another of the five moons that circled Halsey's planet were common; the moons were the mines. Even the weekly liner and freighters from the colony on Sunward, the planet next in from Halsey's, were routine to the Yards workers. But to anybody an interstellar ship was a sensation, a once-or-twice-in-a-lifetime thrill.

Protocols were uncertain. Traders argued about the first crack at the strangers and their goods. A dealer named Aalborg said the only fair system would be to give every trade there an equal opportunity to do business-in alphabetical order. Everybody agreed that under no circumstances should the man from Leverett and Sons be allowed to trade-everybody, except the man from Leverett and Sons. He pointed out that his firm was the logical choice because it had more and fresher experience in handling interstellar goods than any other....

They almost mobbed him.

It wasn't merely money that filled the atmosphere with electric tingles. The glamor of time-travel was on them. The crew aboard that ship were travelers of time as well as space. The crew that had launched the ship was dust. The crew that served it now had never seen a planet.

There was even some humility in the crowd. There were thoughtful ones among them who reflected that it was not, after all, a very great feat to hitch a rocket to a shell and lob it across a few million miles to a neighboring planet. It was eclipsed by the tremendous deed whose climax they were about to witness. The thoughtful ones shrugged and sighed as they thought that even the starship booming down toward Halsey's Planet-fitted with the cleverest air replenishers and the most miraculously efficient waste converters-was only a counter in the game whose great rule was the mass-energy formulation of the legendary Einstein: that there is no way to push a material object past the speed of light.

A report swept the field that left men reeling in its wake. Radar Track confirmed that the ship was of unfamiliar pattern. All hope that it might be a starship launched from this very spot on the last leg of a stupefying round trip was officially dead. The starship was foreign.

"Wonder what they have?" Marconi muttered.

"Trader!" Ross sneered ponderously. He was feeling better; the weight of depression had been lifted for the time being, either by his confession or the electric atmosphere. If every day were like this, he thought vaguely....

"Let's not kid each other," Marconi was saying exuberantly. "This is an event, man! Where are they from, what are they peddling? Do I get a good cut at their wares? It could be fifty thousand shields for me in commission alone. Lurline and I could build a tower house on Great Blue Lake with that kind of money, with a whole floor for her parents! Ross, you just don't know what it is to really be in love. Everything changes."

A jeep roared up and slammed to a stop; Ross blinked and yelled: "Here it comes!"

They watched the ground-controlled approach with the interest of semiprofessionals and concealed their rising excitement with shop talk.

"Whups! There goes the high-power job into action." Marconi pointed as a huge dish antenna swiveled ponderously on its mast. "Seems the medium-output dishes can't handle her."

"Maybe the high-power dish can't either. She might be just plain shot."

"Standard, sealed GCA doesn't get shot, my young friend. Not in a neon-atmosphere tank it doesn't."

"Maybe along about the fifth generation they forgot what it was and cut it open with an acetylene torch to see what was inside."

"Bad luck for us in that case, Ross." The ship steadied on a due-west course and flashed across the heavens and over the horizon.

"Somebody decided a braking ellipse or two was in order. What about line of sight?"

"No sweat. The GCA jockey-and I'd bet it's Delafield himself-pushes a button that hooks him into the high-power dish at every rocket field on Halsey's. It's been all thought out. There's a potential fortune aboard that longliner and Fields Administration wants its percentage for servicing and accommodating."

"Wonder what they have?"

"I already asked that one, Ross."

"So you did."

They lapsed into silence until the rocket boomed in again from the east, high and slow. The big dish swiveled abruptly and began tracking again.

"He'll try to bring her down this time. Yes! There go fore and stabilizing jets."

Flame jutted from the silvery speck high in the blue; its apparent speed slowed to a crawl. It vanished for a second as steering jets turned her slowly endwise. They caught sight of the stern jets when they blasted for the descent.

It was uneventful-just the landing of a very, very big rocket. When a landing is successful it is like every other successful landing ever made.

But the action that the field whirled into immediately following the landing was far from routine. The bullhorns roared that all traders, wipers, rubbernecks, and visitors were to get behind the ready lines and stay there. All Class-Three-and-higher Field personnel were to take stations for longliner clearance. The weapons and decontamination parties were to take their stations immediately. Captain Delafield would issue all future orders and don't let any of the traders talk you out of it, men. Captain Delafield would issue all future orders.

Ross watched in considerable surprise as Field men working with drilled precision broke out half a dozen sleek, needle-nosed guns from an innocent-looking bay of the warehouse and manhandled them into position. From another bay a large pressure tank was hauled and backed against the lock of the starship. Ross could see the station medic bustlingly supervise that, and the hosing of white gunk onto the juncture between tank and ship.

Delafield crossed the stretch from the GCA complex to the tank, vanished into it through a pressure-fitted door and that was that. The tank had no windows.

Ross said to Marconi, wonderingly: "What's all this about? There was Doc Gibbons handling the pressure tank, there was Chunk Blaney rolling out a God-damned cannon I never knew was there-how many more little secrets are there that I don't know about?"

Marconi grinned. "They have gun drill once a month, my young friend, and they never say a word about it. Let the right rabble-rouser get hold of the story and he might sail into office on a platform of 'Keep the bug-eyed monsters off of Halsey's Planet.' You have to have reasonable precautions, military and medical, though-and this is the straight goods-there's never been any trouble of either variety."

The conversation died and there was a long, boring hour of nothing. At last Delafield appeared again. One of the decontamination party ran up in a jeep with a microphone.

"What'll it be?" Ross demanded. "Alphabetic order? Or just a rush?"

The announcement floored him. "Representative of the Haarland Trading Corporation please report to the decontamination tank."

The representative of the Haarland Trading Corporation was Marconi.

"Hell," Ross said bitterly. "Good luck with them, whoever they are."

Marconi brooded for a moment and then said gruffly, "Come on along."

"You mean it?"

"Sure. Uh-naturally, Ross, you'll give me your word not to make any commercial offers or inquiries without my permission."

"Oh. Naturally." They started across the field and were checked through the ready line, Marconi cheerfully presenting his identification and vouching for Ross.

Captain Delafield, at the tank, snapped, "What are you doing here, Ross? You're Oldham's man. I distinctly said — —"

"My responsibility, Captain. Will that do it?" Marconi asked.

Delafield snapped, "It'll be your fundament if Haarland hears about it. Actually it's the damnedest situation-they *asked* for Haarland's."

Marconi looked frightened and his hand involuntarily went to his breast pocket. He swallowed and asked, "Where are they from?"

Delafield grimaced and said, "Home."

Marconi exploded, "Oh, no!"

"That's all I can get out of them. I suppose their trajectory can be analyzed, and there must be books. We haven't been in the ship yet. Nobody goes in until it gets sprayed, rayed, dusted, and busted down into its component parts. Too many places for nasty little mutant bacteria and viruses to lurk."

"Sure, Captain. 'Home,' eh? They're pretty simple?"

"Happy little morons. Fifteen of them, ranging in age from one month to what looks like a hundred and twenty. All they know is 'home' and 'we wish to see the representative of the Haarland Trading Corporation.' First the old woman said it. Then the next in line-he must be about a hundred-said it. Then a pair of identical twins, fifty-year-old women, said it in chorus. Then the rest of them on down to the month-old baby, and I swear to God he tried to say it. Well, you're the Haarland Trading Corporation. Go on in."

CHAPTER II.

They were all naked. Why not? There's no weather in a space ship. All of them laughed when Ross and Marconi came in through the lock except the baby, who was nursing at the breast of a handsome woman. Their laughter was what attracted Ross immediately. Cheerful-no meanness in it. The happy yelping of puppies at play with a red rubber bone.

A stab went through him as the pleasure in their simple happiness turned to recollection and recognition. His wife of a decade ago....Ross studied them with amazement, expecting to find her features in their features, her figure in theirs. And failed. Yet they reminded him inescapably of his miserable year with that half-a-woman, but they were physically no kin of hers. They were just cheerful laughers who he knew were less than human.

The cheerful laughers exposed unblemished teeth in all their mouths, including that of the hundred-and-twenty-year-old matriarch. Why not? If you put calcium and fluorides into a closed system, they stay there.

The old woman stopped laughing at them long enough to say to Marconi, "We wish to see the representative of the Haarland — —"

"Yes, I know. I'm the representative of the Haarland Trading Corporation. Welcome to Halsey's Planet. May I ask what your name is, ma'am?"

"Ma," she said genially.

"Pleased to meet you, Ma. My name's Marconi."

Ma said, bewildered, "You just said you were the representative of the Haarland Trading — —"

"Yes, Ma, but that's all right. Let's say that's my other name. Two names-understand?"

She laughed at the idea of two names, wonderingly.

Marconi pressed, "And what's the name of this gentleman?"

"He isn't Gentleman. He's Sonny."

Sonny was a hundred years old.

"Pleased to meet you, Sonny. And your name, sir?"

"Sonny," said a redheaded man of eighty or thereabouts.

The identical-twin women were named The Kids. The baby was named Him. The rest of the troop were named Girl, Ma, or Sonny. After introductions Ross noticed that Him had been passed to another Ma who was placidly suckling him. She had milk; it dribbled from the corner of the baby's mouth. "There isn't another baby left in the ship, is there?" Ross asked in alarm.

They laughed and the Ma suckling the baby said: "There was, but she died. Mostly they do when you put them into the box after they get born. Ma here was lucky. Her Him didn't die."

"Put them in the box? What box? Why?"

Marconi was nudging him fiercely in the ribs. He ignored it.

They laughed amiably at his ignorance and explained that the box was the box, and that you put your newborn babies into it because you put your newborn babies into it.

A beep tone sounded from the ship.

Ma said, "We have to go back now, The Representative of the Haarland Trading Corporation Marconi."

"What for?"

Ma said, "At regular intervals signaled by a tone of six hundred cycles and an intermittent downward shifting of the ship lights from standard illumination frequency to a signal frequency of 420 millimicrons, ship's operating personnel take up positions at the control boards for recalibration of ship-working meters and instruments against the battery of standard masters. We'll be right back."

They trooped through the hatch, leaving Ross and Marconi staring at each other in the decontamination tank.

"Well," Ross said slowly, "at last I know why the Longliner Departments have their little secrets. 'The box.' I say it's murder."

"Be reasonable," Marconi told him-but his own face was white under the glaring germicidal lamps. "You can't let them increase without limit or they'd all die. And before they died there'd be cannibalism. Which do you prefer?"

"Letting kids be born and then snuffing them out if a computer decides they're the wrong sex or over the quota is inhuman."

"I didn't say I like it, Ross. But it works."

"So do pills!"

"Pills are a private matter. A person might privately decide not to take hers. The box is a public matter and the group outnumbers and overrules a mother who decides not to use it. There's your question of effectiveness answered, but there's another point. Those people are sane, Ross. Preposterously naive, but sane! Saner than childless women or sour old bachelors we both know who never had to love anything small and helpless, and so come to love nobody but themselves. They're sane. Partly because the women get a periodic biochemical shakeup called pregnancy that their biochemical balance is designed to mesh with. Partly because the men find tenderness and protectiveness in themselves toward the pregnant women. Mostly, I think, because-it's something to do.

"Can you imagine the awful monotony of life in the ship? The work is sheer rote and repetition. They can't read or watch screentapes. They were born in the ship, and the books and screentapes are meaningless because they know nothing to compare them with. The only change they see is each other, aging toward death. Frequent pregnancies are a Godsend to them. They compare and discuss them; they wonder who the fathers are; they make bets of rations; the men brag and keep score. The girls look forward to their first and their last. The jokes they make up about them! The way they speculate about twins! The purgative fear, even, keeps them sane."

"And then," Ross said, "'the box.'"

Staring straight ahead at the ship's port Marconi echoed: "Yes. 'The box.' If there were another way-but there isn't."

* * * * *

His breezy young boss, Charles Oldham IV, was not pleased with what Ross had to report.

"Asked for Haarland!" he repeated unbelievingly. "Those dummies didn't know where they were going or where they were from, but they knew enough to ask for Haarland." He slammed a ruler on his desk and yelled: "God-damn it!"

"Mr. Oldham!" Ross protested, aghast. For a superior to lose his temper publicly was unthinkable; it covered you with embarrassment.

"Manners be God-damned too!" Oldham screamed, breaking up fast. "What do you know about the state of our books? What do you know about the overhead I inherited from my loving father? What the hell do you know about the downcurve in sales?"

"These fluctuations — —" Ross began soothingly.

"Fluctuations be God-damned! I know a fluctuation when I see one, and I know a long-term downtrend when I see one. And that's what we're riding, right into bankruptcy, fellow. And now these God-damned dummies blow in from nowhere with a consignment exclusively for Haarland —I don't know why I don't get to hell out of this stupid business and go live in a shack on Great Blue Lake and let the planet go ahead and rot."

Ross's horror at the unseemly outburst was eclipsed by his interest at noting how similarly he and Oldham had been thinking. "Sir," he ventured, "I've had something on my mind for a while — —"

"It can wait," Oldham growled, collecting himself with a visible effort. So there went his chance to resign. "What about customs? I know Haarland hasn't got enough cash to lay out. Who has?"

Ross said glibly: "Usual arrangement, sir. They turn an estimated twenty-five per cent of the cargo over to the port authority for auction, the receipts to be in full discharge of their import tax. And I suppose they enter protective bids. They aren't wasting any time-auction's 2100 tonight."

"You handle it," Oldham muttered. "Don't go over one hundred thousand shields. Diversify the purchases as much as possible. And try to sneak some advance information out of the dummies if you get a chance."

"Yes, sir," Ross said. As he left he saw Oldham taking a plastic bottle from a wall cabinet.

And that, thought Ross as he rode to the Free Port, was the first crack he had ever seen in the determined optimism of the trading firm's top level. They were optimists and they were idealists, at least to hear them tell it. Interplanetary trading was a cause and a mission; the traders kept the flame of commerce alight. Perhaps, thought Ross, they had been able to indulge in the hypocrisy of idealism only so long as a population upcurve assured them of an expanding market. Perhaps now that births were flattening out-some said the dirty word "declining" —they all would drop their optimistic creed in favor of fang-and-claw competition for the favors of the dwindling pool of consumers.

And that, Ross thought gloomily, was the way he'd go himself if he stayed on: junior trader, to senior trader, to master trader, growing every year more paranoidally suspicious of his peers, less scrupulous in the chase of the shield....

But he was getting out, of course. The purser's berth awaited. And then, perhaps, the awful depressions he had been enduring would lift off him. He thought of the master traders he knew: his own man Oldham, none too happy in the hereditary business; Leverett, still smug and fat with his terrific windfall of the Sirius IV starship fifteen years ago; Marconi's boss Haarland-Haarland broke the sequence all to hell. It just wasn't possible to think of Haarland being driven by avarice and fear. He was the oldest of them all, but there was more zest and drive in his parchment body than in the rest of them combined.

In the auction hall Ross found a seat near the velvet ropes. One of the professional bidders lounging against a wall flicked him an almost imperceptible signal, and he answered with another. That was that; he had his man, and a good one. They had often worked together in the commodity pits, but not so often or so exclusively that the bidder would be instantly known as his.

Inside the enclosure Marconi, seated at a bare table, labored over a sheaf of papers with one of the "Sonnies" from the ship. Sonny was wriggling in coveralls, the first clothes he had ever worn. Ross saw they hadn't been able to get shoes onto him.

Who else did he know? Captain Delafield was sitting somberly within the enclosure; Win Fraley, the hottest auctioneer on the Port, was studying a list, his lips moving. Every trading firm was represented; the heads of the smaller firms were there in person, not daring to delegate the bidding job. Plenty of Port personnel, just there for the excitement of the first longliner in fifteen years, even though it was well after close of the business day.

The goods were in sealed cases against the back wall as usual. Ross could only tell that some of them were perforated and therefore ought to contain living animals. Only the one Sonny from the starship crew was there; presumably the rest were back on the ship. He wouldn't be able to follow Oldham's orders to snoop out the nature of the freight from them. Well, damn Oldham; damn even the auction, Ross thought to himself. His mood of gloom did not lift.

The auction was a kind of letdown. All that turmoil and bustle, concentrated in a tiny arc around the velvet ropes, contrasted unpleasantly with the long, vacant rows of dusty seats that stretched to the back of the hall. Maybe a couple of centuries ago Ross would have enjoyed the auction more. But now all it made him think of was the thing he had been brooding about for a night and a day, the slow emptying of the planet, the....

Decay.

But, as usual, no one else seemed to notice or to care.

Captain Delafield consulted his watch and stood up. He rapped the table. "In accordance with the rules of the Trade Commission and the appropriate governing statutes," he droned, "certain merchandise will now be placed on public auction. The Haarland Trading Corporation, consignee, agrees and consents to divest itself of merchandise from Consignment 97-W amounting by estimate of the customs authorities to twenty-five per cent of the total value of all merchandise in said consignment. All receipts of this auction are to be entered as excise duties paid by the consignee on said merchandise, said receipts to constitute payment in full on excise on Consignment 97-W. The clerk will record; if any person here present wishes to enter an objection let him do so thank you." He glanced at a slip of paper in his hand. "I am requested to inform you that the Haarland Trading Corporation has entered with the clerk a protective bid of five thousand shields on each item." There was a rustle in the hall. Five thousand shields was a lot of money. "Your auctioneer, Win Fraley," said Captain Delafield, and sat down in the first row of seats.

The auctioneer took a long, slow swallow of water, his eyes gleaming above the glass at the audience. Theatrically he tossed the glass to an assistant, smacked his hands together and grinned. "Well," he boomed genially, "I don't have to tell you gentlemen that somebody's going to get rich tonight. Who knows-maybe it'll be you? But you can't make money without spending money, so without any further ado, let's get started. I have here," he rapped out briskly, "Item Number One. Now you don't know and I don't know exactly what Item Number One contains, but I can tell you this, they wouldn't have sent it two hundred and thirty-one lights if they didn't think it was worth something. Let's get this started with a rush, folks, and I mean with a big bid to get in the right mood. After all, the more you spend here the less you have to pay in taxes," he laughed. "You ready? Here's the dope. Item Number One — —" His assistant slapped a carton at the extreme left of the line. " — —weight two hundred and fifteen grams, net; fifteen cubic centimeters; one microfilm reel included. Reminds me," he reminisced, "of an item just about that size on the Sirius IV shipment. Turned out to be Maryjane seeds, and I don't suppose I have to tell anybody here how much Mr. Leverett made out of Maryjanes; I bet every one of us has been smoking them ever since. What do you say, Mr. Leverett? You did all right last time-want to say ten thousand as a first big bid on Item Number One? Nine thousand? Do I hear — —?"

One of the smaller traders, not working through a professional bidder, not even decently delegating the work to a junior, bid seventy-five hundred shields. Like the spokesmen for the other big traders, Ross sat on his hands during the early stages. Let the small fry give themselves a thrill and drop out. The big firms knew to a fraction of a shield how much the small ones could afford to bid on a blind purchase, and the easiest way to handle them was to let them spend their budgets in a hurry. Of course the small traders knew all this, and their strategy, when they could manage it, was to hold back as long as possible. It was a matter of sensing emotion rather than counting costs; of recognizing the fraction of a second in which a little fellow made up his mind to acquire an item and bidding him up-of knowing when he'd gone his limit and letting him have it at a ruinous price. It was an art, and Ross, despising it, knew that he did it very, very well.

He yawned and pretended to read a magazine while the first six items went on the block; the little traders seemed desperate enough to force the price up without help. He bid on Item Seven partly to squeeze a runt trader and partly to test his liaison with his professional bidder. It was perfect; the pro caught his signal —a bored inspection of his fingernails-while seeming to peek clumsily at the man from Leverett's.

Ross let the next two pass and then acquired three items in rapid succession. The fever had spread to most of the bidders by then; they were starting at ten thousand and up. One or two of the early birds had spent their budgets and were leaving, looking sandbagged-as indeed they had been. Ross signaled "take five" to his professional and strolled out for a cup of coffee.

On the way back he stopped for a moment outside the hall to look at the stars and breathe. There were the familiar constellations-The Plowman, the Rocket Fleet, Marilyn Monroe. He stood smoking a cigarette and yearning toward them until somebody moved in the darkness near him. "Nice night, Ross," the man said gloomily.

It was Captain Delafield. "Oh, hello, sir," Ross said, the world descending around him again like a too-substantial curtain. "Taking a breather?"

"Had to," the captain growled. "Ten more minutes in that place and I would have thrown. Damned money-grabbing traders. No offense, Ross; just that I don't see how you stand the life. Seems to have got worse in my time. Much worse. You high-rollers goading the pee-wees into shooting their wads-it didn't use to be like that. Gallantry. Not stomping a downed man. I don't see how you stand it."

"I can't stand it," Ross said quietly. "Captain Delafield, you don't know —I'm so sick to death of the life I'm leading and the work I'm doing that I'd do anything to get away. Mr. Fallon offered me a purser's spot on his ship; I've been thinking about it very seriously."

"Purser? A dirty job. There's nothing to do except when you're in port, and then there's so much to do that you never get to see the planet. I don't recommend it, Ross."

Ross grunted, thinking. If even the purser's berth was no way out, what was left for him? Sixty more years of waiting for a starship and scheming how to make a profit from its contents? Sixty more years watching Ghost Town grow by nibbles on Halsey City, watching the traders wax in savagery as they battled for the ever-diminishing pool of consumers, watching obscene comedies like Lurline of the Old Landowners graciously consenting to wed Marconi of the New Nobodies? He said wearily: "Then what shall I do, Captain? Rot here with the rest of the planet?"

Delafield shrugged, suprisingly gentle. "You feel it too, Ross? I'm glad to hear it. I'm not sensitive, thank God, but I know they talk about me. They say I quit the space-going fleet as soon as I had a chance to grab off the port captaincy. They're right; I did. Because I was frightened."

"Frightened? You?" Delafield's ribbons for a dozen heroic rescues gleamed in the light that escaped from the hall.

"Sure, Ross." He flicked the ribbons. "Each one of these means I and my men pulled some people out of a jam they got into because of somebody's damned stupidity or slow reflexes or defective memory. No; I withdraw that. The 'Thetis' got stove in because of mechanical failure, but all the rest were human error. There got to be too many for me; I want to enjoy my old age.

"Ready to face that if you become a purser? I can tell you that if you don't like it here you won't be happy on Sunward and you won't like the moons. And you most especially and particularly won't like being a purser. It's the same job you're doing now, but it pays less, offers you a six-by-eight cubicle to work and live in, and gives you nothing resembling a future to aim at. Now if you'll excuse me I'd better get back inside. I've enjoyed our talk."

Ross followed the captain gloomily. Nothing had changed inside; Ross lounged in the door-way inconspicuously picking up the eye of his bidder. Marconi was gone from the enclosure. Ross looked around hopefully and found his friend in agitated conversation with an unrecognizable but also agitated man at the back of the hall. Ross drifted over. Heads were turning in the front rows. As Ross got within range he heard a couple of phrases. " — —in the ship. Mr. Haarland specially asked for you. Please, Mr. Marconi!"

"Oh, hell," Marconi said disgustedly. "Go on. Tell him I'll be there. But how he expects me to take care of things here and — —" He trailed off as he caught sight of Ross.

"Trouble?" Ross asked.

"Not exactly. The hell with it." Marconi stared indecisively at the auctioneer for a moment. He said obscurely, "Taking your life isn't enough; he wants more. And I thought I'd be able to see Lurline tonight. Excuse me, Ross. I've got to get over to the ship." He hurried out.

Ross looked wonderingly after him, caught the eye of his bidder, and went back to work. By the time the auction was over and dawn was breaking in the west, Oldham Trading had bought nine lots of merchandise: three breathing, five flowering, and one a roll of microfilm. Ross took his prizes to the office where Charles Oldham was waiting, much the better for a few drinks and a long nap.

"How much?" demanded Oldham. Evidently they were both supposed to ignore his hysteria of the night before.

"Fifty-seven thousand," Ross said dully.

"For nine lots? Good man! With any kind of luck at all — —" And Oldham babbled on and on. He wanted Ross to stay and view the microfilm projection, stand by for a report from a zoologist and a botanist on the living acquisitions. He pleaded weariness and Oldham became conciliatory to the wonderful young up-and-comer who had bid in the merchandise at a whopping bargain price.

Ross dragged himself from the building, into a cab, and home. Morosely undressing he lit a cigarette and brooded: well, that was it. What you'd been waiting for since you were a junior apprentice. The starship came, you had the alien prizes in your hands and you realized they were as tawdry as the cheap gimcracks you export every week to Sunward.

He stared out the window, over Ghost Town, to the Field. The sun was high over the surrounding mountains; he imagined he could pick out the reflected glimmer from the starship a dozen miles away. Marconi at least got to examine the ship. Marconi might be there now; he'd been headed that way when Ross saw him last. And evidently not enjoying it much. Ross wondered vaguely if anybody really enjoyed anything. He stubbed out his cigarette.

As he fell asleep he was remembering what Delafield had told him about the moons and the planet ports. His dreams were of the cities of other planets, and every one of them was populated by aloof Delafields and avaricious Oldhams.

CHAPTER III.

"Wake up, Ross," Marconi was saying, joggling him. "Come on, wake up."

Ross thrust himself up on an elbow and opened his eyes. He said with a tongue the size of his forearm in a dust-lined mouth: "Wha' time is it? Wha' the hell are you doing here, for that matter?"

"It's around noon. You've slept for three hours; you can get up."

"Uh." Ross automatically reached for a cigarette. The smoke got in his eyes and he rubbed them; it dehydrated and seared what little healthy tissue appeared to be left in his mouth. But it woke him up a little. "What are you doing here?" he demanded.

Marconi's hand was involuntarily on his breast pocket again, the one in which he carried Lurline's picture. He said harshly: "You want a job? Topside? Better than purser?" He wasn't meeting Ross's eye. His gaze roved around the apartment and lighted on a coffee maker. He filled it and snapped it on. "Get dressed, will you?" he demanded.

Ross sat up. "What's this all about, Marconi? What do you want, anyway?"

Marconi, for his own reasons, became violently angry. "You're the damnedest question-asker I ever did meet, Ross. I'm trying to do you a favor."

"What favor?" Ross asked suspiciously.

"You'll find out. You've been bellyaching to me long enough about how dull your poor little life is. Well, I'm offering you a chance to do something big and different. And what do you do? You crawfish. Are you interested or aren't you? I told you: It's a space job, and a big one. Bigger than being a purser for Fallon. Bigger than you can imagine."

Ross began to struggle into his clothes, no more than half comprehending, but stimulated by the magic words. He asked, puzzling sleepily over what Marconi had said, "What are you sore about?" His guess was that Lurline had broken a date-but it seemed to be the wrong time of day for that.

"Nothing," Marconi said grumpily. "Only I have my own life to live." He poured two cups of coffee. He wouldn't answer questions while they sipped the scalding stuff. But somehow Ross was not surprised when, downstairs, Marconi headed his car along the winding road through Ghost Town that led to the Yards.

Every muscle of Ross's body was stiff and creaky; another six hours of sleep would have been a wonderful thing. But as they drove through the rutted streets of Ghost Town he began to feel alive again. He stared out the window at the flashing ruins, piecing together the things Marconi had said.

"Watch it!" he yelled, and Marconi swerved the car around a tumbled wall. Ross was shaking, but Marconi only drove faster. This was crazy! You didn't race through Ghost Town as though you were on the pleasure parkways around the Great Blue Lake; it wasn't safe. The buildings had to fall over from time to time-nobody, certainly, bothered to keep them in repair. And nobody bothered to pick up the pieces when they fell, either, until the infrequent road-mending teams made their rounds.

But at last they were out of Ghost Town, on the broad highway from Halsey City to the port. The administration building and car park was just ahead.

It was there that Marconi spoke again. "I'm assuming, Ross, that you weren't snowing me when you said you wanted thrills, chills, and change galore."

"That's not the way I put it. But I wasn't snowing you."

"You'll get them. Come on."

He led Ross across the field to the longliner, past a gaggle of laughing, chattering Sonnies and Mas. He ignored them.

The longliner was a giant of a ship, a blunt torpedo a hundred meters tall. It had no ports-naturally enough; the designers of the ship certainly didn't find any reason for its idiot crew to look out into space, and landings and takeoffs would be remote-controlled. Two hundred years old it was; but its metal was as bright, its edges as sharp, as the newest of the moon freighters at the other end of the hardstand. Two hundred years—a long trip, but an almost unimaginably long distance that trip covered. For the star that spawned it was undoubtedly almost as far away as light would travel in two centuries' time. At 186,000 miles per second, sixty seconds in a minute, sixty minutes in an hour. Ross's imagination gave up the task. It was far.

He stared about him in fascination as they entered the ship. He gaped at sterile, gray-walled cubicles, each of which contained the same chair and cot-no screen or projector for longliners. Ross remembered his rash words of the day before about shipping out on a longliner, and shuddered.

"Here we are," said Marconi stopping before a closed door. He knocked and entered.

It was a cubicle like the others, but there were reels stacked on the floor and a projector. Sitting on the cot in a just-awakened attitude was old man Haarland himself. Beady-eyed, Ross thought. Watchful.

Haarland asked: "Ross?"

"Yes, sir," Marconi said. There was tension in his voice and attitude. "Do you want me to stay, sir?"

Haarland growled: "Good God, no. You can get out. Sit down, Ross."

Ross sat down. Marconi, carefully looking neither to right or left, went out and closed the door. Haarland stretched, scratched, and yawned. He said: "Ross, Marconi tells me you're quite a fellow. Sincere, competent, a good man to give a tough job to. Namely, his."

"Junior-Fourth Trader?" Ross asked, bewildered.

"A little more dramatic than that-but we'll come to the details in a minute. I'm told you were ready to quit Oldham for a purser's berth. That's ethical. Would you consider it unethical to quit Oldham for Haarland?"

"Yes—I think I would."

"Glad to hear it! What if the work had absolutely nothing to do with trading and never brings you into a competitive situation with Oldham?"

"Well——" Ross scratched his jaw. "Well, I think that would be all right. But a Junior Fourth's job, Mr. Haarland——" The floor bucked and surged under him. He gasped, "What was that?"

"Blastoff, I imagine," Haarland said calmly. "We're taking off. Better lie down."

Ross flopped to the floor. It was no time to argue, not with the first-stage pumps thundering and the preheaters roaring their threat of an imminent four-G thrust.

It came like thunder, slapping Ross against the floor plates as though he were glued to them. He felt every tiny wrinkle in every weld he lay on, and one arm had fallen across a film reel. He heaved, and succeeded in levering it off the reel. It thwacked to the floor as though sandbags were stacked meters-high atop it.

Blackout came very soon.

He awoke in free fall. He was orbiting aimlessly about the cubicle.

Haarland was strapped to the cot, absorbed in manipulating the portable projector, trying to thread a free-floating film. Ross bumped against the old man; Haarland abstractedly shoved him off.

He careened from a bulkhead and flailed for a grip.

"Oh," said Haarland, looking up. "Awake?"

"Yes, awake!" Ross said bitterly. "What is all this? Where are we?"

The old man said formally, "Please forgive my cavalier treatment of you. You must not blame your friend Marconi; he had no idea that I was planning an immediate blastoff with you. I had an assignment for him which he-he preferred not to accept. Not to mince words, Ross, he quit."

"Quit his job?"

The old man shook his head. "No, Ross. Quit much more than the job of working for me. He quit on an assignment which is—I am sorry if it sounds melodramatic-absolutely vital to the human race." He suddenly frowned. "I—I think," he added weakly. "Bear with me, Ross. I'll try to explain as I go along. But, you see, Marconi left me in the lurch. I needed him and he failed me. He felt that you would be glad to take it on, and he told me something about you." Haarland glowered at Ross and said, with a touch of bitterness, "A recommendation from Marconi, at this particular point, is hardly any recommendation at all. But I haven't much choice-and, besides, I took the liberty of calling that pompous young fool you work for."

"Mister Haarland!" Ross cried, outraged. "Oldham may not be any prize but really — —"

"Oh, you know he's a fool. But he had a lot to say about you. Enough so that, if you want the assignment, it's yours. As to the nature of the assignment itself — —" Haarland hesitated, then said briskly, "The assignment itself has to do with a message my organization received via this longliner. Yes, a message. You'll see. It has also to do with certain facts I've found in its log which, if I can ever get this damned thing working — —There we are."

He had succeeded in threading the film.

He snapped on the projector. On the screen appeared a densely packed block of numerals, rolling up and being replaced by new lines as fast as the eye could take them in. Haarland said, "Notice anything?"

Ross swallowed. "If that stuff is supposed to mean anything to me," he declared, "it doesn't."

Haarland frowned. "But Marconi said — —Well, never mind." He snapped off the projector. "That was the ship's log, Ross. It doesn't matter if you can't read it; you wouldn't, I suppose, have had much call for that sort of thing working for Oldham. It is a mathematical description of the routing of this ship, from the time it was space-launched until it arrived here yesterday. It took a long time, Ross. The reason that it took a long time is partly that it came from far away. But, even more, there is another reason. We were not this ship's destination! Not the original destination. We weren't even the first alternate-or the second alternate. To be exact, Ross, we were the seventh choice for this ship."

Ross let go of his stanchion, floated a yard, and flailed back to it. "That's ridiculous, Mr. Haarland," he protested. "Besides, what has all this to do with — —"

"Bear with an old man," said Haarland, with an amused gleam in his eye.

There was very little he could do but bear with him, Ross thought sourly. "Go on," he said.

Haarland said professorially, "It is conceivable, of course, that a planet might be asleep at the switch. We could believe it, I suppose, if it seemed that the first-choice planet somehow didn't pick the ship up when this longliner came into radar range. In that event, of course, it would orbit once or twice on automatics, and then select for its first alternate target-which it did. It might be a human failure in the GCA station-once." He nodded earnestly. "Once, Ross. Not six times. No planet passes up a trading ship."

"Mr. Haarland," Ross exploded, "it seems to me that you're contradicting yourself all over the place. Did six planets pass this ship up or didn't six planets pass this ship up? Which is it? And why would anybody pass a longliner up anyhow?"

Haarland asked, "Suppose the planets were vacant?"

"What?" Ross was shaken. "But that's silly! I mean, even I know that the star charts show which planets are inhabited and which aren't."

"And suppose the star charts are wrong. Suppose the planets have become vacant. The people have died off, perhaps; their culture decayed."

Decay. Death and decay.

Ross was silent for a long time. He took a deep breath. He said at last, "Sorry. I won't interrupt again."

Haarland's expression was a weft of triumph and relief. "Six planets passed this ship up. Remember Leverett's ship fifteen years ago? Three planets passed that one before it came to us. Nine different planets, all listed on the traditional star charts as inhabited, civilized, equipped with GCA radars, and everything else needed. Nine planets out of communication, Ross."

Decay, thought Ross. Aloud he said, "Tell me why."

Haarland shook his head. "No," he said strongly, "I want you to tell me. I'll tell you what I can. I'll tell you the message that this ship brought to me. I'll tell you all I know, all I've told Marconi that he isn't man enough to use, and the things that Marconi will never learn,

64

as well. But why nine planets that used to be pretty much like our own planet are now out of communication, that you'll have to tell me."

Forward rockets boomed; the braking blasts hurled Ross against the forward bulkhead. Haarland rummaged under the cot for space suits. He flung one at Ross.

"Put it on," he ordered. "Come to the airlock. I'll show you what you can use to find out the answers." He slid into the pressure suit, dived weightless down the corridor, Ross zooming after.

They stood in the airlock, helmets sealed. Wordlessly Haarland opened the pet cocks, heaved on the lock door. He gestured with an arm.

Floating alongside them was a ship, a ship like none Ross had ever seen before.

CHAPTER IV.

Picture Leif's longboat bobbing in the swells outside Ambrose Light, while the twentieth-century liners steam past; a tiny, ancient thing, related to the new giants only as the Eohippus resembles the horse.

The ship that Haarland revealed was fully as great a contrast. Ross knew spaceships as well as any grounder could, both the lumbering interplanet freighters and the titanic longliners. But the ship that swung around Halsey's Planet was a midget (fueled rocket ships must be huge); its jets were absurdly tiny, clearly incapable of blasting away from planetary gravity; its entire hull length was unbroken and sheer (did the pilot dare fly blind?).

The coupling connections were being rigged between the ships. "Come aboard," said Haarland, spryly wriggling through the passage. Ross, swallowing his astonishment, followed.

The ship was tiny indeed. When Ross and Haarland, clutching handholds, were drifting weightlessly in its central control cabin, they very nearly filled it. There was one other cabin, Ross saw; and the two compartments accounted for a good nine-tenths of the cubage of the ship. Where that left space for the combustion chambers and the fuel tanks, the crew quarters, and the cargo holds, Ross could not imagine. He said: "All right, Mr. Haarland. Talk."

Haarland grinned toothily, his expression eerie in the flickering violet light that issued from a gutter around the cabin's wall.

"This is a spaceship, Ross. It's a pretty old one-fourteen hundred years, give or take a little. It's not much to look at, compared with the up-to-date models you're used to, but it's got a few features that you won't find on the new ones. For one thing, Ross, it doesn't use rockets." He hesitated. "Ask me what it does use," he admitted, "and I can't tell you. I know the name, because I read it: nucleophoretic drive. What nucleophoresis is and how it works, I can't say. They call it the Wesley Effect, and the tech manual says something about squared miles of acceleration. Does that mean anything to you? No. How could it? But it works, Ross. It works well enough so that this little ship will get you where you're going very quickly. The stars, Ross-it will take you to the stars. Faster than light. What the top speed is I have no idea; but there is a ship's log here, too. And it has a three-month entry-three months, Ross! —in which this little ship explored the solar systems of fourteen stars."

Wide-eyed, Ross held motionless. Haarland paused. "Fourteen hundred years," he repeated. "Fourteen hundred years this ship has been floating out here. And for all that time, the long-liners have been crawling from star to star, while little hidden ships like this one could have carried a thousand times as much goods a million times faster. Maybe the time has come to get the ships out of hiding. I don't know. I want to find out; I want you to find out for me. I'll be specific, Ross. I need a pilot. I'm too old, and Marconi turned it down. Someone has to go out there — —" he gestured to the blind hull and the unseen stars beyond —"and find out why nine planets are out of communication. Will you do it?"

Ross opened his mouth to speak, and a thousand questions competed for utterance. But what he said, barely aloud, was only: "Yes."

The far-off stars-more than a thousand million of them in our galaxy alone. By far the greatest number of them drifted alone through space, or with only a stellar companion as utterly unlivable by reason of heat and crushing gravity as themselves. Fewer than one in a million had a family of planets, and most even of those could never become a home for human life.

But out of a thousand million, any fraction may be a very large number, and the number of habitable planets was in the hundreds.

Ross had seen the master charts of the inhabited universe often enough to recognize the names as Haarland mentioned them: Tau Ceti II, Earth, the eight inhabitable worlds of Capella. But to realize that this ship-this ship! —had touched down on each of them, and on a hundred more, was beyond astonishment; it was a dream thing, impossible but unquestioned.

Through Haarland's burning, old eyes, Ross looked back through fourteen centuries, to the time when this ship was a scout vessel for a colonizing colossus. The lumbering giant drove slowly through space on its one-way trip from the planet that built it-was it semi-mythical Earth? The records were not clear-while the tiny scout probed each star and solar system as it drew within range. While the mother ship was covering a few hundred million miles, the scout might flash across parsecs to scan half a dozen worlds. And when the scout came back with word of a planet where humans could survive, they christened it with the name of the scout's pilot, and the chartroom labored, and the ship's officers gave orders, and the giant's nose swerved through a half a degree and began its long, slow deceleration.

"Why slow?" Ross demanded. "Why not use the faster-than-light drive for the big ships?"

Haarland grimaced. "I've got to answer that one for you sooner or later," he said, "but let me make it later. Anyway, that's what this ship was: a faster-than-light scout ship for a real longliner. What happened to the longliner the records don't show; my guess is the colonists cannibalized it to get a start in constructing homes for themselves. But the scout ship was exempted. The captain of the expedition had it put in an orbit out here, and left alone. It's been used a little bit, now and then-my great-grandfather's father went clear to 40 Eridani when my great-grandfather was a little boy, but by and large it has been left alone. It had to be, Ross. For one thing, it's dangerous to the man who pilots it. For another, it's dangerous to-the Galaxy."

Haarland's view was anthropomorphic; the danger was not to the immense and uncaring galaxy, but to the sparse fester of life that called itself humanity.

When the race abandoned Earth, it was a gesture of revulsion. Behind them they left a planet that had decimated itself in wars; ahead lay a cosmos that, in all their searches, had revealed no truly sentient life.

Earth was a crippled world, the victim of its playing with nuclear fission and fusion. But the techniques that gave them a faster-than-light drive gave them as well a weapon that threatened solar systems, not cities; that could detonate a sun as readily as uranium could destroy a building. The child with his forbidden matches was now sitting atop a munitions dump; the danger was no longer a seared hand or blinded eye, but annihilation.

And the decision had been made: secrecy. By what condign struggles the secrecy had been enforced, the secrecy itself concealed. But it had worked. Once the radiating colonizers had reached their goals, the nucleophoretic effect had been obliterated from their records and, except for a single man on each planet, from their minds.

Why the single man? Why not bury it entirely?

Haarland said slowly, "There was always the chance that something would go wrong, you see. And-it has."

Ross said hesitantly, "You mean the nine planets that have gone out of communication?"

Haarland nodded. He hesitated. "Do you understand it now?" he asked.

Ross shook his head dizzily. "I'm trying," he said. "This little ship-it travels faster than light. It has been circling out here-how long? Fourteen hundred years? And you kept it secret-you and your ancestors before you because you were afraid it might be used in war?" He was frowning.

"Not 'afraid' it would be used," Haarland corrected gently. "We knew it would be used."

Ross grimaced. "Well, why tell me about it now? Do you expect me to keep it secret all the rest of my life?"

"I think you would," Haarland said soberly.

"But suppose I didn't? Suppose I blabbed all over the Galaxy, and it was used in war?"

Haarland's face was suddenly, queerly gray. He said, almost to himself, "It seems that there are things worse than war." Abruptly he smiled. "Let's find Ma."

They returned through the coupling and searched the longliner for the old woman. A Sonny told them, "Ma usually hangs around the meter room. Likes to see them blinking." And there they found her.

"Hello, Haarland," she smiled, flashing her superb teeth. "Did you find what you were looking for?"

"Perfect, Ma. I want to talk to you under the seal."

She looked at Ross. "Him?" she asked.

"I vouch for him," Haarland said gravely. "Wesley."

She answered, "The limiting velocity is C."

"But C^2 is not a velocity," Haarland said. He turned to Ross. "Sorry to make a mystery," he apologized. "It's a recognition formula. It identifies one member of what we call the Wesley families, or its messenger, to another. And these people are messengers. They were dispatched a couple of centuries ago by a Wesley family whose ship, for some reason, no longer could be used. Why? —I don't know why. Try your luck, maybe you can figure it out. Ma, tell us the history again."

She knitted her brows and began to chant slowly:

"In great-grandfather's time the target was Clyde,
Rocketry firm and ores on the side.
If we hadn't of seen them direct we'd of missed 'em;
There wasn't a blip from the whole damn system.

That was the first.
Before great-grandfather's day was done
We cut the orbit of Cyrnus One.
The contact there was Trader McCue,
But the sons o' bitches missed us too.

That was the second.
My grandpa lived to see the green
Of Target Three through the high-powered screen.
But where in hell was Builder Carruthers?
They let us go by like all the others.
That was the — —"

"Ma," said Haarland. "Thanks very much, but would you skip to the last one?"

Ma grinned.

The Haarland Trading Corp. was last
With the fuel down low and going fast.
I'm glad it was me who saw the day
When they brought us down on GCA.
I told him the message; he called it a mystery,
But anyway this is the end of the history.
And it's about time!

"The message, please," Haarland said broodingly.

Ma took a deep breath and rattled off: "L-sub-T equals L-sub-zero e to the minus-T-over-two-N."

Ross gaped. "That's the message?"

"Used to be more to it," Ma said cheerfully "That's all there is now, though. The darn thing doesn't rhyme or anything. I guess that's the most important part. Anyway, it's the hardest."

"It's not as bad as it seems," Haarland told Ross. "I've asked around. It makes a very little sense."

"It does?"

"Well, up to a point," Haarland qualified. "It seems to be a formula in genetics. The notation is peculiar, but it's all explained, of course. It has something to do with gene loss. Now, maybe that means something and maybe it doesn't. But I know something that does mean something: some member of a Wesley Family a couple of hundred years ago thought it was important enough to want to get it across to other Wesley families. Something's happening. Let's find out what it is, Ross." The old man suddenly buried his face in his hands. In a cracked voice he mumbled, "Gene loss and war. Gene loss or war. God, I wish somebody would take this right out of my hands-or that I could drop with a heart attack this minute. You ever think of war, Ross?"

Shocked and embarrassed, Ross mumbled some kind of answer. One might think of war, good breeding taught, but one never talked about it.

"You should," the old man said hoarsely. "War is what this faster-than-light secrecy and identification rigmarole is all about. Right now war is impossible-between solar systems, anyhow, and that's what counts. A planet might just barely manage to fit an invading multigeneration expedition at gigantic cost, but it never would. The fruits of victory-loot, political domination, maybe slaves-would never come back to the fitters of the expedition but to their remote descendants. A firm will take a flyer on a commercial deal like that, but no nation would accept a war on any such basis-because a conqueror is a man, and men die. With F-T-L —faster-than-light travel-they might invade Curnus or Azor or any of those other tempting dots on the master maps. Why not? Take the marginal population, hop them up with patriotic fervor and lust for booty, and ship them off to pillage and destroy. There's at least a fifty per cent chance of coming out ahead on the investment, isn't there? Much more attractive deal commercially speaking than our present longliners."

Ross had never seen a war. The last on Halsey's planet had been the Peninsular Rebellion about a century and a half ago. Some half a million constitutional psychopathic inferiors had started themselves an ideal society with theocratic trimmings in a remote and unfruitful corner of the planet. Starved and frustrated by an unrealistic moral creed they finally exploded to devastate their neighboring areas and were quickly quarantined by a radioactive zone. They disintegrated internally, massacred their priesthood, and were permitted to disperse. It was regarded as a shameful episode by every dweller on the planet. It wasn't a subject for popular filmreels; if you wanted to find out about the Peninsular Rebellion you went through many successive library doors and signed your name on lists, and were sternly questioned as to your age and scholarly qualifications and reasons for sniffing around such an unsavory mess.

Ross therefore had not the slightest comprehension of Haarland's anxiety. He told him so.

"I hope you're right," was all the old man would say. "I hope you don't learn worse."

* * * * *

The rest was work.

He had the Yard worker's familiarity with conventional rocketry, which saved him some study of the fine-maneuvering apparatus of the F-T-L craft-but not much. For a week under Haarland's merciless drilling he jetted the ship about its remote area of space, far from the commerce lanes, until the old man grudgingly pronounced himself satisfied.

There were skull-busting sessions with the Wesley drive, or rather with a first derivative of it, an insane-looking object which you could vaguely describe as a fan-shaped slide rule taller than a man. There were twenty-seven main tracks, analogues of the twenty-seven main geodesics of Wesley Space-whatever they were and whatever that was. Your cursor settings on the main tracks depended on a thirty-two step computation based on the apparent magnitudes of the twenty-seven nearest celestial bodies above a certain mass which varied according to yet another lengthy relationship. Then, having cleared the preliminaries out of the way, you began to solve for your actual setting on the F-T-L drive controls.

Somehow he mastered it, while Haarland, driving himself harder than he drove the youth who was to be his exploring eyes and ears, coached him and cursed him and-somehow! —kept his own complicated affairs going back on Halsey's Planet. When Ross had finally got the theory of the Wesley Drive in some kind of order in his mind, and had learned all there was to learn about the other worlds, and had cut his few important ties with Halsey's Planet, he showed up in Haarland's planet-based office for a final, repetitive briefing.

Marconi was there.

He had trouble meeting Ross's eyes, but his handclasp was firm and his voice warmly friendly-and a little envious. "The very best, Ross," he said. "I —I wish — —" He hesitated and stammered. He said, in a flood, "Damn it, I should be going! Do a good job, Ross-and I hope you don't hate me." And he left while Ross, disturbed, went in to see old man Haarland.

Haarland spared no time for sentiment. "You're cleared for space flight," he growled. "According to the visa, you're going to Sunward-in case anyone asks you between here and the port. Actually, let's hear where you *are* going."

Ross said promptly, "I am going on a mission of exploration and reconnaissance. My first proposed destination is Ragansworld; second Gemser, third Azor. If I cannot make contact with any of these three planets, I will select planets at random from the master charts until I find some Wesley Drive families somewhere. The contacts for the first three planets are: On Ragansworld, Foley Associates; on Gemser, the Franklin Foundation; on Azor, Cavallo Machine Tool Company. F-T-L contacts on other planets are listed in the appendix to the master charts. The co-ordinates for Ragansworld are — —"

"Skip the co-ordinates," mumbled Haarland, rubbing his eyes. "What do you do when you get in contact with a Wesley Drive family?"

Ross hesitated and licked his lips. "I —well, it's a little hard — —"

"Dammit," roared Haarland, "I've told you a *thousand* times — —"

"Yessir, I know. All I meant was I don't exactly understand what I'm looking for."

"If I knew what you were to look for," Haarland rasped, "I wouldn't have to send you out looking! Can't you get it through your thick head? *Something* is wrong. I don't know what. Maybe I'm crazy for bothering about it-heaven knows, I've got troubles enough right here-but we Haarlands have a tradition of service, and maybe it's so old that we've kind of forgotten just what it's all about. But it's not so old that I've forgotten the family tradition. If I had a son, he'd be doing this. I counted on Marconi to be my son; now all I have left is you. And that's little enough, heaven knows," he finished bitterly.

Ross, wounded, said by rote: "On landing, I will attempt at once to make contact with the local Wesley Drive family, using the recognition codes given me. I will report to them on all the data at hand and suggest the need for action."

Haarland stood up. "All right," he said. "Sorry I snapped at you. Come on; I'll go up to the ship with you."

And that was the way it happened. Ross found himself in the longliner, then with Haarland in the tiny, ancient, faster-than-light ship which had once been tender to the ship that colonized Halsey's Planet. He found himself shaking hands with a red-eyed, suddenly-old Haarland, watching him crawl through the coupling to the longliner, watching the longliner blast away.

He found himself setting up the F-T-L course and throwing in the drive.

Ross was lucky. The second listed inhabited planet was still inhabited.

He had not quite stopped shuddering from the first when the approach radar caught him. The first planet was given in the master charts as "Ragansworld. Pop. 900,000,000; diam. 9400 m.; mean orbit 0.8 AU," and its co-ordinates went on to describe it as the fourth planet of a small G-type sun. There had been some changes made: the co-ordinates now intersected well inside a bright and turbulent gas cloud.

It appeared that suppressing the F-T-L drive had not quite annihilated war.

But the second planet, Gemser-there, he was sure, was a world where nothing was seriously awry.

He left the ship mumbling a name to himself: "Franklin Foundation." And he was greeted by a corporal's guard of dignified and ceremonially dressed men; they smiled at him, welcomed him, shook his hand, and invited him to what seemed to be the local equivalent of the administration building. He noticed disapprovingly that they didn't seem to go in for the elaborate decontamination procedures of Halsey's Planet, but perhaps, he thought, they had bred disease-resistance into their bloodlines. Certainly the four men in his guide party seemed hale and well-preserved, though the youngest of them was not less than sixty.

"I would like," he said, "to be put in touch with the Franklin Foundation, please."

"Come right in here," beamed one of the four, and another said:

"Don't worry about a thing." They held the door for him, and he walked into a small and sybaritically furnished room. The second man said, "Just a few questions. Where are you from?"

Ross said simply, "Halsey's Planet," and waited.

Nothing happened, except that all four men nodded comprehendingly, and the questioner made a mark on a sheet of paper. Ross amplified, "Fifty-three light years away. You know—another star."

"Certainly," the man said briskly. "Your name?"

Ross told him, but with a considerable feeling of deflation. He thought wryly of his own feelings about the longlines and the far stars; he remembered the stir and community excitement that a starship meant back home. Still, Ross told himself. Halsey's Planet might be just a back eddy in the main currents of civilization. Quite possibly on another world-this one, for instance-travelers from the stars were a commonplace. The field hadn't seemed overly busy, though; and there was nothing resembling a spaceship. Unless-he thought with a sudden sense of shock-those rusting hulks clumped together at the edge of the field had once been spaceships. But that was hardly likely, he reassured himself. You just don't let spaceships rust.

"Sex?" the man asked, and "Age?" "Education?" "Marital status?" The questions went on for more time than Ross quite understood; and they seemed far from relevant questions for the most part; and some of them were hard questions to answer. "Tau quotient?" for instance; Ross blinked and said, with an edge to his voice:

"I don't know what a tau quotient is."

"Put him down as zero," one of the men advised, and the interlocutor nodded happily.

"Working-with-others rating?" he asked, beaming.

Ross said with controlled irritation, "Look, I don't know anything about these ratings. Will you take me to somebody who can put me in touch with the Franklin Foundation?"

The man who was sitting next to him patted him gently on the shoulder. "Just answer the questions," he said comfortably. "Everything will be all right."

Ross flared, "The hell everything will — —"

Something with electrified spikes in it hit him on the back of the neck.

Ross yelled and ducked away; the man next to him returned a little rod to his pocket. He smiled at Ross. "Don't feel bad," he said sympathetically. "Go ahead now, answer the questions."

Ross shook his head dazedly. The pain was already leaving his neck, but he felt nauseated by the suddenness and sharpness of it; he could not remember any pain quite like that in his life. He stood up waveringly and said, "Wait a minute, now — —"

This time it was the man on the other side, and the pain was about twice as sharp. Ross found himself on the floor, looking up through a haze. The man on his right kept the rod in his hand, and the expression on his face, while in no way angry, was stern. "Bad boy," he said tenderly. "Why don't you want to answer the questions?"

Ross gasped, "God damn it, all I want is to see somebody! Keep your dirty hands off me, you old fools!" And that was a mistake, as he learned in the blessedly few minutes before he passed out completely under the little rods held by the gentle but determined men.

He answered all the questions-bound to a chair, with two of the men behind him, when he had regained consciousness. He answered every one. They only had to hit him twice.

When they untied him the next morning, Ross had caught on to the local folkways quite well. The fatherly fellow who released him said, "Follow me," and stood back, smiling but with one hand on one of the little rods. And Ross was careful to say:

"Yes, sir!"

They rode in a three-wheeled car, and entered a barracks-like building. Ross was left alone next to a bed in a dormitory with half a hundred beds. "Just wait here," the man said, smiling. "The rest of your group is out at their morning session now. When they come in for lunch you can join them. They'll show you what to do."

Ross didn't have too long to wait. He spent the time in conjecture as confused as it was fruitless; he had obviously done something wrong, but just what was it?

If he had had twice as long he would have got no farther toward an answer than he was: nowhere. But a noise outside ended his speculations. He glanced toward the curiously shaped door-all the doors on this planet seemed to be rectangular. A girl of about eighteen was peering inside.

She stared at Ross and said, "Oh!" Then she disappeared. There were footsteps and whispers, and more heads appeared and blinked at him and were jerked back.

Ross stood up in wretched apprehension. All of a sudden he was fourteen years old again, and entering a new school where the old hands were giggling and whispering about the new boy. He swore sullenly to himself.

A new face appeared, halted for an inspection of Ross, and walked confidently in. The man was a good forty years old, Ross thought; perhaps a kind of overseer in this institution-whatever kind of institution it was. He approached Ross at a sedate pace, and he was followed through the door in single file by a couple score men and women. They ranged in age, Ross thought wonderingly, from the leader's forty down to the late teens of the girl who had first peered in the door, and now was at the end of the procession.

The leader said, "How old are you?"

"Why, uh — —" Ross figured confusedly: this planet's annual orbital period was roughly forty per cent longer than his own; fourteen into his age, multiplied by ten, making his age in their local calculations....

"Why, I'm nineteen of your years old, about. And a half."

"Yes. And what can you do?"

"Look here, sir. I've been through all this once. Why don't you go and ask those gentlemen who brought me here? And can anybody tell me where the Franklin Foundation is?"

The fortyish fellow, with a look of outrage, slapped Ross across the mouth. Ross knocked him down with a roundhouse right.

A girl yelled, "Good for you, Junior!" and jumped like a wildcat onto a slim, gray-haired lady, clawing, and slapping. The throng dissolved immediately into a wild melee. Ross, busily fighting off the fortyish fellow and a couple of his stocky buddies, noted only that the scrap was youth against age, whatever it meant.

"How *dare* you?" a voice thundered, and the rioters froze.

A decrepit wreck was standing in the doorway, surrounded by three or four gerontological textbook cases only a little less spavined than he. "Glory," a girl muttered despairingly. "It would be the minister."

"What is the meaning of this brawl?" rolled from the wreck's shriveled lips in a rich basso-no; rolled, Ross noted, from a flat perforated plate on his chest. There was a small, flesh-colored mike slung before his lips. "Who is responsible here?" asked the golden basso.

Ross's fortyish assailant said humbly: "I am, sir. This new fellow here — —"

"Manners! Speak when you're spoken to."

Abjectly: "Yes, sir. I'm sorry, sir."

"Silly fools!" the senile wreck hectored them. "I'm going to take no official notice of this since I'm merely passing through. Luckily for you this is no formal inspection. But you've lost your lunch hour with your asinine pranks. Now get back to your work and never let me hear of a disgraceful incident like this again from Junior Unit Twenty-Three."

He swept out with his retinue. Ross noted that some of the younger girls were crying and that the older men and women were glaring at him murderously.

"We'll teach you manners, you pup," the foreman-type said. "You go on the dye vats this afternoon. Any more trouble and you'll miss a few meals."

Ross told him: "Just keep your hands off me, mister."

The foreman-type expanded into a beam of pleasure. "I thought you'd be sensible," he said. "Everybody to the plant, now!" He collared a pretty girl of about Ross's age. "Helena here is working out a bit of insolence on the dye vats herself. She'll show you." The girl stood with downcast eyes. Ross liked her face and wondered about her figure. Whatever it was like, it was covered from neck to knee by a loose shirt. But the older women wore fitted clothes.

The foreman-type led a grand procession through the door. Helena told Ross: "I guess you'd better get in front of me in line. I go here — —" She slipped in deftly, and Ross understood a little more of what went on here. The procession was in order of age.

He had determined to drift for a day or two-not that he seemed to have much choice. The Franklin Foundation, supposedly having endured a good many years, would last another week while he explored the baffling mores of this place and found out how to circumvent them and find his way to the keepers of F-T-L on this world. Nobody would go anywhere with his own ship-not without first running up a setting for the Wesley Drive!

The line filed into a factory whose like Ross had never before seen. He had a fair knowledge of and eye for industrial processes; it was clear that the place was an electric-cable works. But why was the concrete floor dangerously cracked and sloppily patched? Why was the big enameling oven rumbling and stinking? Why were the rolling mills in a far corner unsupplied with guards and big, easy-to-hit emergency cutoffs? Why was the light bad and the air full of lint? Why did the pickling tank fume and make the workers around it cough hackingly? Most pointed of all, why did the dye vats to which Helena led him stink and slop over?

There were grimy signs everywhere, including the isolated bay where braiding cord was dyed the standard code colors. The signs said things like: Age is a privilege and not a right. Age must be earned by work. Gratitude is the index of your progress to maturity.

Helena said girlishly as she took his arm and hooked him out of the moving line: "Here's Stinkville. Believe me, I'm not going to talk back again. After all, one's maturity is measured by one's acceptance of one's environment, isn't it?"

"Yeah," said Ross. "Listen, Helena, have you ever heard of a place called the Franklin Foundation?"

"No," she said. "First you climb up here-golly! I don't even know your name."

"Ross."

"All right, Ross. First you climb up here and make sure the yarn's running over the rollers right; sometimes it gets twisted around and then it breaks. Then you take one of the thermometers from the wall and you check the vat temperature. It says right on the thermometers what it should be for the different colors. If it's off you turn that gas tap up or down, just a little. Then you check the wringer rolls where the yarn comes out. Watch your fingers when you do! The yarn comes in different thicknesses on the same thread so you have to adjust the wringer rolls so too much dye doesn't get squeezed out. You can tell by the color; it shouldn't be lighter after it goes through the rolls. But the yarn shouldn't come through sloppy and drip dye on the floor while it travels to the bobbin — —"

There was some more, equally uncomplicated. He took the yellow and green vats; she took the red and blue. They had worked in the choking stench and heat for perhaps three hours before Ross finished one temperature check and descended to adjust a gas tap. He found Helena, spent and gasping, on the floor, hidden from the rest of the shop by the bulky tanks.

"Heat knock you out?" he asked briskly. "Don't try to talk. I'll tote you over by the wall away from the burners. Maybe we'll catch a little breeze from the windows there." She nodded weakly.

He picked her up without too much trouble, carried her three yards or so to the wall, still isolated from the rest of the shop. She was ripely curved under that loose shirt, he learned. He set her down easily, crouching himself, and did not take his hands away.

It's been a long time, he thought-and she was responding! Whether she knew it or not, there was a drowsy smile on her face and her body moved a little against his hands, pleasurably. She was breathing harder.

Ross did the sensible thing and kissed her.

Wildcat!

Ross reeled back from her fright and anger, his face copiously scratched. "I'm dreadfully sorry," he sputtered. "Please accept my sincerest — —"

The flare-up of rage ended; she was sobbing bitterly, leaning against the wall, wailing that nobody had ever treated her like that before, that she'd be set back three years if he told anybody, that she was a good, self-controlled girl and he had no *right* to treat her that way, and what kind of degenerate was he, not yet twenty and going around kissing girls when *everybody* knew you went crazy from it.

He soothed her-from a distance. Her sobbing dropped to a bilious croon as she climbed the ladder to the yellow vat, tears still on her face, and checked its temperature.

Ross, wondering if he were already crazy from too much kissing of girls, mechanically resumed his duties. But she had responded. And how long had they been working? And wasn't this shift ever going to end?

All the shifts ended in time. But there was a catch to it: There was always another shift. After the afternoon shift on the dye vats came dinner-porridge! —and then came the evening shift on the dye vats, and then sleep. The foreman was lenient, though; he let Ross off the vats after the end of the second day. Then it was kitchen orderly, and only two shifts a day. And besides, you got plenty to eat.

But it was a long, long way, Ross thought sardonically to himself, from the shining pictures he had painted to himself back on Halsey's Planet. Ross the explorer, Ross the hero, Ross the savior of humanity....

Ross, the semipermanent KP.

He had to admit it to himself: The expedition thus far had been a bust. Not only was it perfectly clear that there no longer was a Franklin Foundation on Gemser, but more had been lost than time and effort. For Ross himself, he silently admitted, was as close to lost as he ever wanted to be. He was, in effect, a prisoner, in a prison from which there was no easy escape as long as he was cursed with youthfulness....

Of course, the implications of that were that there was a perfectly easy escape in time. All he had to do was get old enough to matter, on this insane planet. Ninety, maybe. And then he would be perfectly free to totter out to the spaceport, dragoon a squad of juniors into lifting him into the ship, and take off....

Helena was some help. But only psychologically; she was pleasant company, but neither she nor anyone else in the roster of forty-eight to whom he was permitted to speak had ever heard of the Franklin Foundation, or F-T-L travel, or anything. Helena said, "Wait for Holiday. Maybe one of the grownups will tell you then?"

"Holiday?" Ross slid back and scratched his shoulder blades against the corner of his bed. Helena was sprawled on the floor, half watching a projected picture on the screen at the end of the dormitory.

"Yes. You're lucky, it's only eight days off. That's when Dobermann — —" she pointed to the foreman — —"graduates; he's the only one this year. And we all move up a step, and the new classes come in, and then we all get everything we want. Well, pretty near," she amended. "We can't do anything *bad*. But you'll see; it's nice."

Then the picture ended, and it was calisthenics time, and then lights out. Forty-eight men and women on their forty-eight bunks-the honor system appeared to work beautifully; there had been no signs of sex play that Ross had been able to see-slept the sleep of the innocent. While Ross, the forty-ninth, lay staring into the dark with rising hope.

In the kitchen the next morning he got more information from Helena. Holiday seemed to be a cross between saturnalia and Boy's Week; for one day of the year the elders slightly relaxed their grip on the reins. On that day alone one could Speak Before Being Spoken To, Interrupt One's Elders, even Leave the Room without Being Excused.

Whee, Ross thought sourly. But still....

The foreman, Dobermann, once you learned how to handle him, wasn't such a bad guy. Ross, studying his habits, learned the proper approach and used it. Dobermann's commonest complaint was of irresponsibility-irresponsibility when some thirty-year-old junior was caught sneaking into line ahead of his proper place, irresponsibility when Ross forgot to make his bed before stumbling out in the dark to his kitchen shift, one awful case of irresponsibility when Helena thoughtlessly poured cold water into the cooking vat while it was turned on. There was a sizzle, a crackle, and a puff of steam, and Helena was weeping over a broken heating element.

Dobermann came storming over, and Ross saw his chance. "That is very irresponsible of you, Helena," he said coldly, back to Dobermann but entirely conscious of his presence. "If Junior Unit Twenty-Three was all as irresponsible as you, it would reflect badly on Mr. Dobermann. You don't know how lucky you are that Mr. Dobermann is so kind to you."

Helena's weeping dried up instantly; she gave Ross one furious glance, and lowered her eyes before Dobermann. Dobermann nodded approvingly to Ross as he waded into Helena; it was a memorable tirade, but Ross heard only part of it. He was looking at the cooking vat; it was a simple-minded bit of construction, a spiral of resistance wire around a ceramic core. The core had cracked and one end of the wire was loose; if it could be reconnected, the cracked core shouldn't matter much-the wire was covered with insulation anyhow. He looked up and opened his mouth to say something, then remembered and merely stood looking brightly attentive.

" — —looks like you want to go back to the vats," the foreman was finishing. "Well, Helena, if that's what you want we can make you happy. This time you'll be by yourself, too; you won't have Ross to help you out when the going's rough. Will she, Ross?"

"No, sir," Ross said immediately. "Sir?"

Dobermann looked back at him, frowning. "What?"

"I think I can fix this," Ross said modestly.

Dobermann's eyes bulged. "Fix it?"

"Yes, sir. It's only a loose wire. Back where I come from, we all learned how to take care of things like that when we were still in school. It's just a matter of — —"

"Now, hold on, Ross"; the foreman howled. "Tampering with a machine is bad enough, but if you're going to turn out to be a liar, too, you're going just too far! School, indeed! You know perfectly well, Ross, that even I won't be ready for school until after Holiday. Ross, I knew you were a troublemaker, knew it the first day I set eyes on you. School! Well, we'll see how you like the school I'm going to send you to!"

The vats weren't so bad the second time. Even though the porridge was cold for two days, until somebody got around to delivering a different though equally worn-out cooking vat.

Helena passed out from the heat three times. And when, on the third time, Ross, goaded beyond endurance, kissed her again, there were no hysterics.

CHAPTER VI.

From birth to puberty you were an infant. From puberty to Dobermann's age, a junior. For ten years after that you went to school, learning the things you had neither the need nor the right to know before.

And then you were Of Age.

Being Of Age meant much, much more than voting, Ross found out. For one thing, it meant freedom to marry-after the enforced sexlessness of the junior years and the directed breeding via artificial insemination of the Scholars. It meant a healthy head start on seniority, which carried with it all offices and all power.

It meant freedom.

As a bare beginning, it meant the freedom to command any number of juniors or scholars. On Ross's last punitive day in the dye vats, a happy ancient commandeered the entire staff to help set shrubs in his front lawn —a good dozen acres of careful landscaping it was, and the prettiest sight Ross had seen on this ugly planet.

When they got back to the dye vats, the yellow and blue had boiled over, and broken strands of yarn had fouled all the bobbins. Dobermann raged-at the juniors.

But then Dobermann's raging came to an end forever. It was the night before Holiday, and there was a pretty ceremony as he packed his kit and got ready to turn Junior Unit Twenty-three over to his successor. Everyone was scrubbed, and though a certain amount of license in regard to neatness was allowed between dinner and lights out, each bunk was made and carefully smoothed free of wrinkles. After half an hour of fidgety waiting, Dobermann called-needlessly-for attention, and the minister came in with his ancient retinue.

The rich mechanical voice boomed out from his breastplate: "Junior Dobermann, today you are a man!"

Dobermann stood with his head bowed, silent and content. Junior Unit Twenty-Three chanted antiphonally: "Good-by, Junior Dobermann!"

The retinue took three steps forward, and the minister boomed, "Beauty comes with age. Age is beauty!"

And the chorus: "Old heads are wisest!" Ross, standing as straight as any of them, faked the words with his lips and tongue, and wondered how many repetitions had drilled those sentiments into Junior Unit Twenty-Three.

There were five more chants, and five responses, and then the minister and his court of four were standing next to Dobermann. Breathing heavily from his exertions, the minister reached behind him and took a book from the hands of the nearest of his retinue. He said, panting, "Scholar Dobermann, in the Book lies the words of the Fathers. Read them and learn."

The chorus cried thrice, "The Word of the Fathers Is Law." And then the minister touched Dobermann's hand, and in solemn silence, left.

As soon as the elders had gone, the juniors flocked around Dobermann to wish him well. There was excited laughter in the congratulations, and a touch of apprehension too: Dobermann, with all his faults, was a known quantity, and the members of Junior Unit Twenty-Three were beginning to look a little fearfully at the short, redheaded youth who, from the next day on, would be Dobermann's successor.

Ross promised himself: He can be good or bad, a blessing or a problem. But he won't be *my* problem. I'm getting out of here tomorrow!

Holiday.

"Oh, it's fun," Helena told him enthusiastically. "First you get up early to get the voting out of the way — —"

"Voting?"

"Sure. Don't they vote where you come from? I thought everybody voted. That's democracy, like we have it here."

He sardonically quoted one of the omnipresent wall signs: "The happiness of the majority means the happiness of the minority." He had often wondered what, if anything, it meant. But Helena solemnly nodded.

They were whispering from their adjoining cots by dim, false dawn filtering through the windows on Holiday morning. They were not the only whisperers. Things were relaxing already.

"Ross," Helena said.

"Yes?"

"I thought maybe you might not know. On Holiday if you, ah, want to do that again you don't have to wait until I faint. Ah, of course you don't do it right out in the open." Overcome by her own daring she buried her head under the coarse blanket.

Fine, thought Ross wearily. Once a year-or did Holiday come once a year? —the kids were allowed to play "Spin The Bottle." No doubt their elders thought it was too cute for words: mere tots of thirty and thirty-five childishly and innocently experimenting with sex. Of course it would be discreetly supervised so that nobody would Get In Trouble.

He was quite sure Helena's last two faints had been unconvincing phonies.

* * * * *

The wake-up whistle blew at last. The chattering members of Junior Unit Twenty-Three dawdled while they dressed, and the new foreman indulgently passed out shabby, smutted ribbons which the girls tied in their hair. They had sugar on their mush for breakfast, and Ross's stomach came near turning as he heard burbles of gratitude at the feast.

With pushing and a certain amount of inexpert horseplay they formed a column of fours and hiked from the hall-from the whole factory complex, indeed, along a rubberized highway.

Once you got out of the factory area things became pleasanter by the mile. Hortatory roadside signs thinned out and vanished. Stinking middens of industrial waste were left behind. And then the landscape was rolling, sodded acres with the road pleasantly springy underfoot, the air clean and crisp.

They oohed and aahed at houses glimpsed occasionally in the distance-always rambling, one-story affairs that looked spanking-new.

Once a car overhauled them on the highway and slowed to a crawl. It was a huge thing, richly upholstered within. A pair of grimlooking youths were respectively chauffeur and footman; the passenger waved at the troop from Junior Twenty-Three and grinned out of a fantastic landscape of wrinkles. Ross gaped. Had he thought the visiting minister was old? This creature, male or female, was *old*.

After the car sped on, to the cheers of the marchers, there was happy twittering speculation. Junior Twenty-Three didn't recognize the Citizen who had graciously waved to them, but they thought he-or she? —was wonderful. So dignified, so distinguished, so learned, so gracious, so democratic!

"Wasn't it sweet of him?" Helena burbled. "And I'm sure he must be somebody important connected with the voting, otherwise he'd just vote from home."

Ross's feet were beginning to hurt when they reached the suburban center. To the best of his recollection, they were no more than eight or ten kilos from the field and his starship. Backtrack on the road to the suburban center about three kilos, take the fork to the right, and that would be that.

Junior Twenty-Three reached a pitch of near-ecstasy marveling at the low, spacious buildings of the center. Through sweeping, transparent windows they saw acres of food and clothing in the shopping center; the Drive-In Theater was an architectural miracle. The Civic Center almost finished them off, with its statue of Equal Justice Under the Law (a dignified beldame whose chin and nose almost met, leaning on a gem-crusted crutch) and Civic Virtue (in a motorized wheelchair equipped with an emergency oxygen tent, Lindbergh-Carrel auxiliary blood pump and an artificial kidney).

Merry oldsters were everywhere in their cars and wheelchairs, gaily waving at the kids. Only one untoward incident marred their prevoting tour of inspection. A thick-headed young man mistakenly called out a cheerful: "Life and wisdom, ma'am!" to a beaming oldster.

"Ma'am, is it?" the oldster roared through his throat mike and amplifier in an unmistakable baritone. "I'll ma'am you, you wise punk!" He spun his wheelchair on a decishield, threw it into high and roared down on the offender, running him over. The boy covered himself as well as he could while the raging old man backed over him again and ran over him again. His ordeal ended when the oldster collapsed forward in the chair, hanging from his safety belt.

The boy got up with tire marks on him and groaned: "Oh, lord! I've hurt him." He appealed hysterically: "What'll I do? Is he dead?"

Another Senior Citizen buzzed up and snapped: "Cut in his L-C heart, you booby!"

The boy turned on the Lindbergh-Carrel pump, trembling. The white-faced juniors of Twenty-Three watched as the tubes to the oldster's left arm throbbed and pulsed. A massive sigh went up when the old man's eyes opened and he sat up groggily. "What happened?"

"You died again, Sherrington," said the other elder. "Third time this week-good thing there was a responsible person around. Now get over to the medical center this minute and have a complete checkup. Hear me?"

"Yes, Dad," Sherrington said weakly. He rolled off in low gear.

His father turned to the youngster who stood vacantly rubbing the tire marks on his face. "Since it's Holiday," he grated, "I'll let this pass. On any other day I would have seen to it that you were set back fifteen years for your disgraceful negligence."

Ross knew by then what that meant, and shuddered with the rest. It amounted to a death sentence, did fifteen additional years of the grinding toil and marginal diet of a junior.

Somewhat dampened they proceeded to the Hall of Democracy, a glittering place replete with slogans, statues, and heroic portraits of the heroic aged. Twenty-Three huddled together as it joined with a stream of juniors from the area's other factory units. Most of them were larger than the cable works; many of them, apparently, involved more wearing and hazardous occupations. Some groups coughed incessantly and were red-eyed from the irritation of some chemical. Others must have been heavy-manual-labor specialists. They were divided into the hale, whose muscles bulged amazingly, and the dying-men and women who obviously could not take the work but who were doing it anyway.

They seated themselves at long benches, with push buttons at each station. Helena, next to him, explained the system to Ross. Voting was universal and simultaneous, in all the Halls of Democracy around the planet and from all the homes of the Senior Citizens who did not choose to vote from a Hall. Simultaneously the votes were counted at a central station and the results were flashed to screens in the Centers and homes. She said a number of enthusiastic things about Democracy while Ross studied a sheet on which the candidates and propositions were listed.

The names meant nothing to him. He noted only that each of three candidates for Chief of State was one hundred thirty years old, that each of three candidates for First Assistant Chief was one hundred and twenty-seven years old, and so on. Obviously the nominating conventions by agreement named candidates of the same age for each office to keep it a contest.

Proposition One read: "To dismantle seven pediatric centers and apply the salvage value to the construction of, and the funds no longer required for their maintenance to the maintenance of, a new wing of the Gerontological Center, said wing to be devoted to basic research in the extension of human life."

Proposition Two was worse. Ross didn't bother to read the rest of them. He whispered hoarsely to Helena, "What next?"

"Ssh!" She pointed to a screen at the front of the Hall. "It's starting."

A Senior Citizen of a very high rank (his face was entirely hidden by an oxygen mask) was speaking from the screen. There was what seemed to be a ritual speech of invocation, then he got down to business. "Citizens," he said through his throat mike, "behold Democracy in

Action! I give you three candidates for Chief of State-look them over, and make up your minds. First, Citizen Raphael Flexner, age one century, three decades, seven months, ten days." Senior Citizen Flexner rolled on screen, spoke briefly through his throat mike and rolled off. The first speaker said again, "Behold Democracy in Action! See now Citizen Sheridan Farnsworth, age one century, three decades, ten months, forty-two days." Applause boomed louder; some of the younger juniors yelled hysterically and drummed their heels on the floor.

Helena was panting with excitement, eyes bright on the screen. "Isn't it *wonderful*?" she gasped ecstatically. "Oh, look at *him*!"

"Him" was the third candidate, and the first oldster Ross had seen whose gocart was a wheeled stretcher. Prone and almost invisible through the clusters of tubing and chromed equipment, Senior Citizen Immanuel Appleby acknowledged his introduction —"Age one century, three decades, eleven months and five days!" The crowd went mad; Helena broke from Ross's side and joined a long yelling snake dance through the corridors.

Ross yelled experimentally as protective coloration, then found himself yelling because everybody was yelling, because he couldn't help it. By the time the speaker on the screen began to call for order, Ross was standing on top of the voting bench and screaming his head off.

Helena, weeping with excitement, tugged at his leg. "Vote now, Ross," she begged, and all over the hall the cry was "Vote! Vote!"

Ross reached out for the voting buttons. "What do we do now?" he asked Helena.

"Push the button marked 'Appleby,' of course. Hurry!"

"But why Appleby?" Ross objected. "That fellow Flexner, for instance ——"

"Hush, Ross! Somebody might be listening." There was sickening fright on Helena's face. "Didn't you hear? We *have* to vote for the best man. 'Oldest Is Bestest,' you know. That's what Democracy *means*, the freedom of choice. They read us the ages, and we choose which is oldest. Now please, Ross, hurry before somebody starts asking questions!"

The voting was over, and the best man had won in every case. It was a triumph for informed public opinion. The mob poured out of the hall in happy-go-lucky order, all precedences and formalities suspended for Holiday.

Helena grasped Ross firmly by the arm. The crowd was spreading over the quiet acres surrounding the Center, each little cluster heedlessly intent on a long-planned project of its own. Under the pressure of Helena's arm, Ross found himself swerving toward a clump of shrubbery.

He said violently, "No! That is, I mean I'm sorry, Helena, but I've got something to do."

She stared at him with shock in her eyes. "On Holiday?"

"On Holiday. Truly, Helena, I'm sorry. Look, what you said last night-from now till tomorrow morning, I can do what I want, right?"

Sullenly, "Yes. I *thought*, Ross, that I *knew* what ——"

"Okay." He jerked his arm away, feeling like all of the hundred possible kinds of a skunk. "See you around," he said over his shoulder. He did not look back.

Three kilos back, he told himself firmly, then the right-hand fork in the road. And not more than a dozen kilos, at the most, to the spaceport. He could do it in a couple of hours.

One thing had been established for certain: If ever there had been a "Franklin Foundation" on this planet, it was gone for good now. Dismantled, no doubt, to provide building materials for an eartrumpet plant. No doubt the little F-T-L ship that the Franklin Foundation was supposed to cover for was still swinging in an orbit within easy range of the spaceport; but the chance that anybody would ever find it, or use it if found, was pretty close to zero. If they bothered to maintain a radar watch at all-any other watch than the fully automatic one set to respond only to highvelocity interstellar ships-and if anyone ever took time to look at the radar plot, no doubt the F-T-L ship was charted. As an asteroid, satellite, derelict or "body of unknown origin." Certainly no one of these smug oldsters would take the trouble to investigate.

The only problem to solve on this planet was how to get off it-fast.

On the road ahead of him was what appeared to be a combination sex orgy and free-for-all. It rolled in a yelling, milling mob of half a hundred excited juniors across the road toward him, then swerved into the fields as a cluster of screaming women broke free and ran, and the rest of the crowd roared after them.

Ross quickened his step. If he ever did get off this planet, it would have to be today; he was not fool enough to think that any ordinary day would give him the freedom to poke around the spaceport's defenses. And it would be just his luck, he thought bitterly, to get involved in a gang fight on the way to the port.

There was a squeal of tires behind him, and a little vehicle screeched to a halt. Ross threw up a defensive arm in automatic reflex.

But it was only Helena, awkwardly fumbling open the door of the car. "Get in," she said sourly. "You've spoiled *my* Holiday. Might as well do what *you* want to do."

* * * * *

"What's that?"

Helena looked where he was pointing, and shrugged. "Guard box," she guessed. "How would I know? Nobody's in it, anyhow."

Ross nodded. They had abandoned the car and were standing outside a long, seamless fence that surrounded the spaceport. The main gates were closed and locked; a few hundred feet to the right was a smaller gate with a sort of pillbox, but that had every appearance of being locked too.

"All right," said Ross. "See that shed with the boxes outside it? Over we go."

The shed was right up against the fence; the metal boxes gave a sort of rough and just barely climbable foothold. Helena was easy enough to lift to the top of the shed; Ross, grunting, managed to clamber after her.

They looked down at the ground on the other side, a dozen feet away. "You don't have to come along," Ross told her.

"That's just *like* you!" she flared. "Cast me aside-trample on me!"

"All right, all right." Ross looked around, but neither junior nor elder was anywhere in sight. "Hang by your hands and then drop," he advised her. "Get moving before somebody shows up."

"On Holiday?" she asked bitterly. She squirmed over the narrow top of the fence, legs dangling, let herself down as far as she could, and let go. Ross watched anxiously, but she got up quickly enough and moved to one side.

Ross plopped down next to her, knocking the wind out of himself. He got up dizzily.

His ship, in lonesome quiet, was less than a quarter of a mile away. "Let's go," Ross panted, and clutched her hand. They skirted another shed and were in the clear, running as fast as they could.

Almost in the clear.

Ross heard the whine of the little scooter before he felt the blow, but it was too late. He sprawled on the ground, dragging Helena after him.

A Senior Citizen with a long-handled rod of the sort Ross remembered all too well was scowling down at them. "Children," he rumbled through his breast-speaker in a voice of awful disgust, "is this the way to act on Holiday?"

Helena, gibbering in terror, was beyond words. Ross croaked, "Sorry, sir. We-we were just — —"

Crash! The rod came down again, and every muscle in Ross's body convulsed. He rolled helplessly away, the elder following him. Crash! "We give you Holiday," the elder boomed, "and — —" crash " — —you act like animals. Terrible! Don't you know that freedom of play on Holiday — —" crash " — —is the most sacred right of every junior — —" crash " — —and heaven help you — —" crash " — —if you abuse it!"

The wrenching punishment and the caressing voice stopped together. Ross lay blinking into the terrible silence that followed. He became conscious of Helena's weeping, and forced his head to turn to look at her.

She was standing behind the elder's scooter, a length of wire in her hand. The senior lay slumped against his safety strap. "Ross!" she moaned. "Ross, what have I done? *I turned him off!*"

He stood up, coughing and retching. No one else was in sight, only the two of them and the silent, slack form of the old man. He grabbed her arm. "Come on," he said fuzzily, and started toward the starship.

She hung back, mumbling to herself, her eyes saucers. She was in a state of grievous shock, it was clear.

Ross hesitated, rubbing his back. He knew that she might never pull out of it. Even if she did, she was certain to be a frightful handicap. But it was crystal-clear that she had declared herself on his side. Even if the elder could be revived, the punishment in store for Helena would be awful to contemplate....

Come what may, he was now responsible for Helena.

He towed her to the starship. She climbed in docilely enough, sat staring blankly as he sealed ship and sent it blasting off the face of the planet.

* * * * *

She didn't speak until they were well into deep space. Then the blank stare abruptly clouded and she exploded in a fit of tears. Ross said ineffectually, "There, there." It had no effect; until, in its own time, the storm ended.

Helena said hoarsely, "Wh-what do I do now?"

"Why, I guess you come right along with me," Ross said heartily, cursing his luck.

"Where's that?"

"Where? You mean, where?" Ross scratched his head. "Well, let's see. Frankly, Helena, your planet was quite a disappointment to me. I had hoped — —Well, no matter. I suppose the best thing to do is to look up the next planet on the list."

"What list?"

Ross hesitated, then shrugged and plunged into the explanation. All about the longliners and the message and faster-than-light travel and the Wesley Families-and none of it, while he was talking, seemed convincing at all. But perhaps Helena was less critical; or perhaps Helena simply did not care. She listened attentively and made no comment. She only said, at the end, "What's the name of the next planet?"

He consulted the master charts. Haarland's listing showed a place called Azor, conveniently near at hand in the strange geodesics of the Wesley Effect, where the far galaxies might be near at hand in the warped space-lines, and the void just beyond the viewplates be infinitely distant. The F-T-L family of Azor was named Cavallo; when last heard from, they had been builders of machine tools.

Ross told Helena about it. She shrugged and watched curiously as he began to set up the F-T-L problem on the huge board.

CHAPTER VII.

They were well within detection range of Azor's radar, if any, and yet there had been no beeping signal that the planet's GCA had taken over and would pilot them down. Another blank? He studied the surface of the world under his highest magnification and saw no signs that it had been devastated by war. There were cities-intact, as far as he could tell, but not very attractive. The design ran to huge, gloomy piles that mounted toward central towers.

Azor was a big world which showed not much water and a great deal of black rock. It was the fifth of its system and reportedly had colonized its four adjacent neighbors and their moons.

His own search radar pinged. The signal was followed at once by a guarded voice from his ship-to-ship communicator: "What ship are you? Do you receive me? The band is 798.44."

He hastily dialed the frequency on his transmitter and called, "I receive you. We are a vessel from outside your solar system, home planet Halsey. We want to contact a family named Cavallo of the planet Azor believed to be engaged in building machine tools. Can you help us?"

"You are a male?" the voice asked cautiously. "In command or simply the communicator?"

"I'm a male and I'm in command of this vessel."

The voice said: "Then sheer off this system and go elsewhere, my friend."

"What is this? Who are you?"

"My name does not matter. I happen to be on watch aboard the prison orbital station 'Minerva.' Get going, my friend, before the planetary GCA picks you up."

Prison orbital station? A very sensible idea. "Thanks for the advice," he parried. "Can you tell me anything about the Cavallo family?"

"I have heard of them. My friend, your time is running out. If you do not sheer off very soon they will land you. And I judge from the tone of your voice that it will not be long before you join the rest of us criminals aboard 'Minerva.' It is not pleasant here. Good-by."

"Wait, please!" Ross had no intention at all of committing any crimes that would land him aboard a prison hulk, and he had every intention of fulfilling his mission. "Tell me about the Cavallo family-and why you expect me to get in trouble on Azor."

"The time is running out, my friend, but-the Cavallo family of machine tool builders is located in Novj Grad. And the crime of which all of us aboard 'Minerva' were convicted is conspiracy to advocate equality of the sexes. Now go!"

The carrier-wave hum of the communicator died, but immediately there was another electronic noise to fill the cabin-the beep of a GCA radar taking over the sealed landing controls of the craft.

Helena had been listening with very little comprehension. "Who was your friend, Ross?" she asked. "Where are we?"

"I think," Ross said, "he *was* my friend. And I think we are-in trouble."

The ship began to jet tentative bursts of reaction mass, nosing toward the big, gloomy planet.

"That's all right," Helena said comfortably. "At least they won't know I disconnected a Senior Citizen." She thought a moment. "They won't, will they? I mean, the Senior Citizens here won't know about the Senior Citizens there, will they?"

He tried to break it to her gently as the ship picked up speed. "Helena, it's possible that the old people here won't be Senior Citizens-not in your planet's sense. They may just be old people, with no special authority over young people. I think, in fact, that we may find you outranking older people who happen to be males."

She took it as a joke. "You are funny, Ross. Old means Senior, doesn't it? And Senior means better, wiser, abler, and in charge, doesn't it?"

"We'll see," he said thoughtfully as the main reaction drive cut in. "We'll see very shortly."

* * * * *

The spaceport was bustling, busy, and efficient. Ross marveled at the speed and dexterity with which the anonymous ground operator whipped his ship into a braking orbit and set it down.

And he stared enviously at the crawling clamshells on treads, bigger than houses, that cupped around his ship; the ship was completely and hermetically surrounded, and bathed in a mist of germicides and prophylactic rays.

A helmeted figure riding a little platform on the inside of one of the clamshells turned a series of knobs, climbed down, and rapped on the ship's entrance port.

Ross opened it diffidently, and almost strangled in the antiseptic fumes. Helena choked and wheezed behind him as the figure threw back its helmet and said, "Where's the captain?"

"I am he," said Ross meticulously. "I would like to be put in touch with the Cavallo Machine-Tool Company of Novj Grad."

The figure shook its long hair loose, which provided Ross with the necessary clue: it was a woman. Not a very attractive-looking woman, for she wore no makeup; but by the hair, by the brows and by the smoothness of her chin, a woman all the same. She said coldly, "If you're the captain, who's that?"

Helena said in a small voice, "I'm Helena, from Junior Unit Twenty-Three."

"Indeed." Suddenly the woman smiled. "Well, come ashore, dear," she said. "You must be tired from your trip. Both of you come ashore," she added graciously.

She led the way out of the clamshells to a waiting closed car. Azor's sun had an unpleasant bluish cast to it, not a type-G at all; Ross thought that the lighting made the woman look uglier than she really had to be. Even Helena looked pinched and bloodless, which he knew well was not the case at all.

All around them was activity. Whatever this planet's faults, it was not a stagnant home for graybeards. Ross, craning, saw nothing that was shoddy, nothing that would have looked out of place in the best-equipped port of Halsey's Planet. And the reception lounge, or whatever it was, that the woman took them to was a handsome and prettily furnished construction. "Some lunch?" the woman asked, directing her attention to Helena. "A cup of tribrew, maybe? Let me have the boy bring some." Helena looked to Ross for signals, and Ross, gritting his teeth, nodded to her to agree. Too young the last time, too male this time; was there ever going to be a planet where he mattered to anyone?

He said desperately, "Madam, forgive my interruption, but this lady and myself need urgently to get in touch with the Cavallo company. Is this Novj Grad?"

The woman's pale brows arched. She said, with an effort, "No, it is not."

"Then can you tell us where Novj Grad is?" Ross persisted. "If they have a spaceport, we can hop over there in our ship——"

The woman gasped something that sounded like, "Well!" She stood up and said pointedly to Helena, "If you'll excuse me, I have something to attend to." And swept out.

Helena stared wide-eyed at Ross. "She must've been a real Senior Citizen, huh?"

"Not exactly," said Ross despairingly. "Look, Helena, things are different here. I need your help."

"Help?"

"Yes, help!" he bellowed. "Get a grip on yourself, girl. Remember what I told you about the planet I came from? It was different from yours, remember? The old people were just like anybody else." She giggled in embarrassment. "They were!" he yelled. "And they are here, too. Old people, young people, doesn't matter. On my planet, the richest people were—well, never mind. On this planet, women are the bosses. Get it? Women are like elders. So you'll have to take over, Helena."

She was looking at him with a puzzled frown. She objected, "But if women are——"

"They are. Never mind about that part of it now; just remember that for the purposes of getting along here, you're going to be my boss. You tell me what to do. You talk to everybody. And what you have to say to them is this: You must get to Novj Grad immediately, and talk to a high-ranking member of the Cavallo Machine-Tool Company. Clear? Once we get there, I'll take over; everything will be under control then." He added prayerfully, "I hope."

Helena blinked at him. "I'm going to be your boss?" she asked.

"That's right."

"Like an elder bosses a junior? And it's legal?"

Ross started to repeat, "That's right," impatiently again. But there was a peculiar look in Helena's round eyes. "Helena!" he said warningly.

She was all concern. "Why, what is it, Ross?" she asked solicitously. "You look upset. Just leave everything to me, dear."

* * * * *

They got started on the way to Novj Grad-not in their ship (the woman had said there was no spaceport in Novj Grad), and not alone, so that Ross could not confirm his unhappy opinion of Helena's inner thoughts. But at least they were on their way to Novj Grad in the Azorian equivalent of a chartered aircraft, with Helena chatting happily with the female pilot, and Ross sitting uncomfortably on a narrow, upholstered strip behind.

Everything he saw in Azor confirmed his first impressions. The planet was busy and prosperous. Nobody seemed to be doing anything very productive, he thought, but somehow everything seemed to get done. Automatic machinery, he guessed; if women were to have any chance of gaining the upper hand on a planet, most of the hard physical work would have to be fairly well mechanized anyhow. And particularly on this planet. They had been flying for six hours, at a speed he guessed to be not much below that of sound, and fully half of the territory they passed over was bare, black rock.

The ship began losing altitude, and the pilot, who had been curled up in a relaxed position, totally ignoring the aircraft, glanced at her instrument panel. "Coming in for a landing," she warned. "Don't distract me right now, dear, I've got a thousand things to do."

She didn't seem to be doing any of them, Ross thought disapprovingly; all she did was watch varicolored lights blink on and off. But no doubt the ship landing, too, was as automatic as the piloting.

Helena turned and leaned back to Ross. "We're coming in for a landing," she relayed.

Ross said sourly, "I heard."

Helena gave him a look of reprimand and forgiveness. "I'm hungry," she mused.

The pilot turned from her controls. "You can get something at the airport," she offered eagerly. "I'll show you."

Helena looked at Ross. "Would you like something?"

But the pilot frowned. "I don't believe there's any place for men," she said disapprovingly. "Perhaps we can get something sent out for him if you like. Although, really, it's probably against the rules, you know."

Ross started to say with great dignity, "Thank you, but that won't be necessary." But he didn't quite get it out. The ship came in for its landing. There was an enormous jolt and a squawk of alarm bells and flashing lights. The ship careened crazily, and stopped.

"Oh, darn," complained the pilot mildly. "It's always doing that. Come on, dear, let's get something to eat. We'll come back for *him* later."

And Ross was left alone to stare apprehensively at the unceasingly flashing lights and to listen to the strident alarms for three-quarters of an hour.

His luck was in, though. The ship didn't explode. And eventually a pallid young man in a greasy apron appeared with a tray of sandwiches and a vacuum jug.

"Up here, boy," Ross called.

He gaped through the port. "You mean come in?"

"Sure. It's all right."

The young man put down the tray. Something in the way he looked at it prompted Ross to invite him: "Have some with me? More here than I can handle."

"Thanks; I believe I will. I, uh, was supposed to take my break after I brought you this stuff." He poured steaming brew into the cup that covered the jug, politely pushed it to Ross and swigged from the jug himself. "You're with the starship?" he asked, around a mouthful of sandwich.

"Yes. I —the captain, that is-wants to contact an outfit called Cavallo Machine-Tool. You know where they are?"

"Sure. Biggest firm on the south side. Fifteen Street; you can't miss them. The captain-is she the lady who was with Pilot Breuer?"

"Yes."

The youngster's eyes widened. "You mean you were in space-alone-with a lady?"

Ross nodded and chewed.

"And she didn't —uh-there wasn't —well-any problem?"

"No," said Ross. "You have much trouble with that kind of thing?"

The boy winced. "If I've asked once I've asked a hundred times for a transfer. Oh, those jet pilots! I used to work in a roadside truck stop. I know truckers are supposed to be rough and tough; maybe they are. But you can't tell me that deep down a trucker isn't a lady. When you tell them no, that's that. But a pilot-it just eggs them on. Azor City today, Novj Grad tomorrow-what do they care?"

Ross was fascinated and baffled. It seemed to him that they should care and care plenty. Back where he came from, it was the woman who paid and he couldn't imagine any cultural setup which could alter that biological fact. He asked cautiously: "Have you ever been-in trouble?"

The boy stiffened and looked disapproving. Then he said with a sigh: "I might as well tell you. It's all over the station anyway; they call me 'Bernie the Pullover.' Yes. Twice. Pilots both times. I can't seem to say no — —" He took another long pull from the jug and a savage bite from a second sandwich.

"I'm sure," Ross said numbly, "it wasn't your fault."

"Try telling that to the judge," Bernie the Pullover said bitterly. "The pilot speaks her piece, the medic puts the blood group tests in evidence, the doctor and crèche director depose that the child was born and is still living. Then the judge says, without even looking up, 'Paternity judgment to the plaintiff, defendant ordered to pay one thousand credits annual support, let this be a warning to you, young man, next case.' I shouldn't have joined you and eaten your sandwiches, but the fact is I was hungry. I had to sell my meal voucher yesterday to meet my payment. Miss three payments and — —" He jerked his thumb heavenward.

Ross thought and realized that the thumb must indicate the orbiting prison hulk "Minerva." It *was* the man who paid here.

He demanded: "How did all this happen?"

Bernie, having admitted his hunger, had stopped stalling and seized a third sandwich. "All what?" he asked indistinctly.

Ross thought hard and long. He realized first that he could probably never explain what he meant to Bernie, and second that if he did they'd probably both wind up aboard "Minerva" for conspiracy to advocate equality. He shifted his ground. "Of course everybody agrees on the natural superiority of women," he said, "but people seem to differ from planet to planet as to the reasons. What do they say here on Azor?"

"Oh-nothing special or fancy. Just the common-sense, logical thing. They're smaller, for one thing, and haven't got the muscles of men, so they're natural supervisors. They accumulate money as a matter of course because men die younger and women are the beneficiaries. Then, women have a natural aptitude for all the interesting jobs. I saw a broadcast about that just the other night. The biggest specialist on the planet in vocational aptitude. I forget her name, but she proved it conclusively."

He looked at the empty platter before them. "I've got to go now. Thanks for everything."

"The pleasure was mine." Ross watched his undernourished figure head for the station. He swore a little, and then buckled down to some hard thinking. Helena was his key to this world. He'd have to have a long skull-session or two with her; he couldn't be constantly prompting her or there would be serious trouble. She would be the front and he would be the very inconspicuous brains of the outfit, trailing humbly behind. But was she capable of absorbing a brand-new, rather complicated concept? She seemed to be, he told himself uncomfortably, in love with him. That would help considerably....

Helena and Pilot Breuer showed up, walking with a languor that suggested a large and pleasant meal disposed of. Helena's first words disposed with shocking speed of Ross's doubts that she was able to acquire a brand-new sociological concept. They were: "Ah, there you are, my dear. Did the boy bring you something or other to eat?"

"Yes. Thanks. Very thoughtful of you," he said pointedly, with one eye on Breuer's reaction. There was none; he seemed to have struck the right note.

"Pilot Breuer," said Helena blandly, "thinks I'd enjoy an evening doing the town with her and a few friends."

"But the Cavallo people — —"

"Ross," she said gently, "don't *nag*."

He shut up. And thought: wait until I get her out into space. *If* I get her out into space. She'd be a damned fool to leave this wacked-up culture....

Breuer was saying, with an altogether too-innocent air, "I'd better get you two settled in a hotel for the night; then I'll pick up Helena and a few friends and we'll show her what old Novj Grad has to offer in the way of night life. Can't have her batting around the universe saying Azor's sidewalks are rolled up at 2100, can we? And then she can do her trading or whatever it is with Cavallo bright and early tomorrow, eh?"

Ross realized that he was being jollied out of an attack of the sulks. He didn't like it.

* * * * *

The hotel was small and comfortable, with a bar crowded by roistering pilots and their dates. The glimpses Ross got of social life on Azor added up to a damnably unfair picture. It was the man who paid. Breuer roguishly tested the mattress in their room, nudging Helena, and then announced, "Get settled, kids, while I visit the bar."

When the door rolled shut behind her Ross said furiously: "Look, you! Protective mimicry's fine up to a point, but let's not forget what this mission is all about. We seem to be suckered into spending the night, but by hell tomorrow morning bright and early we find those Cavallo people — "

"There," Helena said soothingly. "Don't be angry, Ross. I promise I won't be out late, and she really did insist."

"I suppose so," he grumbled. "Just remember it's no pleasure trip."

"Not for you, perhaps," she smiled sweetly.

He let it drop there, afraid to push the matter.

Breuer returned in about ten minutes with a slight glow on. "It's all fixed," she told Helena. "Got a swell crowd lined up. Table at Virgin Willie's —oops!" She glanced at Ross. "No harm in it, of course," she said. "Anything you want, Ross, just dial service. It's on my account. I fixed it with the desk."

"Thanks."

They left, and Ross went grumpily to bed.

* * * * *

A secretive rustle in the room awoke him. "Helena?" he asked drowsily.

Pilot Breuer's voice giggled drunkenly, "Nope. Helena's passed out at Virgin Willie's, kind of the way I figured she would be on triple antigravs. Had my eye on you since Azor City, baby. You gonna be nice to me?"

"Get out of here!" Ross hissed furiously. "Out of here or I'll yell like hell."

"So yell," she giggled. "I got the house dick fixed. They know me here, baby — —"

He fumbled for the bedside light and snapped it on. "I'll pitch you right through the door," he announced. "And if you give me any more lip I won't bother to open it before I do."

She hiccupped and said, "A spirited lad. That's the way I like 'em." With one hand she drew a nasty-looking little pistol. With the other she pulled a long zipper and stepped out of her pilot's coveralls.

Ross gulped. There were three ways to play this, the smart way, the stupid way, and the way that all of a sudden began to look attractive. He tried the stupid way.

He got the pistol barrel alongside his ear for his pains. "Don't jump me," Pilot Breuer giggled. "The boys that've tried to take this gun away from me are stretched end to end from here to Azor City. By me, baby."

Ross blinked through a red-spotted haze. He took a deep breath and got smart. "You're pretty tough," he said admiringly.

"Oh, sure." She kicked the coveralls across the room and moved in on him. "Baby," she said caressingly, "if I seem to sort of forget myself in the next couple of minutes, don't get any ideas. I *never* let go of my gun. Move over."

"Sure," Ross said hollowly. This, he told himself disgustedly, was the damnedest, silliest, ridiculousest....

There was a furious hiccup from the door. "So!" Helena said venomously, pushing the door wide and almost falling to the floor. "So!"

Ross flailed out of the bed, kicking the pistol out of Pilot Breuer's hand in the process. He cried enthusiastically, "Helena, dear!"

"Don't you 'Helena-dear' me!" she said, moving in and kicking the door shut behind her. "I leave you alone for one little minute, and what happens? And *you!*"

"Sorry," Pilot Breuer muttered, climbing into her coveralls. "Wrong room. Must've had one anti-grav too many." She licked her lips apprehensively, zipping her coveralls and sidling toward the door. With one hand on the knob, she said diffidently, "If I could have my gun back — —? No, you're right! I'll get it tomorrow." She got through the door just ahead of a lamp.

"Hussy!" spat Helena. "And you, Ross — —"

It was the last straw. As Ross lurched toward her he regretted only one thing: that he didn't have a hairbrush.

Pilot Breuer had been right. Nobody paid any attention to the noise.

* * * * *

"Yes, Ross." Helena had hardly touched her breakfast; she sat with her eyes downcast.

"'Yes, Ross'," he mimicked bitterly. "It better be 'Yes, Ross.' This place may look all right to you, but it's trouble. You don't want to find yourself stuck here all your life, do you? Then do what I tell you."

"Yes, Ross."

He pushed the remains of his food away. "Oh, the hell with it," he said dispiritedly. "I wish I'd never started out on this fool's errand. And I double damn well wish I'd left you in the dye vats."

"Yes, Ro — —I mean, I'm glad you didn't, Ross," she said in a small voice.

He stood up and patted her shoulder absently. "Come on," he said, "we've got to get over to the Cavallo place. I wish you had let me talk to them on the phone."

She said reasonably, "But you said — —"

"I know what I said. When we get there, remember that I do the talking."

They walked through green-lit streets, filled with proud-looking women and sad-eyed men. The Cavallo Machine-Tool Corporation was only a few intersections away, by the map the desk clerk had drawn for Helena; they found it without trouble. It was a smallish sort of building for a factory, Ross thought, but perhaps that was how factories went on Azor. Besides, it was well constructed and beautifully landscaped with the purplish lawns these people seemed to prefer.

Helena led him through the door, as was right and proper. She said to the busy little bald-headed man who seemed to be the receptionist, "We're expected. Miss Cavallo, please."

"Certainly, Ma'am," he said with a gap-toothed smile, and worked a combination of rods and buttons on the desk beside him. In a moment, he said, "Go right in. Three up and four over; can't miss it."

They passed through a noisy territory of machines where metal was sliced, spun, hacked, and planed; no one seemed to be paying any attention to them. Ross wondered who had built the machines, and had a sudden flash of realization as to where those builders were now: On "Minerva," staring at the unattainable free sky.

Miss Cavallo was a motherly type with a large black cigar. "Sit right down," she said heartily. "You, too, young man. Tell me what we in Cavallo Company can do for you."

Helena opened her mouth, but Ross stopped her with a gesture. "That's enough," he said quietly. "I'll take over. Miss Cavallo," he declaimed from memory, "what follows is under the seal."

"Is it indeed! What do you know," she said.

Ross said, "Wesley."

Miss Cavallo slapped her thigh admiringly. "Son of a gun," she said admiringly. "How this takes me back-those long-ago childhood days, learning these things at my mother's knee. Let's see. Uh-the limiting velocity is C."

"But C^2 is not a velocity," Ross finished triumphantly. And, from the heart, "Miss Cavallo, you don't begin to know how happy this makes me."

Miss Cavallo reached over and pumped his hand, then Helena's. To the girl she said, "You've got a right to be a proud woman, believe me. The way he got through it, without a single stumble! Never saw anything like it in my life. Well, just tell me what I can do for you, now that that's over."

Ross took a deep, deep breath. He said earnestly, "A great deal. I don't know where to begin. You see, it all goes back to Halsey's Planet, where I come from. This, uh, this ship came in, a longliner, and it got some of us a little worried because, well, it seemed that some of the planets were no longer in communication. We-uh, Miss Cavallo?" She was smiling pleasantly enough, but Ross had the crazy feeling that he just wasn't getting through to her.

"Go right ahead," she boomed. "God knows, I've got nothing against men in business; that's old-fashioned prejudice. Take your time. I won't bite you. Get on with your proposition, young man."

"It isn't exactly a proposition," Ross said weakly. All of a sudden the words seemed hard to find. What did you say to a potential partner in the salvation of the human race when she just nodded and blew cigar smoke at you?

He made an effort. "Halsey's Planet was the seventh alternate destination for this ship, and so we figured — —That is, Miss Cavallo, it kind of looked like there was some sort of trouble. So Mr. Haarland-he's the one who has the F-T-L secret on Halsey, like you do here on Azor-he passed it on to me, of course-well, he asked me to, well, sort of take a look around." He stopped. The words by then were just barely audible anyhow; and Miss Cavallo had been looking furtively at her watch.

Miss Cavallo shrugged sympathetically to Helena. "They're all like that under the skin, aren't they?" she observed ambiguously. "Well, if men could take our jobs away from us, what would we do? Stay home and mind the kids?" She roared and poked a box of cigars at Helena.

"Now," she said briskly, "let's get down to cases. I really enjoyed hearing those lines from you, young man, and I want you to know that I'm prepared to help you in any possible way because of them. Open a line of credit, speed up deliveries, send along some of our technical people to help you get set up-anything. Now, what can I do for you? Turret lathes? Grinders? Screw machines?"

"Miss Cavallo," Ross said desperately, "don't you know anything about the faster-than-light secret?"

She said impatiently, "Of course I do, young man. Said the responses, didn't I? There's no call for that item, though."

"I don't want to *buy* one," Ross cried. "I have one. Don't you realize that the human race is in danger? Populations are dying out or going out of communication all over the galaxy. Don't you want to do something about it before we all go under?"

Miss Cavallo dropped all traces of a smile. Her face was like flint as she stood up and pointed to the window. "Young man," she said icily, "take a look out there. That's the Cavallo Machine-Tool Company. Does that look as if we're going under?"

"I know, but Clyde, Cyrnus One, Ragansworld-at least a dozen planets I can name-are *gone*. Didn't you ever think that you might be next?"

Miss Cavallo kept her voice level, but only with a visible effort.

She said flatly, "No. Never. Young man, I have plenty to do right here on Azor without bothering my head about those places you're talking about. Seventy-five years ago there was another fellow just like you; Flarney, some name like that; my grandmother told me about him. He came bustling in here causing trouble, with that old silly jingle about Wesley and C-square and so on, with some cock-and-bull story about a planet that was starving to death, stirring up a lot of commotion. Well, he wound up on 'Minerva,' because he wouldn't take no for an answer. Watch out that you don't do the same."

She marched majestically to the door. "And now," she said, "if you've wasted quite enough of my time, kindly leave."

CHAPTER VIII.

"Stupid old bat," Ross muttered. They were walking aimlessly down Fifteen Street, the nicely-landscaped machine tool works behind them.

Helena said timidly: "You really shouldn't talk that way, Ross. She *is* older than you, after all. Old heads are — —"

" — —wisest," he wearily agreed. "Also the most conservative. Also the most rigidly inflexible; also the most firmly closed to the reception of new ideas. With one exception."

She reeled under the triple blasphemy and then faintly asked: "What's the exception?"

Ross became aware that they were not alone. Their very manner of walking, he a little ahead, obviously leading the way, was drawing unfavorable attention from passers-by. Nothing organized or even definite-just looks ranging from puzzled distaste to anger. He said, "Somebody named Haarland. Never mind," and in a lower voice: "Straighten up. Step out a little ahead of me. Scowl."

She managed it all except the scowl. The expression on her face got some stupefied looks from other pedestrians, but nothing worse.

Helena said loudly and plaintively: "I don't like it here after all, Ross. Can't we get away from all these women?"

Should the impulse seize you, placard ancient Brooklyn with twenty-four sheets proclaiming the Dodgers to be cellar-dwelling bums. Mount a detergent box and inform a crowd of Altairians that they are degenerate slith-fondlers if you must. Announce in a crowded Cephean bar room that Sadkia Revall is no better than she should be. From these situations you have some chance of emerging intact. But never, never pronounce the word "women" as Helena pronounced it on Fifteen Street, Novj Grad, Azor.

The mob took only seconds to form.

Ross and Helena found themselves with their backs to the glass doors of a food store. The handful of women who had actually heard the remark were all talking to them simultaneously, with fist-shaking. Behind them stood as many as a dozen women who knew only that something had happened and that there were comfortably outnumbered victims available. The noise was deafening, and Helena began to cry. Ross first wondered if he could bring himself to knock down a woman; then realized after studying the hulking virago in their foreground that he might bring himself to try but probably would not succeed.

She seemed to be accusing Helena of masquerading, of advocating equality, of uttering obscenely antisocial statements in the public road, to the affront of all decent-minded girls.

There was violence in the air. Ross was on the point of blocking a roundhouse right when the glass doors opened behind them. The small diversion distracted the imbecile collective brain of the mob.

"What's going on here?" a suety voice demanded. "Ladies, may I please get through?"

It was a man trying to emerge from the food shop with a double armful of cartons. He was a great fat slob, quite hairless, and smelling powerfully of kitchen. He wore the gravy-spotted whites of any cook anywhere.

The virago said to him, "Keep out of this, Willie. This fellow here's a masquerader. The thing I heard him say — —!"

"I'm not," Helena wept. "I'm not!"

The cook stooped to look into her face and turned on the mob. "She isn't," he said definitely. "She's a lady from another system. She was slopping up triple antigravs at my place last night with a gang of jet pilots."

"That doesn't prove a thing!" the virago yelled.

"Madam," the cook said wearily, "after her third antigrav I had to trip her up and crown her. She was about to climb the bar and corner my barman."

Ross looked at her fixedly. She stopped crying and nervously cleared her throat.

"So if you'll just let us through," the cook bustled, seizing the psychological moment of doubt. His enormous belly bulldozed a lane for them. "Beg pardon. Excuse us. Madam, will you-thank you. Beg pardon — —"

The lynchers were beginning to drift away, embarrassed. The party had collapsed. "Faster," the cook hissed at them. "Beg pardon — —" And they were in the clear and well down the street.

"Thank you, Sir," Helena said humbly.

"Just 'Willie', *if* you please," the fat man said.

One hand descended on Ross's shoulder and another on Helena's. They both belonged to the virago. She spun them around, glaring. "*I'm* not satisfied with the brush-off," she snapped. "Exactly what did you mean by that remark you made?"

Helena wailed, "It's just that you and all these other women here seem so *young*."

The virago's granite face softened. She let go and tucked in a strand of steel-wool hair. "Did you really think so, dear?" she asked, beaming. "There, I'm sorry I got excited. A wee bit jealous, were you? Well, we're broad-minded here in Novj Grad." She patted Helena's arm and walked off, smiling and jaunty.

Virgin Willie led off and they followed him. Ross's knees were shaky. The virago had not known that to Helena "young" meant "stupid."

The cook absently acknowledged smiles and nods as they walked. He was, obviously, a character. Between salutes he delivered a low-voiced, rapid-fire reaming to Ross and Helena. "Silly stunt. Didn't you hear about the riots? Supposed to be arms caches somewhere here on the south side. Everybody's nerves absolutely ragged. Somebody gets smashed up in traffic, they blame it on us. Don't care *where* you're from. Watch it next time."

"We will, Willie," Helena said contritely. "And I think you run an awfully nice restaurant."

"Yeah," said Ross, looking at her.

Willie muttered, "I guess you're clear. You still staying at that hot pilot's hangout? This is where we say good-by, then. You turn left."

He waddled on down the street. Helena said instantly, "I don't remember a thing, Ross."

"Okay," he said. "You don't remember a thing."

She looked relieved and said brightly, "So let's get back to the hotel."

"Okay," he said. Climbed the bar and tried to corner the....Halfway to the hotel he slowed, then stopped, and said, "I just thought of something. Maybe we're not staying there any more. After last night why should Breuer carry us on her tab? I thought we'd have some money to carry us from the Cavallos by now — —"

"The ship?" she asked in a small voice.

"Across the continent. Hell! Maybe Breuer forgave and forgot. Let's try, anyway."

They never got as far as the hotel. When they reached the square it stood on, there was a breathless rush and Bernie stood before them, panting and holding a hand over his chest. "In here," he gasped, and nodded at a shopfront that announced hot brew. Ross thoughtlessly started first through the door and caught Bernie's look of alarm. He opened the door for Helena, who went through smiling nervously.

They settled at a small table in an empty corner in stiff silence. "I've been walking around that square all morning," Bernie said, with a cowed look at Helena.

Ross told her: "This young man and I had a talk yesterday at the plane while you were eating. What is it, Bernie?"

He still couldn't believe that he was doing it, but Bernie said in a scared whisper: "Wanted to head you off and warn you. Breuer was down at the field cafe this morning, talking loud to the other hot-shots. She said you-both of you-talked equality. Said she got up with a hangover and you were gone. But she said there'd be six policewomen waiting in your room when you got back." He leaned forward on the table. Ross remembered that he had been forced to sell his ration card.

"Here comes the waiter," he said softly. "Order something for all of us. We have a little money. And thanks, Bernie."

Helena asked, "What do we *do*?"

"We eat," Ross said practically. "Then we think. Shut up; let Bernie order."

* * * * *

They ate; and then they thought. Nothing much seemed to come from all the thinking, though.

They were a long, long way from the spaceship. Ross commandeered all of Helena's leftover cash. It was almost, not quite, enough for one person to get halfway back to Azor City. He and Bernie turned out their pockets and added everything they had, including pawnable valuables. That helped. It made the total almost enough for one person to get three-quarters of the way back.

It didn't help enough.

Ross said, "Bernie, what would happen if we, well, stole something?"

Bernie shrugged. "It's against the law, of course. They probably wouldn't prosecute, though."

"They wouldn't?"

"Not if they can prove egalitarianism on you. Stealing's against the law; preaching equality is against the *state*. You get the maximum penalty for that."

Helena choked on her drink, but Ross merely nodded. "So we might as well take a chance," he said. "Thanks, Bernie. We won't bother you any more. You'll forget you heard this, won't you?"

"The hell I will!" Bernie squawked. "If you're getting out of here, I want to go with you! You aren't leaving *me* behind!"

"But Bernie — —" Ross started. He was interrupted by the manager, a battleship-class female with a mighty prow, who came scowling toward them.

"Pipe down," she ordered coarsely. "This place is for decent people; we don't want no disturbances here. If you can't act decent, get out."

"Awk," said Helena as Ross kicked her under the table. "I mean, yes ma'am. Sorry if we were talking too loud." They watched the manager walk away in silence.

As soon as she was fairly away, Ross hissed, "It's out of the question, Bernie. You might be jumping from the frying-pan into the fire."

Bernie asked, startled, "The what?"

"The-never mind, it's just an expression where I come from. It means you might get out of this place and find yourself somewhere worse. We don't know where we're going next; you might wish to God you were back here within the next three days."

"I'll take that chance," Bernie said earnestly. "Look, Ross, I played square with you. I didn't have to stick my neck out and warn you. How about giving me a break too?"

Helena interrupted, "He's right, Ross. After all, we owe him that much, don't we? I mean, if a person does that much for a person, a person ought to — —"

"Oh, shut up." Ross glared at both of them. "You two seem to think this is a game," he said bitterly. "Let me set you straight, both of you. It isn't. More hangs on what happens to me than either of you realize. The fate of the human race, for instance."

Helena flashed a look at Bernie. "Of *course*, Ross," she said soothingly. "Both of us know that, don't we, Bernie?"

Bernie stammered, "Sure-sure we do, Ross." He rubbed his ankle. He went on, "Honest, Ross, I want to get the hell away from Azor once and for all. I don't care *where* you're going. Anything would be better than this place and the damned female bloodsuckers that — —"

He stopped, petrified. His eyes, looking over Ross's shoulder, were enormous.

"Go on, sonny," said a rich female voice from behind Ross. "Don't let me and the lieutenant stop you just when you're going good."

* * * * *

"It must have been that damn manager," Bernie said for the fifteenth time.

Ross uncrossed his legs painfully and tried lying on the floor on his side. "What's the difference?" he asked. "They got us; we're in the jug. And face it: somebody would have caught us sooner or later, and we might have wound up in a worse jail than this one." He shifted uncomfortably. "If that's possible, I mean. Why don't they at least have beds in these places?"

"Oh," said Bernie immediately, "some do. The jails in Azor City and Nuevo Reykjavik have beds; Novj Grad, Eleanor, and Milo don't. I mean, that's what they tell me," he added virtuously.

"Sure," Ross growled. "Well, what do they tell you usually happens next?"

Bernie spread his hands. "Different things. First there's a hearing. That's all over by now. Then an indictment and trial. Maybe that's started already; sometimes they get it in on the same day as the hearing, sometimes not. Then-tomorrow sometime, most likely-comes the sentencing. We'll know about that, though, because we'll be there. The law's very strict on that-they always have you in the court for sentencing."

Ross cried, "You mean the trial might be going on right now without us?"

"Of course. What else? Think they'd take a chance on having the prisoners creating a disturbance during the trial?"

Ross groaned and turned his face to the wall. For this, he thought, he had come the better part of a hundred light years; for this he had left a comfortable job with a brilliant future. He spent a measurable period of time cursing the memory of old Haarland and his double-jointed, persuasive tongue.

Back in the days of Ross's early teens he had seen a good many situations like this in the tri-dis, and the hero had never failed to extricate himself by a simple exercise of superhuman strength, intellect, and ingenuity. That, Ross told himself, was just what he needed now. The trouble was, he didn't have them.

All he had was the secret of faster-than-light travel. And, here on Azor as on the planet of the graybeards, it had laid a king-sized egg. Women, Ross thought bitterly, women were basically inward-directed and self-seeking; trust them with the secret of F-T-L; make them, like the Cavallos, custodians of a universe-racking truth; and see the secret lost or embalmed in sterile custom. What, he silently demanded of himself, did the greatest of scientific discoveries mean to a biological baby-foundry? How could any female-no single member of which class had ever painted a great picture, written a great book, composed a great sonata, or discovered a great scientific truth-appreciate the ultimate importance of the F-T-L drive? It was like entrusting a first-folio Shakespeare to a broody hen; the shredded scraps would be made into a nest. For the egg came first. Motherhood was all.

That explained it, of course. That, Ross told himself moodily, explained everything except why the F-T-L secret had fallen into apparently equal or worse desuetude on such planets as Gemsel, Clyde, Cyrnus One, Ragansworld, Tau Ceti II, Capella's family of eight, and perhaps a hundred others.

Ragansworld was gone entirely, drowned in a planetary nebula.

The planet of the graybeard had gone to seed; nothing new, nothing not hallowed by tradition had a chance in its decrepit social order.

His home, Halsey's Planet, was rapidly, calmly, inevitably depopulating itself.

And Azor had fallen into a rigid, self-centered matriarchal order that only an act of God could break.

Was there a pattern? Were there any similarities?

Ross searched desperately in his mind; but without result. The image of Helena kept intruding itself between him and his thoughts. Was he getting sentimental about that sweet little chucklehead? Who, he hastily added, had come near to criminally assaulting him, who had climbed the....

He turned to the little waiter and demanded: "Will she-Helena-be on the orbital station with us if we're all convicted?"

"Hmm-no, I should think not. As a responsible person, she gets the supreme penalty."

Ross numbly asked after a long pause, "How? Nothing-painful?" It was hard to think of Helena dangling grotesquely at a rope's end or jolting as she sat strapped in a large, ugly chair. But there were things he had heard of which were horribly worse.

Bernie had been watching him. "I'm sorry," the little man said soberly. "It's up to the judge. She's a foreigner, so they may consider that an extenuating circumstance and place some quick-acting poison aboard for her to take. Otherwise it's slow starvation."

A faint, irrational hope had begun to dawn in Ross's mind. "Aboard what? Exactly how does it work?"

"They'll put her aboard some hulk with the rockets disabled, fire it off into space-and that's that. I suppose they'll use the ship she came in — —"

Ross was frantically searching his pockets. He had a stylus. "Got any paper?" he briskly demanded of Bernie.

"Yes, but — —?" The waiter blankly passed over an order book. Ross sprawled on the floor and began to scribble: "Never mind how or why this works. Do it. You saw me work the big fan-shaped computer in the center room and you can do it too. Find the master star maps in the chart room. Look up the co-ordinates of Halsey's System. Set these co-ordinates on the twenty-seven dials marked Proximate Mass. Take the readings on the windows above the dials and set them on the cursors of the computer — —" He scribbled furiously, from time to time forcing himself deliberately to slow down as the writing became an unreadable scrawl. He filled the ruled fronts of the order pages and then the backs-perhaps ten thousand closely-written words, and not one of them wasted. Haarland's precise instructions, mercilessly drilled into him, flowed out again.

He flung the stylus down at last and read through the book again, ignoring the gaping Bernie. It was all there, as far as he could tell. Grant her a lot of luck and more brains than he privately credited her with, and she had a fighting chance of winding up within radar range of Halsey's Planet. GCA could take her down from there; an annoying ship-like object hanging on the radarscopes would provoke a reconnaissance.

She knew absolutely nothing about F-T-L or the Wesley drive, but then-neither did he. That fact itself was no handicap.

He might rot on "Minerva," but some word might get back to Haarland. And so would the ship. And Helena would not perish miserably in a drifting hulk.

Bernie saw the mysterious job was ended and dared to ask, "A letter?"

"No," Ross said jubilantly. "By God, if things break right they won't get her. It's like this — —"

He happily began to explain that his F-T-L ship's rockets were only auxiliaries for fine ma-neuvering, but he counted on the court not knowing that. If he and Helena could persuade....

As he went on the look on Bernie's face changed very slowly from hope to pity to politely-simulated interest. Correspondingly Ross's accounting became labored and faulty. The pauses became longer and at last he broke off, filled with self-contempt at his folly. He said bitterly, "You don't think it'll work."

"Oh, no!" Bernie protested with too much heartiness. "I could see she's awfully mechanically-minded for a woman, even if it wouldn't be polite to say so. Sure it'll work, Ross. Sure!"

The hell it would.

At least he had disposed of a few hours. And-perhaps some bungling setting would explode the ship, or end a Wesley Jump in the heart of a white dwarf star-sudden annihilation, whiffing Helena out of existence before her body could realize that it had died, before the beginning of apprehension could darken happy absorption with a task she thought would bring her to safety.

For that reason alone he had to carry the scheme through.

* * * * *

The courtroom was a chintzy place bright with spring flowers. Ross and Helena looked numbly at one another from opposite corners while the previous order of business was cleared from the docket. A wedding.

The judge, unexpectedly sweet-faced and slender though gray, obviously took such parts of her work seriously. "Marylyn and Kent," she was saying earnestly to the happy couple, "I suppose you know my reputation. I lecture people a bit before I tie the knot. Evidently it's not such a bad idea because my marriages turn out well. Last week in Eleanor one of my girls was arrested and reprimanded for gross infidelity and a couple of years ago right here in Novj Grad one of my boys got five hundred lashes for nonsupport. Let's hope it did them some good, but the cases were unusual. My people, I like to think, know their rights and responsibilities when they walk out of my court, and I think the record bears me out.

"Marylyn, you have chosen to share part of your life with this man. You intend to bear his children. This should not be because your animal appetites have overcome you and you can't win his consent in any other way but because you know, down deep in your womanly heart, that you can make him happy. Never forget this. If you should thoughtlessly conceive by some other man, don't tell him. He would only brood. Be thrifty, Marylyn. I have seen more marriages broken up by finances than any other reason. If your husband earns a hundred Eleanors a week, spend only that and no more. If he makes *fifty* Eleanors a week spend only that and no more. Honorable poverty is preferable to debt. And, from a practical standpoint, if you spend more than your husband earns he will be jailed for debt sooner or later, with resulting loss to your own pocket.

"Kent, you have accepted the proposal of this woman. I see by your dossier that you got in just under the wire. In your income group the antibachelor laws would have caught up with you in one more week. I must say I don't like the look of it, but I'll give you the benefit of the doubt. I want to talk to you about the meaning of marriage. Not just the wage assignment, not just the insurance policy, not just the waiver of paternity and copulation 'rights', so-called. Those, as a good citizen, you will abide by automatically-Heaven help you if you don't. But there is more to marriage than that. The honor you have been done by this woman who sees you as desirable and who wishes to make you happy over the years is not a sterile legalism. Marriage is like a rocket, I sometimes think. The brute, unreasoning strength of the main jets representing the husband's share and the delicate precise steering and stabilizing jets the wife's. We have all of us seen too many marriages crash to the ground like a rocket when these roles were reversed. It is not reasonable to expect the wife to provide the drive-that is, the income. It is not reasonable to expect the husband to provide the steering-that is, the direction of the personal and household expenditures. So much for the material side of things. On the spiritual side, I have little to say. The laws are most explicit; see that you obey them-and if you don't, you had better pray that you wind up in some court other than mine. I have no patience with the obsolete doctrine that there is such a legal entity as seduction by female, despite the mouthings of certain so-called jurists who disgrace the bench of a certain nearby city.

"Having heard these things, Marylyn and Kent, step forward and join hands."

They did. The ceremony was short and simple; the couple then walked from the courtroom under the beaming smile of the judge.

A burly guard next to Ross pointed at the groom. "Look," she said sentimentally. "He's crying. Cute!"

"I don't blame the poor sucker," Ross flared, and then, being a man of conscience, wondered suddenly if that was why, on Halsey's Planet, women cried at weddings.

A clerk called: "Dear, let's have those egalitarians front and center, please. Her honor's terribly rushed."

Helena was escorted forward from one side, while Ross and Bernie were jostled to the fore from the other. The judge turned from the happy couple. As she looked down at the three of them the smile that curved her lips turned into something quite different. Ross, quailing, suddenly realized that he had seen just that expression once before. It was when he was very,

very young, when a friend of his mother's had come bustling into the kitchen where he was playing, just after she had smelled, and just before she had seen, the long-dead rat he had fetched up from the abandoned cellar across the street.

While the clerk was reading the orders and indictment, the judge's stare never wavered. And when the clerk had finished, the judge's silent stare remained, for a long, terrible time.

In the quietest of voices, the judge said, "So."

Ross caught a flicker of motion out of the corner of his eye. He turned just in time to see Bernie, knees buckling, slip white-faced and unconscious to the floor. The guards rushed forward, but the judge raised a peremptory hand. "Leave him alone," she ordered soberly. "It is kinder. Defendants, you are charged with the gravest of crimes. Have you anything to say before sentence is passed on you?"

Ross tried to force words-any words, to protest, to plead, to vilify-through his clogged throat. All he managed was a croaking sound; and Helena, by his side, nudged him sharply to silence. He turned to her sharply, and realized that this was the best chance he'd be likely to get. He clutched at her, rolled up his eyes, slumped to the floor in as close an imitation of Bernie's swoon as he could manage.

The judge was visibly annoyed, and this time she didn't stop the attendants when they rushed in to kick him erect. But he had the consolation of seeing a flash of understanding cross Helena's face, and her hand dart to a pocket with the paper he had handed her. In the confusion no one saw.

The rest of the courtroom scene was kaleidoscopic in Ross's recollection. The only part he remembered clearly was the judge's voice as she said to him and Bernie, " — —for the rest of your lives, as long as Almighty God shall, in Her infinite wisdom, permit you the breath of life, be banished from Azor and all of its allied worlds to the prison hulk in 'Orbit Minerva.'"

And they were hustled out as the judge, even more wrathful than before, turned to pronounce sentence on Helena.

CHAPTER IX

The guard spat disgustedly. "Fine lot of wrecks we're getting," she complained. "Not like the old days. They used to send real men here." She glowered at Ross and Bernie, holding their commitment papers loosely in her hand. "And for treason, too!" she added. "Used to be it took guts to commit a crime against the state." She shook her head, then made a noise of distaste and scribbled initials on the commitment papers. She handed them back to the pilot who had brought them up from Azor, who grinned, waved, and got out of there. "All right," said the guard, "we have to take what we get. I'll have to put you two on construction; you'll never stand up under hard work. Keep your noses clean, that's all. Up at 0500; breakfast till 0510; work detail till 1950; dinner and recreation till 2005; then lights out. Miss a formation and you miss a meal. Miss two, and you get punishment detail. Nobody misses three."

Ross and Bernie found themselves sharing a communal cell. They had all of five minutes to look around and get oriented; then they were out on their first work detail.

It wasn't so bad as it sounded. Their shiftmates were a couple of dozen ragged-looking wrecks, half-heartedly assembling a sort of meccano-toy wall out of sheets of perforated steel and clip-spring bolts. All the parts seemed well worn; some of the bolts hardly closed. It took Ross the better part of his first detail, whispering when the guards were looking the other way, to find out why. Their half of the prisoners were Construction; the other half was Demolition. What Construction in the morning put up, Demolition in the evening tore down. Neither side was anxious to set any speed records, and the guards without exception were too bored to care.

With any kind of luck, Ross found, he could hope eventually to get a real job-manning the "Minerva's" radar, signal, or generating facilities, working in the kitchens or service shops, perhaps even as an orderly in the guard quarters. (Although Ross quite by accident chanced to see a guard's orderly as he passed through a corridor near the work area, a handkerchief held daintily to his nose. And though the orderly's clothing was neat and his plump cheeks indicated good eating, the haunted expression in his eyes made Ross think twice.)

The one thing he could not do, according to the testimony of every man he spoke to, was escape.

The fifth time Ross got that answer, the guard had stepped out of the room. Ross took the opportunity to thrash the thing through. "Why?" he demanded. "Back where I come from we've got lots of prisons. I never heard of one nobody escaped from."

The other prisoner laughed shortly. "Now you have," he said. "Go ahead, try. Every one of us has tried, one time or another. There's only one thing stopping you-there's no place to go. You can get past the guards easy enough-they're lazy, when they're not either drunk or boy-chasing. You can roam around 'Minerva' all you like. You can even get to the spacelock, and if you want to you can walk right through it. But not in a spacesuit, because there aren't any on board. And not into the tender that brings us up from Azor, because you aren't built right."

Ross looked puzzled. "Not built right?"

"That's right. There's telescreens and remote-control locks built into that tender. The pilot brings you up, but once she couples with 'Minerva' the controls lock. And the only way they get unlocked is when three women, in three different substations down on Azor, push the RC releases. And they don't do that until they look in their screens, and see that everybody who has turned up in the tender has stripped down to nothing at all, and every one of them is by-God female. Any further questions?" He grinned wryly. "Don't even think about plastic surgery, if that happens to cross your mind," he said. "We have two men here who tried it. You don't have much equipment here; you can't do a neat enough job."

Ross gulped. "Hadn't given it a thought," he assured the other man. "You can't even hide away in a trunk or something?"

The prisoner shook his head. "Aren't any trunks. Everything's one way-Azor to 'Minerva' — except pilots and guards. No men ever go back. When you die, you go out the lock-without a ship. Same with everything else that they want to get rid of."

Ross thought hard. "What if they-well, what if you're sent up here and all, and then some new evidence turns up and you're found innocent? Don't they send you back then?"

"Found innocent?" The man looked at Ross pityingly. "Man, you *are* new. Hey," he called. "Hey, Chuck! This guy wants to know what happens if they find out back on Azor that he's innocent!"

Chuck exploded into laughter. Wiping his eyes, he walked over to Ross. "Thanks," he grinned. "Haven't had a good laugh in fifteen years."

"I don't see that that's so funny," Ross said defensively. "After all, the judge can make a mistake, none of us is per-awk!"

"Shut up!" Chuck hissed, holding a hand over Ross's mouth. "Do you want to get us all in *real* trouble? Some of these guys would rat to the guards for an extra hunk of bread! The judges never make a mistake." And his lips formed the silent word: "Officially."

He let go of Ross and stood back, but didn't walk away. He scratched his head. "Say," he said, "you ask some stupid questions. Where are you from, anyhow?"

Ross said bitterly, "What's the use? You won't believe me. I happen to be from a place called Halsey's Planet, which is a good long distance from here. About as far as light will travel in two hundred years, if that gives you an idea. I came here in an F-T-L —that is, a faster-than-light ship. You don't know what that is, of course, but I did. It was a mistake, I admit it. But here I am."

Somewhat to Ross's surprise, Chuck didn't laugh again. He looked dubious, and he scratched his head some more, but he didn't laugh. To the other prisoner he said, "What do you think, Sam?"

Sam shrugged. "So maybe we were wrong," he observed.

Ross demanded, "Wrong about what?"

"Well," Chuck said hesitantly, "there's a guy here named Flarney. He's a pretty old son-of-a-gun by now, must be at least ninety, and he's been here a good long time. Dunno how long. But he talks crazy, just like you. No offense," he added, "it's just that we all thought he'd gone space-happy. But maybe we're wrong. Unless — —" his eyes narrowed "unless the two of you are both space-happy, or trying to kid us, or something."

Ross said urgently, "I swear, Chuck, there's no such thing. It's true. Who's this Flarney? Where does he say he came from?"

"Who can make sense out of what he says? All I know is, he talked a lot about something faster than light. That's crazy; that's like saying slower than dark, or bigger than green, or something. But I don't know, maybe it means something."

"Believe me, Chuck, it does! Where is this man-can I see him?"

Chuck looked uncertain. "Well, sure. That is, you can see him all right. But it isn't going to do you a whole hell of a lot of good, because he's dead. Died yesterday; they're going to pitch him out into space sometime today."

Sam said, "This is when Whitker flips. One week without his old pal Flarney and he'll begin to look funny. Two weeks and he starts acting funny. Three and he's talking funny and the guards begin to crack down. I give him a month to get shot down and heaved through the locker."

Old pal? Ross demanded, "Who's this Whitker? Where can I get in touch with him?"

"Him and Flarney were both latrine orderlies. That's where they put the feeble old men, mopping and polishing. Number Two head, any hour of the day or night. Old buzzard has his racket-we're supposed to get a hank of cellosponge per man per day, but he's always 'fresh out' —unless you slip him your saccharine ration every once in a while."

Ross asked the way to Number Two head and the routine. But it was an hour before he could bring himself to ask the hulking guard for permission.

"Sure, sonny," she boomed. "I'll show you the way. Need any help?"

"No, thanks, ma'am," he said hastily, and she roared with laughter. So did the members of the construction gang; it must have been an ancient gag. He hurried on his way thinking dark and bloody thoughts.

"Whitker?" he asked a tottering ancient who nodded and drowsed amid the facilities of the head.

The old man looked up blearily and squeaked: "Fresh out. Fresh out. You should've saved some from yesterday."

"That's all right. I'm a new man here. I want to ask you about your friend Flarney ——"

Whitker bowed his head and began to cry noiselessly.

"I'm sorry, Mr. Whitker. I heard. But there's something we can do about it-maybe. Flarney was a faster-than-light man. He must have told you that. So am I. Ross, from Halsey's Planet."

He hadn't the faintest idea as to whether any of this was getting through to the ancient.

"It seems Flarney and I were both on the same mission, finding out how and why planets were dropping out of communication. You and he used to talk a lot, they tell me. Did he ever tell you anything about that?"

Whitker looked up and squeaked dimly. "Oh, yes. All the time. I humored him. He was an old man, you know. And now he's dead." The tears leaked from his rheumy eyes and traced the sad furrows beside his nose.

Was he getting through? "What did he *say*, Mr. Whitker? About faster-than-light?"

The old man said, "L-sub-T equals L-sub-zero e to the minus T-over-two-N."

That damned formula again! "But what does it mean, Mr. Whitker? What did he say it meant?" Ross softly urged.

The old man looked surprised. "Genes?" he asked himself hazily. "Generations? I don't remember. But you go to Earth, young man. Flarney said *they'd* know, and know what to do about it, too, which is more than he did. His very words, young man!"

Ross didn't dare stay longer. Furthermore he suspected that the old man's attention span had been exhausted. He started from the room with a muttered thanks, and was stopped at the door by Whitker's hand on his shoulder.

"You're a good boy," Whitker squeaked. "Here."

Ross found himself walking down the corridor with an enormous wad of cellosponge in his hand.

The bunks were hard, but that didn't matter. Dormitories were the outermost layer of the hulk, pseudogravity varies inversely as the fourth power of the distance, and the field generator was conventionally located near "Minerva's" center. When your relative weight is one-quarter normal you can sleep deliciously on a gravel driveway. This was the dormitory's only attractive feature. Otherwise it was too many steel slabs, tiered and spotted too close, too many unwashed males, too much weary snoring. The only things in short supply were headroom and air.

Not everybody slept. Insomniacs turned and grunted; those who had given up the struggle talked from bunk to bunk in considerably low tones.

Bernie muttered from a third-tier bunk facing Ross's: "I wonder if she made it."

Ross knew what he meant. "Unlikeliest thing in the world," he said. "But I think she went fast and never knew what hit her." He thought of the formula and "They'd know on Earth-and know what to do about it too." Earth the enigma, from which all planetary peoples were supposed to be derived. Earth-the dot on the traditional master charts, Earth-from which and to which no longliners ever seemed to travel. Haarland had told him no F-T-L ship had in recent centuries ever reported again after setting out for Earth. Another world sunk in barbarism? But Flarney had said-no; that was not data. That was the confused recollections of a very old man, possibly based on the confused recollections of another very old man. Perhaps it had got mixed up with the semilegendary origin story.

Poor sweet Helena! He hoped it had happened fast, that she had been thinking of some pleasant prospect on Halsey's Planet. In her naïve way she'd think it just around the corner, a mere matter of following instructions....

* * * * *

So thought Ross, the pessimist.

In his gloom he had forgotten that this was exactly what it was. In his snobbishness he never realized that he was guilty of the most frightful arrogance in assuming that what he could do, she could not. In his ignorance he was not aware that since navigation began, every new instrument, every technique, has drawn the shuddery warnings of savants that uneducated skippers, working by rote, could not be expected to master these latest fruits of science-or that uneducated skippers since navigation began have cheerfully adopted new instruments and techniques at the drop of a hat and that never once have the shuddery warnings been justified by the facts.

Up the aisle somebody was saying in a low, argumentative tone, "I saw the drum myself. Naturally it was marked Dulsheen Creme, but the guards here never did give a damn whether their noses were dull or bright enough to flag down a freighter and I don't think they've suddenly changed. It was booze, I tell you. Fifty liters of it."

"Gawd! The hangovers tomorrow."

"We'll all have to watch our steps. I hope they don't do anything worse than getting quietly drunk in their quarters. Those foot-kissing orderlies'll get a workout, but who cares what happens to an orderly?"

"They haven't been on a real tear since I've been here."

"Lucky you. Let's hope they don't bust loose tonight. It's a break in the monotony, sure-but those girls play rough. Five prisoners died last time."

"They beat them up?"

"One of them."

"What about the others? Oh! Oh, Gawd-fifty liters, you said?"

Bernie began to whimper: "Not again! Not those plug-uglies! I swear I'll throw myself through the spacelock if they make a pass at me. Ross, isn't there anything we can do?"

"Seems not, Bernie. Maybe they won't come in. Or if they do, maybe they'll pass you by. There certainly isn't any place to hide."

A raucous female voice roared through the annunciator: "Bed check five minutes, boys. Anybody got any li'l thing to do down the hall, better do it now. See you lay-terrr!" Hiccup and drunken giggle.

For the first time in his life Ross suddenly and spontaneously acted like a tri-di hero, with the exception that he felt like a silly ass through it all.

"Got an idea," he muttered. "Get out of your bunk." He pulled the wad of cellosponge, old Whitker's present, from his pocket and yanked it in half, one for him and one for Bernie.

The Pullover said faintly: "Thanks, but I don't have to — —"

Ross didn't bother to answer. He was carefully fluffing the stuff out to its maximum dimensions. He unzipped his coveralls and began wadding them with cellosponge.

"I get it," Bernard said softly. He stepped out of his one-piece garment and followed suit. In less than a minute they had creditable dummies lying on their bunks.

The others watched their activity with emotions ranging between awe and envy. One giant of a man proclaimed grimly to whoever cared to listen: "These are a couple of smart guys. I wish them luck. And I want you guys to know that I will personally break the back of any sneaking rat who tips off a guard about this."

"Sure, Ox. Sure," came a muted chorus.

Arranged in a fetal sleeping position, face down, the dummies astonished even their creators. It would take a lucky look in a fair light to note that the heads were earless, fibrous globes.

"They'll do," Ross snapped. "Come on, Bernie."

They walked quietly from the dormitory in their singlet underwear toward the dormitory latrine-and past it. Into the corridor. Through a doorless opening into a storeroom piled with crates of rations. "This'll do," Ross said quietly. They ducked into a small cavern formed by sloppy issuing of stock and hunched down.

"The dummies will fool the bed check. It's only a sweep with a hundred-line TV system. If the guards do raid the dormitory tonight we'll have to count on them ignoring the dummies or thinking they're a joke or being too busy with other things to care. They'll be drunk, after all. Then in the morning things'll be plenty disorganized. We'll be able to sneak back into formation-and that'll be that for a matter of years. They can't often bribe the pilots with enough to guarantee a real ripsnorting drunk. Now try and get some sleep. There's nothing more we can do."

They actually did doze off for a couple of hours, and then were awakened by drunken war whoops.

"It's them!" Bernie wailed.

"Shut up. They're heading for the dormitory. We're safe."

"Safe!" Bernie echoed derisively. "Safe until when?"

Ross threatened him with the side of his hand and Bernie was quiet, though his lips were mumbling soundlessly. The guards lurched giggling past and Ross said:

"We'll sneak into the lockroom. There won't be anybody there tonight; at least we'll get a night's sleep."

"Big deal," grumbled Bernie, but he followed, complaining inarticulately to himself. Ross thought tiredly: All this work for a night's sleep! And saw, half-formed, the dreadful procession of days and nights and years ahead....

They reached the lockroom and stumbled in breathlessly.

"Dearie!" Two guards, playing a card game on the floor with a ring of empty bottles around them, looked up in drunken delight. "Dearie!" repeated the bigger of the two. "Angela, *look* what *we've* got!"

Ross said stupidly. "But you shouldn't be here ——"

The guard made a clumsy pass at fluffing up her back hair and giggled. "Duty comes first, dearie. Angela, just lock that door, will you?" The other guard scrambled unevenly to her feet and weaved over to the door. It was locked before Ross or Bernie could move.

The big guard stood up too, leering at Bernie. "Wow!" she said. "New merchandise. Just be patient, dearie. We've got a little something to attend to in a couple of minutes, but we'll have *lots* of time after that."

Then things began to happen rapidly. There was Angela the guard, inarticulate, falling-down drunk; she waved bonelessly at a brightly flickering light on the far side of the lockroom. There was the other guard, reaching out for Bernie with one hand, pawing at a bottle with the other. There was Ross, a paralyzed spectator.

And there was Bernie.

Bernie's eyes bulged wide as the guard came toward him. He babbled hysterically, "No! Nonononono! I said I'd kill myself and I ——"

He stiff-armed the big guard and leaped for the lock door. Ross suddenly came to life. "Bernie!" he bellowed. "Hold it! Don't jump!"

But it was too late. The one guard sprawling, the other staggering helplessly across the floor, Bernie was clear. He scrabbled at the lockwheels, spun them open. Ross tensed himself for the sudden, awful rush of expanding air; he leaped after Bernie just as Bernie flung the lock door open and jumped.

Ross jumped after.

There was no rush of air. They were not in space. Around them was no ripping, sucking void, no flaming backdrop of stars; around them were six walls and a Wesley board, and Helena peering at them wide-eyed and delighted.

"Well!" she said. "*That* was fast!"

* * * * *

Ross said, "But ——"

Helena, hanging from the acceleration loops, smiled maternally. "Oh, it was nothing," she said. "Ross don't you think we're far enough away yet?"

Ross said hopelessly, "All right," and cut the drive. The starship hung in space in the limbo between stars. Azor, "Minerva," and the rest were light-years behind, far out of range of challenge.

Helena wriggled free from the loops and rubbed her arms where the retaining straps had gripped them. "After all," she said demurely, "you *told* me how to run the ship, and *really*, Ross, I'm not quite *stupid*."

Ross said, "But — —"

"But what, Ross? It isn't as if I were some sort of brainless little thing that had never run a machine in her life. My goodness, Ross — —" She wrinkled her nose. "*You* should remember. All those days in the dye vats? Don't you think I had to learn a little something about machines *there*?"

Ross swore incredulously. To compare those clumsy constructs of wheels and rollers with the subtle subelectronic flows of the Wesley force-and to make it work! He said, unbelievingly, "And the 'Minerva' helped you vector in? They gave you the co-ordinates and radared your course?"

"Certainly." Helena turned to Bernie, who was staring dazedly around him. "Are you all right, dear?" she asked.

Ross turned his back on them and faced the Wesley Christmas tree of controls. Don't question it, he told himself; take a miracle for what it is. God wanted you out of "Minerva" —and God moves in most mysterious ways His wonders to perform.

Anyway, they had to get going. When the court had exiled Helena in the starship they had gone through the customary rituals; not only was everything that looked like a weapon gone, along with all but a teacup of fuel for the auxiliary jets, but the food locker was stripped entirely. He put everything else out of his mind and began to calculate a setting.

Bernie said over his shoulder, "Home, huh? That place you call Halsey's Planet?"

Ross shook his head. "Not this time. I got this far and I'm still alive; maybe I can finish the job. Anyway, I'll try. The first solid suggestion I've had ever since I took off was what that half-witted old moron — —" He ignored a little gasp from Helena. " — —said back on 'Minerva.' If Flarney had lived, he would have gone there; we'll go there now." He finished manipulating the calculator and began to set it up on the board. He said, "The name of the place is-Earth."

CHAPTER X.

It took Ross a while to learn a lesson, but when he learned it, it stuck. This time, he promised himself, *no spaceport*.

They sneaked into the solar system that held fabulous old Earth from far outside the ecliptic, where the chance of radar detection was least; they came to a relative dead halt millions of miles from the planet and cautiously scanned the surrounding volume of space with their own radar.

No ships seemed to be in space. Earth's solar system turned out to be a trivial affair, only five planets, scarcely a half-dozen moons among them. None of the planets except Earth itself was anything like inhabitable.

"Hold tight," said Ross grimly, "I'm not so good at this fine navigation." He cautiously applied power along a single vector; the starship leaped and bucked. He corrected with another; and the distant sun swelled in their view plates with frightening rapidity. The alarm beeps bleated furiously, and the automatic cutoff restored all controls to neutral.

Ross, sweating, picked himself up from the floor and staggered back to the panel. Helena said carefully, "You're doing *fine*, Ross, but if you'd like *me* to take over for a minute ——"

Ross swallowed his pride and stood back. After one wide-eyed stare of shock-she wasn't even calculating! —he gripped the loops and closed his eyes and waited for death.

There was a punishing bump and his eyes flew open. Helena was looking at him apologetically. "You would have done it better," she lied, "but anyway we're down."

Ross lied, "Of course, but I'm glad you had the practice. Where-uh, where are we?"

Helena silently showed him the radar plot. Earth, it seemed, had a confusing multiplicity of continents; they were on one in the northern hemisphere, a large one as Earth's continents went, and smack in the middle of it. It was night on their side of Earth just then; and, by the plot, a largish city was only a dozen or so miles away.

"Okay," said Ross wearily, "landing party away. Helena, you stay here while Bernie and I ——"

Helena said simply, "No."

Ross stared at her a minute, then shrugged. "All right. Then Bernie will stay while ——"

"I will not!" said Bernie.

Clearly it was time for a showdown. Ross roared: "Who's the captain here, anyway?"

"You are," Helena said promptly. "As long as I don't have to stay here alone."

"Yeah," said Bernie.

Ross said, "Oh." He thought for a while and then said, "Well, let's all go." They thought it was a wonderful idea.

Earth wasn't a very unusual planet-lots of green sand and purple vegetation. Either the master star chart was wrong or the gravity meter was off; the former, strangely enough, gave Earth's gravity as 1.000000 and the latter as 0.8952, a whopping ten per cent discrepancy. Further, the principal inert gas in Earth's atmosphere was, according to the master chart's planetary supplement, nitrogen; and according to the ship's instruments was indubitably neon. A terrific aurora polaris display constantly flickering in the northern sky bore that out.

But the gap between the chart and the facts didn't particularly worry Ross as they swung along overland. So the chart was off, or perhaps things had changed. This was-according to Flarney via Whitker-the place where people knew about the formula, where his questions would be answered. After this, he thought happily, it's off to Halsey's Planet and an unspecified glorious future, revered as the savior of humanity instead of a lousy Yards clerk pushing invoices around. And Helena, he thought sentimentally....

He turned to smile at her and found she and Bernie were giggling.

"Listen, you two!" Captain Ross roared. "Haven't you learned anything yet? What's the good of us exploring if we stroll along with our silly heads in the clouds, not paying attention? Do you realize that this place may be as dangerous as Azor or worse?"

"Ross ——" Helena said.

"Don't interrupt! What this outfit needs is some discipline-tightening up. You two have got to accept your responsibilities. Keep alert! Be on the lookout! Any single thing out of the ordinary may be a deathtrap. Watch for — —"

Helena was looking not at Ross but over his shoulder. Bernie was making strangled noises and pointing.

Ross turned. Behind him stood a mechanical monstrosity vaguely recognizable as a heavily-armed truck, its motor faintly humming. A man leaned darkly from the cab and transfixed them to the ground with a powerful spotlight. From the dazzling circle of light his voice came, hasty and furtive. "Thought it was two women and a man, but I guess you're the ones. Ugh, those faces on you! Yes, you're the ones. Get in. Fast."

The light blinked out. When their eyes adjusted to the dimmer illumination of the stars and the aurora display they saw a side door in the body of the truck standing open. Too, one of the long, slim gun barrels with which the truck seemed copiously supplied swiveled to cover them.

Ross stupidly read aloud a sign on the truck: "Jones Floor-Cover Company. Finest Tile on Jones. Wall-to-Wall a Specialty. 'Rugs Fit For a Jones'."

"Yeah," the man said. "Yeah, yeah. Just don't try to buy any. Get in, for Jones' sake! If I'd of known you were half-wits I wouldn't of taken this job for a million Joneses, cash. Get in!" His voice was hysterical and the gun covering them moved ominously. "If this is a frame — —" he began to shrill.

"Get in," Ross said shakily to the others. They climbed in and the door slammed violently and automatically. Helena began to cry in a preoccupied sort of way and Bernie began a long, mumbling inventory of his own mental weaknesses for ever getting involved in this crackbrained, imbecilic, feeble-minded....

There were windows in the truck body and Ross turned from one to another. He saw the guns on the cab telescope into stubs, the stubs fold into the mounts, the mounts smoothly descend flush with the sheet metal. He saw the cursing driver manipulate a dozen levers as the car began to glide across the green sand, purple-dotted with vegetation. Finally, through the rear window, he saw three figures racing across the sand waving their arms, rapidly being left behind. All he could make out was that they seemed to be two women and a man.

Helena was wailing softly, " — —and I am *not* ugly and just because we're young and we're strangers isn't any reason to go around insulting people — —"

From Bernie: " — —fatheaded, goggly-eyed, no-browed, slobber-lipped, dim-witted — —"

"Shut up," Ross said softly. "Before I bang both your heads together."

They stared.

"Thank you. We've got to think. What's this spot we're in? What can we do about it? I don't have any F-T-L contact name for Earth and obviously this fellow picked us up by mistake. I saw two women and a man-remember what he said? —just now trying to catch up with us. He seems to be some kind of criminal. Otherwise why a disguised gun-carrier? Why floor coverings 'but don't try to buy any'? And Jones seems to be the name of the local political subdivision, the name of the local deity and the currency. That's important. It points to a rigid one-man dictatorship-Jones, of course, or possibly his dynasty. What course of action should we take? Kick it around. Helena, what do you think?"

"He shouldn't have said we were ugly," she pouted. "Isn't *that* important?"

"Women!" Ross said grimly. "If you'll kindly forget the trivial affront to your vanity perhaps we can figure something out."

Helena said stubbornly: "But he *shouldn't*. We're not. What if they just *think* we are because they all look alike and we don't look like them?"

Ross collapsed. After a long pause during which he tried and almost failed to control his temper he said slowly: "Thank you, Helena. You're wrong, of course, but it was a contribution. You see, you can't build up such a wild, far-fetched theory from the few facts available." His voice was beginning to choke with anger. "It isn't reasonable and it isn't really any help. In fact it's the God-damndest stupidest imitation of reasoning I have ever — —"

"City," Bernard croaked, pointing. The jolting ride had become smoother, and gliding past the windows were green tiled buildings and street lights.

"Fine," Ross said bitterly. "We had a few clear minutes to think and now we find they were wasted by the crackpot dissertation of a female and my reasonable attempt to show her the elements of logical thinking." He put his head in his hands and tried to ignore them, tried to reason it out. But the truck made a couple of sharp turns and jolted to a stop.

The door opened and the voice of their driver said, again from behind a flashlight's dazzling circle: "Out. Walk ahead of me."

They did, into a fair-sized, well-lighted room with eight people in it whom they studied in amazement. Every one of the eight was exactly the same height-six feet. Every one had straight red hair of exactly the same shade, sprouting from an identical hairline. Every one had precisely the same build-gangling but broad-shouldered. Their sixteen eyes were the identical blue under sixteen identical eyebrows. Head to toe, they were duplicates. One of them spoke-in exactly the same voice as the truckdriver's.

"So you want to be Joneses, do you?" he said.

"Absolutely impossible."

"But we took their money."

"Give it back. Reasonable changes, yes, but look at them!"

"We can't give it back. Look what we spent already. Anyway, Sam, — —" It sounded like "Sam" to Ross. " — —anyway, Sam, look at some of the work you've done already. You can do it. I doubt if anybody else could, but you can."

Ross felt his eyes crossing, and gave up the effort of trying to tell which Jones was speaking to which. Even the clothing was nearly identical-purple pantaloons, scarlet jacket, black cummerbund sash, black shoes. Then he noticed that Third-from-the-left Jones-the one who seemed to be named Sam-wore a frilly shirt of white under the scarlet jacket. Only a lacy edge showed at the open collar; but where his was white, the others were all muted pastels of pink and green.

Sam said coldly, "I know nobody else can do it. Anybody else! Who else *is* there?"

A Jones with a frill of chartreuse pursed his lips. "Well," he said thoughtfully, "there's Northside Tim Jones — —"

"Northside Tim Jones," Sam mimicked. "Eight of his jobs are in the stockade right now! Paraffin, for Jones's sake-he still uses paraffin to mold a face!"

"I know, Sam, but after all, these people need help. If you won't do it for them, what's left?"

Sam shrugged morosely. "Well — —" he said. Then he shook his head, sighed, and came forward to look at the three travelers. With an expression of revulsion he said, "Strip."

Ross hesitated. "Hold it!" he said sharply to Helena, already half out of her coveralls. "Sir, there may have been some mistake. Would you mind explaining just what you propose to do?"

"The usual thing," Sam said irritably. "Fix your hair, build up your frames, level you off at standard Jones height. The works. Though I must say," he added bitterly, "I never saw such unpromising specimens in my life. How the Jones have you managed to stay out of trouble this long? Whose garrets have you been hiding in?"

Ross licked his lips. "You mean," he said, "you want to make us look more like you gentlemen, is that it?"

"*I* want!" Sam repeated in bafflement. Over his shoulder he roared, "Ben, what kind of creeps are you saddling me with?"

Ben, looking worried, said, "Holy Jones, Sam, I don't get it either. It was a perfectly normal deal. This guy came up to me in Jones's Joint and made a pitch. He knew the setup all right, and he had the money with him. Six hundred Joneses, cold cash; and it wasn't funny money, either." His face clouded. "I did think, though," he mentioned, "that he said two women and one man. But Paul Jones picked them up right at the rendezvous, so it must've been the right ones."

He glowered suspiciously at Ross and the others. "Come to think of it," he said, "maybe not. Tell you what, Sam, you just sit tight here for twenty minutes or so." And he hurried out of the room.

One of the other Joneses said curtly, "Sit down." Ross, Bernie, and Helena found chairs lined up against a wall; they sat. A different Jones rummaged in a stack of papers on a table; he handed something to each of them. "Relax," he advised. Obediently the three spacefarers opened the magazines he gave them. When they were settled, most of the Joneses, after a whispered conference, went out. The one that was left said, "No talking. If we made a mistake, we're sorry. Meanwhile, you do what you're told."

Ross found that his magazine was called *By Jones*; it seemed to be a periodical devoted to entertaining news and gossip of sports, fashion, and culture. He stared at an article headed "Be Glad the People's Police Are Watching YOU!", but the words made little sense. He tried to think; but somehow he couldn't find a point at which to grasp the flickering mass of impressions that were circling through his brain. Nothing seemed to make a great deal of sense any more; and Ross suddenly realized that he was very, very tired.

His mind an utter blank, he sat and waited.

It was twenty minutes and a bit more. Then the door flew open and half a dozen Joneses burst in. Even at first sight, Ross could tell that three of them were newcomers. For one thing, two were women; and the third, though red-haired, tall and gangling, had a nose a full centimeter shorter than any of the others, and his hair was crisply curled.

"All right, you Peepeece!" snarled the first Jones. "You found what you were looking for-now try to get out!"

Helena did the talking. It wasn't Ross's idea, but when her heel crunched down on his instep he was too startled to object, and from then on he didn't get a chance to get a word in edgewise.

He had to admit that her act was getting across with the audience. Long before she had finished reporting their meeting, their flight to Azor, the escape from "Minerva," and the flight here, most of the Joneses had put their guns away, and all were showing signs of stupefaction. "— —And then," she finished, "we saw this truck, and that very good-looking man picked us up. And so we're here on Earth; and, honest to goodness, that's the exact truth."

There was silence while the Joneses looked at each other. Then the plastic-surgeon-type Jones, Sam with the white shirt front, stepped forward. "Hold still, my dear," he ordered. Helena bravely stood rigid while the surgeon raked searchingly through the roots of her hair, peered into her eyes, expertly traced the configuration of her ribs.

He stepped back, shaken. "One thing is for sure," he told the others, "they're not Peepeece. Not with those bones. They'd never get in."

Ben Jones beat his forehead and moaned. "How do I get into these things?" he demanded.

One of the female Joneses said shrilly, "We didn't expect anything like this. We're honest Jones-fearing Joneses and — —"

"Shut up!" Ben Jones roared. "What about the other two, Sam? They all right too?"

"Oh, for Jones's sake, Ben," Sam said disgustedly, "just look at them, will you? Do you think the police would take in a five-inch height deviation like that one — —" he pointed to Bernie — —"or a half-bald scarecrow like that?" Ross, stung, opened his mouth to object; but swiftly closed it again. Nobody was paying much attention to him, anyhow, except as Exhibit A.

"So what do we do?" Ben demanded.

Sam shrugged. "The first thing we do," he said wearily, "is to take care of our, uh, clients here. We get them out of the way, and then we decide what to do next." He looked around at the other Joneses. "If you three will come this way," he said, "we'll finish up your job and get you back home. I needn't remind you, of course, that if you should happen to mention anything you've seen here tonight to the Peepeece it would — —" His voice was cut off by the closing door before Ross could catch the nature of the threat.

Ben Jones stayed behind, scowling to himself. "You people got any Joneses?" he demanded abruptly.

"You mean money? Not any at all," Helena said honestly. Ross could have kicked her.

Ben Jones growled deep in his throat. "Always it happens to me!" he complained. "I suppose we're going to have to feed you, too."

"Well," Helena said diffidently, "we haven't eaten in a long time — —"

Ben Jones swore to his god, whose name was Jones, but he stepped to the door and ordered food. When it came it was surprisingly good; each of the three, with their diverse backgrounds, found it delicious. While they were eating, Ben Jones sat watching them, refreshing himself from time to time with a greenish bubbling liquid out of a jug. He offered some to Ross; who clutched his throat as though he'd swallowed molten steel.

Ben Jones guffawed till his eyes ran. "First taste of Jones's Juice, hey? Kind of gets right down inside, doesn't it?" He wiped his eyes, then sobered. "I guess you people are all right," he admitted. "What I'm going to do with you I don't know. I can't take you to Earth, and I can't keep you here, and I can't throw you out on the street-the Peepeece would have you in the stockade in ten minutes."

Ross, startled, said, "Aren't we on Earth?"

"Naw," Ben Jones said disgustedly. "Didn't you hear me? You're on Jones, halfway between Jones's Forks and Jonesgrad. But you came pretty close, at that. Earth's about fifty miles out the Jones Pike past Jonesgrad, turn right at Jonesboro Minor."

Ross said bewilderedly, "The planet Earth is fifty miles along the Pike?"

"Not a planet," Ben Jones said. "It's an old city, kind of. Nobody lives there any more; the Peepeece don't permit it. I've never been there, but they say it's kind of, you know, different. Some of the buildings — —" he seemed actually to be blushing — —"are as much as fifteen, twenty stories high; and the walls aren't even all green. Excuse me," he added, looking at Helena.

Sam Jones returned and said to Ben, "It's all right. All finished. Trivial alterations. Maybe they could have gone along for the rest of their lives on wigs and pads-but we don't tell them that, do we? And anyway now they won't worry. Healy Jones, the older man, for instance. Very bright fellow, but it seems he was working as a snathe-handler's apprentice. Afraid to take the master's test, afraid to change his line of work-might be noticed and questioned." He heaved a tremendous sigh and poured himself a tremendous slug of the green fluid. Ben Jones gave Ross a cynical wink and shrug.

"Look at my hand!" the surgeon exploded. It was shaking. He gulped the Jones Juice and poured himself another. "Nothing physical," he said. "Neurosis. The subconscious coldly counting up my crimes and coldly imposing and executing sentence. I'm a surgeon, so my hand trembles." He drank. "Jones is not mocked," he said broodingly. "Jones is not mocked. Think those three are going to be happy? Think they're going to be folded in Jones's bosom just because they're Joneses externally now? No. Watch them five years, ten years. Maybe they'll sentence themselves to be hateful, vitriol-tempered lice and wonder why nobody loves them. Maybe they'll sentence themselves to penal servitude and wonder why everybody pushes them around, why they haven't the guts to hit back-Jones is not mocked," he told the jug of green liquid, ignoring the others, and drank again.

Ben Jones said softly to them, "Come on," and led them into an adjoining room furnished with sleeping pads. He said apologetically, "The doctor's nerves are shot tonight. Trouble is, he's too Jones-fearing. Me, I can take it or leave it alone." His laugh had a little too much bravado in it. "There's a little bit of nonJones in the best of us, I always say-but not to the doctor. And not when he's hitting the Jones juice." He shrugged cynically and said, "What the hell? L-sub-T equals L-sub-zero e to the minus T-over-two-N."

Ross had him by his shirt frill. "Say that again!"

Ben Jones shoved him away. "What's the matter with you, boy?"

"I'm sorry. Would you please repeat that formula? What you said?" he hastily amended when the word "formula" obviously failed to register.

Ben Jones repeated the formula wonderingly.

"What does it mean?" Ross demanded. "I've been chasing the damned thing across the Galaxy." He hastily filled Ben Jones in on its previous appearances.

"Well," Ben Jones said, "it means what it says, of course. I mean, it's obvious, isn't it?" He studied their faces and added uncertainly, "Isn't it?"

"What does it mean to *you*, Ben?" Ross asked softly.

"Why, what it means to anybody, pal. Right's right, wrong's wrong, Jones is in his Heaven, conform or else-it means morality, man. What else could it mean?"

Ross then proceeded to make an unmannerly nuisance of himself. He grilled their involuntary host mercilessly, shrugging aside all attempted diversions of the talk into what they were going to do with the three visitors. He ignored protestations that Ben was no Jonesologist, Jones knew, and drilled in. By the time Ben Jones exploded, stamped out, and locked them in for the night, he had elicited the following:

Everybody knew the formula; they were taught it at their mother's knee. It was recited antiphonally before and after Jones Meetings. Ben knew it was right, of course, and some day he was going to get right with Jones and live up to it, but not just yet, because if he didn't make money in the prosthesis racket somebody else would. The formula was everywhere: on the lintels of public buildings, hanging in classrooms, and on the bedroom walls of the most Jones-fearing old ladies where they could see its comforting message last thing at night and first thing in the morning.

From a book? Well yes, he guessed so; sure it was in the Book of Joneses, but who could say whether that was where it started. Most people thought it was just Handed Down. Way back during the war-what war? The War of the Joneses, of course! Anyway, in the war the last of the holdouts against the formula had been destroyed. No, he didn't know anything about the war. No, not his grandfather's time or his grandfather's grandfather's time. Long ago, that war was. Maybe there were records in the old museum in Earth. The city, of course, not some damn planet he never heard of!

After Ben Jones slammed out and the room darkened Helena and Bernie exchanged comforting words from adjoining sleeping pads, to Ross's intense displeasure. They fell asleep and at last he fell asleep still churning over the problem.

When he woke he found that evidently the doctor, Sam Jones, had stumbled in during the night and passed out on the pad next to him. The white frill was stiff and green with dried Jones Juice. Helena and Bernie still slept. He tried the door.

It was locked, but there was a tantalizing hum of voices beyond it. He put his ear to the cold steel. The fruits of his eavesdropping were scanty but alarming.

" — —cut 'em down mumble found someplace mumble."

" — —mumble never killed yet mumble prosthesis racket."

" — —Jones's sake, it's their lives or mumble mumble time to get scared mumble Peepeece are you?"

And then apparently the speakers moved out of range. Ross was cold with sweat, and there was an abnormal hollow in the pit of his stomach that breakfast would never fill.

He spun around as a Jones voice croaked painfully: "Hear anything good, stranger?"

The surgeon, looking very dilapidated, was sitting up and regarding him through bloodshot eyes. "They're talking about killing us," he said shortly.

"They are not really intelligent," Sam Jones said wearily. "They were just bright enough to entangle me to the point where I had to work for them-and to keep me copiously supplied with that green stuff I haven't the intelligence to use in moderation."

Ross said, "How'd you like to break away from this?"

Sam Jones mutely extended his hand. It trembled like a leaf. He said, "For his own inscrutable reason, Jones grants me steadiness of hand during an operation designed to frustrate his grand design. He then overwhelms me with a titanic thirst for oblivion to my shame."

"There's no design," Ross said. "Or if there is, luckily this planet is a trifling part of it. I have never heard of such arrogant pip-squeakery in my life. You flyspecks in your shabby corner of the Galaxy think your own fouled-up mess is the pattern of universal life. You're wrong! I've seen life elsewhere and I know it isn't."

The doctor passed his trembling hand over his eyes. "Jones is not mocked," he croaked. "L-sub-T equals L-sub-zero e to the minus T-over-two-N. You can't fight *that*, stranger. You can't fight that."

Ross realized he was silently crying behind his covering hand.

He said, much more gently, "It's nothing you have to fight. It's something you have to understand." He told Sam Jones of his two previous encounters with the formula. The doctor looked up, his eyes full of wonder. Ross said, "How would you like to be free, doctor? Free of your shaking hands, free of your guilt, free of these killers? How would you like to know the truth?"

The doctor said faintly, "If I dared —— "

Ross pressed, "The museum in Earth city. Get me records, facts, anything about the War of the Joneses. If there's any meaning to the formula it'll have to lie in that. It seems there was a battle about its interpretation and we know who won. Let's find out what the other side said. Get me in there." He was thinking of the disgraceful war of fanaticism that had marred his own planet's history. The doctor's weak Jones jaw was firming up, though his eyes were still haunted. "Stall your killer friends, doctor," Ross urged. "Tell them you can use us for experiments that'll cut the cost of the operations. That ought to bring them around. And get me the facts!"

"To be free," the doctor said wistfully. He said after a pause, "I'll try. But —— " And rapped a code series on the steel door.

CHAPTER XI.

The doctor said with weak belligerence, "Who do you think I am? Jones? I *had* to leave your friends behind. I had enough trouble getting those hoods to let me take *you* along. After all, I'm not a miracle-worker."

Ross said sullenly, "Okay, okay." He glowered out of the car window and spat out a tendril of red hair that had come loose from the fringe surrounding his mouth. The trouble with a false beard was that it itched, worse than the real article, worse than any torment Ross had ever known. But at least Ross, externally and at extreme range, was enough of a Jones to pass a casual glance.

And what would Helena and Bernie be thinking now? He hadn't had a chance to whisper to them; they'd been just waking when the doctor dragged him out. Ross put that problem out of his mind; there were problems enough right on hand.

He cautiously felt his red wig to see if it was on straight. The doctor didn't seem to look away from his driving, but he said: "Leave it alone. That's the first thing the Peepeece look for, somebody who obviously isn't sure if his hair is still on or not. It won't come off."

"Umph," said Ross. The road was getting worse, it seemed; they had passed no houses for several miles now. They rounded a rutted turn, and ahead was a sign.

Stop!
Restricted Area Ahead
Warning: This Road Is Mined
No Traffic Allowed! Detour
"Trespassers beyond this point will be shot
without further notice." Decree #404-5
People's Commissariat of
Culture and Solidarity.

The doctor spat contemptuously out the window and roared past. Ross said, "Hey!"

"Oh, relax," said the doctor. "That's just the Cultureniks. Nobody pays any attention to *them.*"

Ross swallowed and sat as lightly as possible on the green leather cushion of the car. By the time they had gone a quarter of a mile, he began to feel a little reassured that the doctor knew what he was talking about. Then the doctor swerved sharply to miss a rusted hulk and almost skidded off the road. He swore and manhandled the wheel until they were back on the straightaway.

White lipped, Ross asked, "What was that?"

"Car," grunted the doctor. "Hit a mine. Silly fools!"

Ross squawked, "But you said — —"

"Shut up," the doctor ordered tensely. "That was weeks ago; they haven't had a chance to lay new mines since then." Pause. "I hope."

The car roared on. Ross closed his eyes, limply abandoning himself to what was in store. But if it was bad to see what was going on, the roaring, swerving, jolting race was ten times worse with his eyes closed. He opened them again in time to see another sign flash past, gone before he could read it.

"What was that?" he demanded.

"What's the difference?" the doctor grunted. "Want to go back?"

"Well, no — —" Ross thought for a moment. "Do we have to go this fast, though?"

"If we want to get there. Crossed a Peepeece radar screen ten miles back; they'll be chasing us by now."

"Oh, I see," Ross said weakly. "Look, Doc, tell me one thing-why do they make this place so hard to get to?"

"Tabu area," the doctor said shortly. "Not allowed."

"Why not allowed?"

"Because it's not allowed. Don't want people poking through the old records."

"Why not just put the old records in a safe place-or burn the damn things up?"

"Because they didn't, that's why. Shut up! Expect me to tell you why the Peepeece do anything? They don't know themselves. It isn't Jonesly to destroy, I guess."

Ross shut up. He leaned against the window, letting the air rush over his head. They were moving through forest, purplish squatty trees with long, rustling leaves. The sky overhead was crisp and cool looking; it was still early morning. Ross exhaled a long breath. Back on Halsey's Planet he would be getting up about now, rising out of a soft, warm bed, taking his leisurely time about breakfast, climbing into a comfortable car to make his way to the spaceport where he was safe, respected, and at home....Damn Haarland!

At least, Ross thought, some sort of a pattern was beginning to shape up. The planets were going out of communication each for its own reason; but wasn't there a basic reason-for-the-reasons that was the same in each case? Wasn't there some overall design-some explanation that covered all the facts, pointed to a way out?

He sat up straight as they approached a string of little signs. He scanned them worriedly as they rolled past.

"Workers, Peasants, Joneses all — —"
"By these presents know ye — —"
"If you don't stop in spite of all — —"
"This to hell will blow ye!"

"Duck!" the doctor yelled, crouching down in the seat and guiding the careening car with one hand. Ross, startled, followed his example, but not before he saw that "THIS" was an automatic, radar-actuated rapid-fire gun mounted a few yards past the last sign. There was a stuttering roar from the gun and a splatter of metal against the armored sides of the car. The doctor sat up again as soon as the burst had hit; evidently only one was to be feared. "Yah, yah," he jeered at the absent builders of the gun. "Lousy fifty-millimeters can't punch their way through a tin can!"

Ross, gasping, got up just in time to see the last sign in the series:

"By order of People's Democratic Council
Of Arts & Sciences, Small Arms Division."

He said wildly, "They can't even write a poem properly. Did you notice the first and third line rhyme-words?"

Surprisingly, the doctor glanced at him and laughed with a note of respect. He took a hand off the wheel to pat Ross on the shoulder. "You'll make a Jones yet, my boy," he promised. "Don't worry about these things; I told you this place was restricted. This stuff isn't worth bothering about."

Ross found that he was able to smile. There was a point, he realized with astonishment, where courage came easily; it was the only thing left. He sat up straighter and breathed the air more deeply. Then it happened.

They rounded another curve; the doctor slammed on the brakes. Suspended overhead across the road was a single big sign:

That's All, Jones!
— —People's Police

The car bucked, slewed around, and skidded. The wheels locked, but not in time to keep it from sliding into the pit, road wide and four feet deep, that was dug in front of them.

Ross heard the axles crack and the tires blow; but the springing of the car was equal to the challenge. He was jarred clear in the air and tumbled to the floor in a heap; but no bones were broken.

Painfully he pushed the door open and crawled out. The doctor limped after and the two of them stood on the edge of the pit, looking at the ruin of their car.

"That one," said the doctor, "was worth bothering about." He motioned Ross to silence and cocked an ear. Was there a distant roaring sound, like another car following on the road they had traveled? Ross wasn't sure; but the doctor's expression convinced him. "Peepeece," he said briefly. "From here on it's on foot. They won't follow beyond here; but let's get out of sight. They'll by-Jones *shoot* beyond here if they see us!"

Ross stared unbelievingly. "This is Earth?" he asked.

The doctor fanned himself and blew. "That's it," he said, looking around curiously. "Heard a lot about it, but I've never been here before," he explained. "Funny-looking, isn't it?" He nudged Ross, indicating a shattered concrete structure beside them on the road. "Notice that toll booth?" he whispered slyly. "Eight sides!"

Ross said wearily, "Yes, mighty funny! Look, Doc, why don't you sort of wander around by yourself for a while? That big thing up ahead is the museum you were talking about, isn't it?"

The doctor squinted. His eyes were unnaturally bright, and his breathing was fast, but he was making an attempt to seem casual in the presence of these manifold obscenities of design. He licked his lips. "*Round pillars,*" he marveled. "Why, yes, I think that's the museum. You go on up there, like you say. I'll, uh, sort of see what there is to see. Jones, yes!" He staggered off, staring from ribald curbing to scatological wall in an orgy of prurience.

Ross sighed and walked through the deserted, weed-grown streets to the stone building that bore on its cracked lintel the one surviving word, "Earth." This was all wrong, he was almost certain; Earth *had* to be a planet, not a city. But still....

The museum had to have the answers.

On its moldering double doors was a large lead seal. He read: "Surplus Information Repository. Access denied to unauthorized personnel." But the seal had been forced by somebody; one of the doors swung free, creaking.

Ross invoked the forcer of the door. If *he* could do it....

He went in and stumbled over a skeleton, presumably that of the last entrant. The skull had been crushed by a falling beam. There was some sort of mechanism involved —a trigger, a spring, a release hook. All had rusted badly, and the spring had lost its tension over the years. A century? Two? Five? Ross prayed that any similar mantraps had likewise rusted solid, and cautiously inched through the dismal hall of the place, ready for a backward leap at the first whisper of a concealed mechanism in action.

It was unnecessary. The place was-dead.

Exploring room after room, he realized slowly that he was stripping off history in successive layers. The first had been the booby-trapped road, lackadaisically planned to ensure that mere inquisitiveness would be discouraged. There had been no real denial of access, for there was almost no possibility that anybody would care to visit the place.

Next, the seal and the mantraps. An earlier period. Somebody had once said: "This episode is closed. This history is determined. We have all reached agreement. Only a dangerous or frivolous meddler would seek to rake over these dead ashes."

And then, prying into the museum, Ross found the era during which agreement had been reached, during which it still was necessary to insist and demonstrate and cajole.

The outer rooms and open shelves were testimonials to Jones. There were books of Jonesology-ingenious, persuasive books divided usually into three sections. Human Jonesology would be a painstaking effort to determine the exact physical and mental tolerances of a Jones. Anatomical atlases minutely gave femur lengths, cranial angles, eye color to an angstrom, hair thickness to a micron. Moral Jonesology treated of the dangers of deviating from these physical and more elastic mental specifications. (Here the formula appeared again, repeatedly invoked but never explained. Already it was a truism.) And Sacred Jonesology was a series of assertions concerning the nature of The Jones in whose image all other Joneses were created.

Subdivisions of the open shelves held works on Geographical Jonesology (the distribution across the planet of Joneses) and similar works.

Ross went looking for a lower layer of history and found it in a bale of crumbling pamphlets. "Comrades, We Must Now Proceed to Consolidate Our Victory"; "Ultra-Jonesism, An Infantile Political Disorder"; "On The Fallacy of 'Jonesism In One Country'." These Ross devoured. They added up to the tale of a savage political battle among the victors of a greater war. Clemency was advocated and condemned; extermination of the opposition was casually mentioned; the Cultural Faction and the Biological Faction had obviously been long locked in a death struggle. Across the face of each pamphlet stood a similar logotype: the formula. It was enigmatically mentioned in one pamphlet, which almost incomprehensibly advanced the claims of the Biological faction to supremacy among the Joneses United: "Let us never forget, comrades, that the initiation of the great struggle was not caused by our will or by the will of our sincere and valiant opponents, the Culturists. The inexorable law of nature, $L_T = L_O e^{-T/2N}$, was the begetter of that holocaust from which our planet has emerged purified — —"

Was it now?

The entrance to a musty, airless wing had once been bricked up. The mortar was crumbling and a few bricks had fallen. Above the arched doorway a sign said Military Archives. On the floor was a fallen metal plaque whose inscription said simply Dead Storage. He kicked the loose bricks down and stepped through.

That was it. The place was lightless, except for the daylight filtering through the violated archway. Ross hauled maps and orders and period newspapers and military histories and handbooks into the corridor in armfuls and spread them on the floor. It took only minutes for him to realize that he had his answer. He ran into the street and shouted for the doctor.

Together they pored over the papers, occasionally reading aloud choice bits, wonderingly.

The simplest statement of the problem they found was in the paper-backed "Why We Fight" pamphlet issued for the enlisted men of the Provisional North Continent Government Army.

"What is a Jones?" the pamphlet asked rhetorically. "A Jones is just a human being, the same as you and I. Dismiss rumors that a Jones is supernatural or unkillable with a laugh when you hear them. They arose because of the extraordinary resemblance of one Jones to another. Putting a bullet through one Jones in a skirmish and seeing another one rise up and come at you with a bayonet is a chilling experience; in the confusion of battle it may seem that the dead Jones rose and attacked. But this is not the case. Never let the rumor pass unchallenged, and never fail to report habitual rumor-mongers.

"How did the Joneses get that way? Many of you were too young when this long war began to be aware of the facts. Since then, wartime disruption of education and normal communications facilities has left you in the dark. This is the authoritative statement in simple language that explains why we fight.

"This planet was colonized, presumably from the quasi-legendary planet Earth. (The famous Earth Archives Building, incidentally, is supposed to derive its puzzling name from this fact.) It is presumed that the number of colonists was originally small, probably in the hundreds. Though the number of human beings on the planet increased enormously as the generations passed, genetically the population remained small. The same ones (heredity units) were combined and reshuffled in varying combinations, but no new ones were added. Now, it is a law of genetics that in small populations, variations tend to smooth out and every member of the population tends to become like every other member. So-called unfixed genes are lost as the generations pass; the end product of this process would theoretically be a population in which every member had exactly the same genes as every other member. This is a practical impossibility, but the Joneses whom we fight are a tragic demonstration of the fact that the process need not be pushed to its ultimate extreme to dislocate the life of a planet and cause endless misery to its dwellers.

"From our very earliest records there have been Joneses. It is theorized that this gangling redheaded type was well represented aboard the original colonizing ship, but some experts believe one Jones type and the workings of chance would be sufficient to produce the unhappy situation of type-dominance.

"Some twenty-five years ago Joneses were everywhere among us and not, as now, withdrawn to South Continent and organized into a ruthless aggressor nation. They made up about thirty per cent of the population and had become a closely knit organization devoted to mutual help. They held the balance of political power in every election from the municipal to the planetary level and virtually monopolized production and finance. There were fanatics and rabble-rousers among them who readily exploited a rising tide of discontent over a series of curbing laws, finally pushed through by a planetary majority, united at last in self-defense against the rapacity and ruthless self-interest of the Joneses.

"The Joneses withdrew en masse to South Continent. Some sincerely wished them well; others scoffed at the secession as a sulky and childish gesture. Only a handful of citizens guessed the terrible truth, and were laughed at for their pains. Five years after their withdrawal the Joneses returned across the Vandemeer Peninsula and the war had begun.

"A final word. There has been much loose talk among the troops about the slogan of the Joneses, which goes $L_T = L_O e^{-T/2N}$. Some uninformed people actually believe it is an invocation which gives the Joneses supernatural power and invulnerability. It is not. It is merely an ancient and well-known formula in genetics which quantitatively describes the loss of unfixed genes from a population. By mouthing this formula, the Joneses are simply expressing in a compact way their ruthless determination that all genes except theirs shall disappear from the planet and the Joneses alone survive. In the formula L_T means the number of genes after the lapse of T years, L_O means the original number of genes, e means the base of the natural system of logarithms and N means number of generations."

The surgeon said slowly and with wonder: "So *that* was my God!" He stretched out his hands before him. The fingers were rock-steady.

Ross left him and paced the corridor uneasily. Fine. Now he knew. Lost genes in genetically small populations. On Halsey's Planet, some fertility gene, no doubt. On Azor, a male-sex-linked gene that provides men with the backbone required to come out ahead in the incessant war of the genders? Bernie was a gutless character. Here, all too many genes determining somatotype. On the planets that had dropped out of communication, who knew? Scientific-thought genes? Sex-drive-determining genes?

One thing was clear: any gene-loss was bad for the survival of a planetary colony. Evolution had — —on Earth — —worked out in a billion trial-and-error years a working mechanism, man. Man exhibited a vast range of variation, which was why he survived almost any conceivable catastrophe.

Reduce man to a single type and he is certain to succumb, sooner or later, to the inevitable disaster that his one type cannot cope with.

The problem, now stated clearly, was bigger than he had dreamed. And now he knew only the problem-not the solution.

Go to Earth.

Well, he had tried. There had been no flaw in his calculations, no failure in setting up the Wesley panel. Yet-this was Jones, not Earth; the city was only a city, not the planet that the star charts logged. And the planet, beyond all other considerations, was less like Earth than any conceivable chart error could account for. Gravitation, wrong; atmosphere, wrong; flora and fauna, wrong.

So. Eliminate the impossible, and what remains, however unlikely, is true. So there had been a flaw in his calculations. And the way to check that, once and for all, was to get back to the starship.

Ross wheeled and went back into the book room. "Doc," he called, "how do we get out of here?"

The answer was: on their bellies. They trudged through the forest for hours, skirting the road, hiding whenever a suspicious noise gave warning that someone might be in the vicinity. The Peepeece knew they were in the woods; there was no doubt of that. And as soon as they got past the tabu area, they had to crawl.

It was well past dark before Ross and the doctor, scratched and aching, got to the tiny hamlet of Jonesie-on-the-Pike. By the light from the one window in the village that gave any signs of life, the doctor took a single horrified look at Ross and shuddered. "You wait here," he ordered. "Hide under a bush or something—your beard rubbed off."

Ross watched the doctor rap on the door and be admitted. He couldn't hear the conversation that followed, but he saw the doctor's hand go to his pocket, then clasp the hand of the figure in the doorway. That was the language all the galaxy understood, Ross realized; he only hoped that the householder was an honest man —i. e., one who would stay bribed, instead of informing the Peepeece on them. It was beyond doubt that their descriptions had long since been broadcast; the road must have been lined with TV scanners on the way in.

The door opened again, and the doctor walked briskly out. He strode out into the street, walked half a dozen paces down the road, and waited for Ross to catch up with him. "Okay," the doctor whispered. "They'll pick us up in half an hour, down the road about a quarter of a mile. Let's go."

"What about the man you were talking to?" Ross asked. "Won't he turn us in?"

The doctor chuckled. "I gave him a drink of Jones's Juice out of my private stock," he said. "No, he won't turn anybody in, at least not until he wakes up."

Ross nodded invisibly in the dark. He had a thought, and suppressed it. But it wouldn't stay down. Cautiously he let it seep through his subconscious again, and looked it over from every angle.

No, there wasn't any doubt of it. Things were definitely looking up!

* * * * *

Ben Jones roared, "Just what the hell do you think you're doing, Doc?"

The doctor pushed Ross through the doorway and turned to face the other Jones. He asked mildly, "What?"

"You heard me!" Ben Jones blustered. "I let you out with this one, and maybe I made a mistake at that. But I by-Jones don't intend to let you get out of here with all three of them. What are you trying to get away with anyhow?"

The doctor didn't change his mild expression. He took a short, unhurried step forward. *Smack.*

Ben Jones reeled back from the slap, his mouth open, hand to his face. "Hey!" he squawked.

The doctor said levelly, "I'm telling you this just one time, Ben. *Don't cross me.* You've got the guns, but I've got these." He held up his spread hands. "You can shoot me, I won't deny that. But you can't make me do your dirty work for you. From now on things go my way—with these three people, with my own life, with the bootleg plastic surgery we do to keep you in armored cars. Or else there won't *be* any plastic surgery."

Ben Jones swallowed, and Ross could see the man fighting himself. He said after a moment, "No reason to act sore, Doc. Haven't we always got along? The only thing is, maybe you don't realize how dangerous these three — —"

"Shut up," said the doctor. "Right, boys?"

The other two Joneses in the room shuffled and looked uncomfortable. One of them said, "Don't get mad, Ben, but it kind of looks as if he's right. We and the doc had a little talk before you got here. It figures, you have to admit it. He does the work; we ought to let him have something to say about it."

116

The look that Ben Jones gave him was pure poison, but the man stood up to it, and in a minute Ben Jones looked away. "Sure," he said distantly. "You go right ahead, Doc. We'll talk this over again later on, when we've all had a chance to cool off."

The doctor nodded coldly and followed Ross out. Helena and Bernie, suitably Jonesified for the occasion, were already in the car; Ross and the doctor jumped in with them, and they drove away. Now that the strain was relaxed a bit the doctor was panting, but there was a grin on his lips. "Son-of-a-Jones," he said happily, "I've been waiting five years for this day!"

Ross asked, "Is it all right? They won't chase after us?"

"No, not Ben Jones. He has his own way of handling things. Now if we were stupid enough to go back there, after he had a chance to talk to the others without me around, that would be something different. But we aren't going back."

Ross's eyes widened. "Not even you, Doc?"

"Especially not me." The doctor concentrated on his driving. Presently: "If I take you to the rendezvous, can you find your ship from there?" he asked.

"Sure," said Ross confidently. "And Doc-welcome to our party."

* * * * *

Space had never looked better.

They hung half a million miles off Jones, and Ross fumbled irritatedly with the Wesley panel while the other three stood around and made helpful suggestions. He set up the integrals for Earth just as he had set them up once before; the plot came out the same. He transferred the computations to the controls and checked it against the record in the log. The same. The ship should have gone straight as a five-dimensional geodesic arrow to the planet Earth.

Instead, he found by cross-checking the star atlas, it had gone in almost the other direction entirely, to the planet of Jones.

He threw his pencil across the room and swore. "I don't get it," he complained.

"It's probably broken, Ross," Helena told him seriously. "You know how machines are. They're *always* doing something funny just when you least expect it."

Ross bit down hard on his answer to that. Bernie contributed his morsel, and even Dr. Sam Jones, whose race had lost even the memory of spaceflight, had a suggestion. Ross swore at them all, then took time to swear at the board, at the starship, at Haarland, at Wesley, and most of all at himself.

Helena turned her back pointedly. She said to Bernie, "The way Ross acts sometimes you'd honestly think he was the *only* one who'd *ever* run this thing. Why, my goodness, I *know* you can't *rely* on that silly board! Didn't I have just exactly the same experience with it myself?"

Ross gritted his teeth and doggedly started all over again with the computations for Earth. Then he did a slow double-take.

"Helena," he whispered. "What experience did you have?"

"Why, just the same as now! Don't you *remember*, Ross? When you and Bernie were in jail and I had to come rescue you?"

"What happened?" Ross shouted.

"My goodness, Ross don't *yell* at me! There was that silly light flashing all the time. It was driving me out of my *mind*. Well, I knew *perfectly* well that I wasn't going to get anywhere if it was going to act like *that*, so I just — —"

Ross, eyes glazed, robotlike, lifted the cover off the main Wesley unit. Down at the socket of the alarm signal, shorting out two delicately machined helices that were a basic part of the Wesley drive, wedged between an eccentric vernier screw and a curious crystalline lattice, was-the hairpin.

He picked it out and stared at it unbelievingly. He marveled, "It says in the manual, 'On no account should any alterations be made in any part of the Wesley driving assembly by any technician under a C-Twelve rating.' She didn't like the alarm going off. So she fixed it. With a hairpin."

Helena giggled and appealed to Bernie. "Doesn't he *kill* you?" she asked.

Ross's eyes were glazed and his hands worked convulsively. "Kill," he muttered, advancing on Helena. "Kill, kill, kill — —"

"Help!" she screamed.

The two men managed to subdue Ross with the aid of a needle from Dr. Jones's kit-pocket.

Helena was in tears and tried to explain to the others: "Just for no reason at *all* — —"

She got only icy stares. After a while she sulkily began setting up the Wesley board for the Earth jump.

CHAPTER XII.

Ross awoke, clearheaded and alert. Helena and Bernie were looking at him apprehensively.

He understood and said grudgingly, "Sorry I flipped. I didn't mean to scare you. Everything seemed to go black — —"

They smothered him with relieved protestations that they understood perfectly and Helena wouldn't stick hairpins into the Wesley Drive ever again. Even if the ship hadn't blown up. Even if she had rescued the men from "Minerva."

"Anyway," she said happily, "we're off Earth. At least, it's *supposed* to be Earth, according to the charts."

He unkinked himself and studied the planet through a vision screen at its highest magnification. The apparent distance was one mile; nothing was hidden from him.

"Golly," he said, impressed. "Science! Makes you realize what backward gropers we were."

Obviously they had it, down there on the pleasant, cloud-flecked, green and blue planet. Science! White, towering cities whose spires were laced by flying bridges-and inexplicably decorated with something that looked like cooling fins. Huge superstreamlined vehicles lazily coursing the roads and skies. Long, linked-pontoon cities slowly heaving on the breasts of the oceans. Science!

Ross said reverently, "We're here. Flarney was right. Helena, Bernie, Doc-maybe this is the parent planet of us all and maybe it isn't. But the people who built those cities *must* know all the answers. Helena, will you please land us?"

"Sure, Ross. Shall I look for a spaceport?"

Ross frowned. "Of course. Do you think *these* people are savages? We'll go in openly and take our problem to them. Besides, imagine the radar setup they must have! We'd never sneak through even if we wanted to."

Helena casually fingered the controls; there was the sickening swoop characteristic of her ship-handling, several times repeated. As she jerked them wildly across the planet's orbit she explained over her shoulder, "I had the darnedest time finding a really big spaceport on that little radar thing-oops! —but there's a nice-looking one near that coastal city. Whee! That was close! There was one-sorry, Ross-on a big lake inland, but I didn't like — —Now everybody be very quiet. This is the hard part and I have to concentrate."

Ross hung on.

Helena landed the ship with her usual timber-shivering crash. "Now," she said briskly, "we'd better allow a little time for it to cool down. This *is* nice, isn't it?"

Ross dragged himself, bruised, from the floor. He had to agree. It was nice. The landing field, rimmed by gracious, light buildings (with the cooling fins), was dotted with great, silvery ships. They didn't, Ross thought with a twinge of irritation, seem to be space vessels, though; leave it to Helena to get them down at some local airport! Still-the ships also, he noticed, were liberally studded with the fins. He peered at them with puzzlement and a rising sense of excitement. Certainly they had a function, and that function could only be some sort of energy receptor. Could it be-dared he imagine that it was the long-dreamed-of cosmic energy tap? What a bonus that would be to bring back with him! And what other marvels might this polished technology have to give them....

Bernie distracted him. He said, "Hey, Ross. Here comes somebody."

But even Bernie's tone was awed. A magnificent vehicle was crawling toward them across the field. It was long, low, bullet-shaped —and with cooling fins. Multiple plates of silvery metal contrasted with a glossy black finish. All about its periphery was a lacy pattern of intricate crumples and crinkles of metal, as though its skirts had been crushed and rumpled. Ross sighed and marveled: What a production problem these people had solved, stamping those forms out between dies.

Then he saw the faces of the passengers.

He drew in his breath sharply. Godlike. Two men whose brows were cliffs of alabaster, whose chins were strong with the firmness of steady, flamelike wisdom. Two women whose calm, lovely features made the heart within him melt and course.

The vehicle stopped ten yards from the open spacelock of the ship. From its tip gushed upward a ten-foot fountain of sparks that flashed the gamut of the rainbow. Simultaneously one of the godlike passengers touched the wheel, and there was a sweet, piercing, imperative summons like a hundred strings and brasses in unison.

Helena whispered, "They want us to come out. Ross-Ross —I can't face *them*!" She buried her face in her hands.

"Steady," he said gravely. "They're only human."

Ross gripped that belief tightly; he hardly dared permit himself to think, even for a second, that perhaps these people were no longer merely human. Hoarsely he said, "We need their help. Maybe we should send Doc Jones out first. He's the oldest of us, and he's the only one you could call a scientist; he can talk to them. Where is he?"

A raucous Jones voice bellowed through the domed control room: "Who wansh ol' doc, hargh? Who wansh goo' ol' doc?"

Good old doc staggered into the room, obviously loaded to the gills by a very enjoyable backslide. He began to sing:

> "In A. J. seven thirty-two a Jones from Jones's Valley, He wandered into Jones's Town to hold a Jonesist Rally. He shocked the gents and ladies both; his talk was most disturbing; He spoke of seven-sided doors and purple-colored curbing — —"

Jones's eyes focused on Helena. He flushed. "'m deeply sorry," he mumbled. "Unf'rgivable vulgararrity. Mom'ntarily f'rgot ladies were present."

Again that sweet summons sounded.

"Pull yourself together, doctor," Ross begged. "This is Earth. The people seem-very advanced. Don't disgrace us. Please!"

Jones's face went pale and perspiration broke out. "'Scuse me," he mumbled, and staggered out again.

Ross closed the door on him and said, "We'll leave him. He'll be all right; nothing's going to happen here." He took a deep breath. "We'll all go out," he said.

Unconsciously Ross and Helena drew closer together and joined hands. They walked together down the unfolding ramp and approached the vehicle.

One of the coolly lovely women scrutinized them and turned to the man beside her. She remarked melodiously, "Yuhsehtheybebems!", and laughed a silvery tinkle.

Panic gripped Ross for a long moment. A thing he had never considered, but a thing which he should have realized would be inevitable. Of course! These folk-older and incomparably more advanced than the rest of the peoples in the universe-would have evolved out of the common language into a speech of their own, deliberately or naturally rebuilt to handle the speed, subtlety, and power of their thoughts.

But perhaps the older speech was merely disused and not lost.

He said formally, quaking: "People of Earth, we are strangers from another star. We throw ourselves on your mercy and ask for your generosity. Our problem is summed up in the genetic law L-sub-T equals L-sub-zero e to the minus T-over-two-N. Of course — —"

One of the men was laughing. Ross broke off.

The man smiled: "Wha's that again?"

They understood! He repeated the formula, slowly, and would have explained further, but the man cut him off.

"Math," the man smiled. "We don' use that stuff no more. I got a lab assistant, maybe he uses it sometimes."

They were beyond mathematics! They had broken through into some mode of symbolic reasoning that must be as far beyond mathematics as math was beyond primitive languages!

"Sir," he said eagerly, "you must be a scientist. May I ask you to — —"

"Get in," he smiled. Gigantic doors unfolded from the vehicle. Thought-reading? Had the problem been snatched from his brain even before he stated it? Mutely he gestured at Helena and Bernie. Jones would be all right where he was for several hours if Ross was any judge of blackouts. And you don't quibble with demigods.

The man, the scientist, did something to a glittering control panel that was, literally, more complex than the Wesley board back on the starship. Noise filled the vehicle-noise that Ross identified as music for a moment. It was a starkly simple music whose skeleton was three thumps and a crash, three thumps and a crash. Then followed an antiphonal chant —a clear tenor demanding in a monotone: "Is this your car?" and a tremendous chorally-shouted: "No!"

Too deep for him, Ross thought forlornly as the car swerved around and sped off. His eyes wandered over the control board and fixed on the largest of its dials, where a needle crawled around from a large forty to a large fifty and a red sixty, proportional to the velocity of the vehicle. Unable to concentrate because of the puzzling music, unable to converse, he wondered what the units of time and space were that gave readings of fifty and sixty for their very low rate of speed-hardly more than a brisk walk, when you noticed the slow passage of objects outside. But there seemed to be a whistle of wind that suggested high speed-perhaps an effect peculiar to the cooling-fin power system, however it worked. He tried to shout a question at the driver, but it didn't get through. The driver smiled, patted his arm and returned to his driving.

They nosed past a building-cooling fins-and Ross almost screamed when he saw what was on the other side: a curve of highway jammed solid with vehicles that were traveling at blinding speed. And the driver wasn't stopping.

Ross closed his eyes and jammed his feet against the floorboards waiting for the crash which, somehow, didn't come. When he opened his eyes they were in the traffic and the needle on the speedometer quivered at 275. He blew a great breath and thought admiringly: reflexes to match their superb intellects, of course. There *couldn't* have been a crash.

Just then, across the safety island in the opposing lane, there was a crash.

The very brief flash of vision Ross was allowed told him, incredibly, that a vehicle had attempted to enter the lane going the wrong way, with the consequences you'd expect. He watched, goggle-eyed, as the effects of the crash rippled down the line of oncoming traffic. The squeal of brakes and rending of metal was audible even above the thumping music: "Is this your car?" "No!"

Thereafter, as they drove, the opposing lane was motionless, but not silent. The piercing blasts of strings and trumpets rose to the heavens from each vehicle, as did the brilliant py-rotechnic jets. A call for help, Ross theorized. The music was beginning to make his head ache. It had been going on for at least ten minutes. Suddenly, blessedly, it changed. There was a great fanfare of trombones in major thirds that seemed to go on forever, but didn't quite. At the end of forever, the same tenor chanted: "You got a Roadmeister?" and the chorus roared: "*Yes!*"

Ross realized forlornly that the music must contain values and subtleties which his coarser senses and undeveloped esthetic background could not grasp. But he wished it would stop. It was making him miss all the scenery. After perhaps the fifteenth repetition of the Roadmeister motif, it ended; the driver, with a look of deep satisfaction, did something to the control board that turned off a subsequent voice before it could get out more than a syllable.

He turned to Ross and yelled above the suddenly-noticeable rush of air, "Talk-talk-talk," and gave a whimsical shrug.

During the moment his attention wandered from the road, his vehicle rammed the one ahead, decelerated sharply and was rammed by the one behind, accelerated and rammed the one ahead again and then fell back into place.

Ross suddenly realized that he knew what had caused those crumples and crinkles around the periphery of the car.

"Subtle," the driver yelled. "Indirection. Sneak it in."

"What?" Ross screamed.

"The commersh," the driver yelled.

It meant nothing to Ross, and he felt miserable because it meant nothing. He studied the roadside unhappily and almost beamed when he saw a sign coming up. Not advertising, of course, he thought. Perhaps some austere reminder of a whole man's duty to the race and himself, some noble phrase that summed up the wisdom of a great thinker....

But the sign-and it had cooling fins-declared:

Be Smug! Smoke Smogs!

And the next one urged:

Beat Your Sister
Cheat Your Brother
But Send Some Smogs
To Dear Old Mother.

It said it on four signs which, apparently alerted by radar, zinged in succession along a roadside track even with the vehicle.

There were more. And worse. They were coming to a city.

Turmoil and magnificence! White pylons, natty belts of green, lacy bridges, the roaring traffic, nimble-skipping pedestrians waving at the cars and calling-greetings? It sounded like "Suvvabih! Suvvabih! Bassa-bassa!" The shops were packed and radiant, dazzling. Ross wondered fleetingly how one parked here, and then found out. A car pulled from the curb and a hundred cars converged on the spot, shrilling their sweet message and spouting their gay sparkles. Theirs too! There were a pair of jolting crashes as it shouldered two other vehicles aside and parked, two wheels over the curb and on the sidewalk.

"Suvvabih-bassa!" shouted drivers, and the man beside Ross gaily repeated the cry. The vehicle's doors opened and they climbed out into the quick tempo of the street.

It was loud with a melodious babble from speaker horns visible everywhere. The driver yelled cheerfully at Ross: "C'mon. Party." He followed, dazed and baffled, assailed by sudden doubts and contradictions.

* * * * *

It was a party, all right-twenty floors up a shimmering building in a large, handsome room whose principal decorative motif seemed to be cooling fins.

Perhaps twenty couples were assembled; they turned and applauded as they made their appearance.

The vehicle driver, standing grandly at the head of a short flight of stairs leading to the room, proclaimed: "I got these rocket flyers like on the piece of paper you guys read me. Right off the field. Twenny points. How about that?"

A tall, graying man with a noble profile hurried up and beamed: "Good show, Joe. I knew we could count on you to try for the high-point combo. You was always a real sport. You got the fish?"

"Sure we got the fish." Joe turned and said to one of the lovely ladies, "Elna, show him the fish."

She unwrapped a ten-pound swordfish and proudly held it up while Ross, Bernie, and Helena stared wildly.

The profile took the fish and poked it. "Real enough, Joe. You done great. Now if the rocket flyers here are okay you're okay. Then you got twenny points and the prize.

"You're a rocket flyer, ain't you, Buster?"

Ross realized he was being addressed. He croaked: "Men of Earth, we come from a far-distant star in search of— —"

The profile said, "Just a minute, Buster. *Just* a minute. You ain't from Earth?"

"We come from a far-distant star in search of — —"

"Stick to the point, Buster. You ain't a rocket flyer from Earth? None of you?"

"No," Ross said. He furtively pinched himself. It hurt. Therefore he must be awake. Or crazy.

The profile was sorrowfully addressing a downcast Joe. "You should of asked them, Joe. You really should of. Now you don't even get the three points for the swordfish, because you went an' tried for the combo. It reely is a pity. Din't you ask them at all?"

Joe blustered, "He did say sump'm, but I figured a rocket flyer was a rocket flyer, and they come out of a rocket." His lower lip was trembling. Both of the ladies of his party were crying openly. "We tried," Joe said, and began to blubber. Ross moved away from him in horrified disgust.

The profile shook its head, turned and announced: "Owing to a unfortunate mistake, the search group of Dr. Joseph Mulcahy, Sc.D., Ph.D., got disqualified for the combination. They on'y got three points. So that's all the groups in an' who got the highest?"

"I got fifteen! I got fifteen!" screamed a gorgeous brunette in a transport of joy. "A manhole cover from the museum an' a las' month *Lipreaders Digest* an' a steering wheel from a police car! I got fifteen!"

The others clustered about her, chattering. Ross said to the profile mechanically: "Man of Earth, we come from a far-distant star in search of — —"

"Sure, Buster," said the profile. "Sure. Too bad. But you should of told Joe. You don't have to go. You an' your friends have a drink. Mix. Have fun. I gotta go give the prize now." He hurried off.

A passing blonde, stacked, said to Ross: "Hel-looo, baldy. Wanna see my operation?" He began to shake his head and felt Helena's fingers close like steel on his arm. The blonde sniffed and passed on.

"I'll operate her," Helena said, and then: "Ross, what's *wrong* with everybody? They act so young, even the old people!"

"Follow me," he said, and began to circulate through the party, trailing Bernie and a frankly terrified Helena, button-holing and confronting and demanding and cajoling. Nothing worked. He was greeted with amused tolerance and invited to have a drink and asked what he thought of the latest commersh with its tepid trumpets. Nobody gave a damn that he was from a far-distant star except Joe, who sullenly watched them wander and finally swaggered up to Ross.

"I figured something out," he said grimly. "You made me lose." He brought up a roundhouse right, and Ross saw the stars and heard the birdies.

* * * * *

Bernie and Helena brought him to on the street. He found he had been walking for some five minutes with a blanked-out mind. They told him he had been saying over and over again, "Men of Earth, I come from a far-distant star." It had got them ejected from the party.

Helena was crying with anger and frustration; she had also got a nasty scare when one of the vehicles had swerved up onto the sidewalk and almost crushed the three of them against the building wall.

"And," she wailed, "I'm hungry and we don't know where the ship is and I've got to sit down and-and go someplace."

"So do I," Bernie said weakly.

So did Ross. He said, "Let's just go into this restaurant. I know we have no money-don't nag me please, Helena. We'll order, eat, not pay, and get arrested." He held up his hand at the protests. "I said, get arrested. The smartest thing we could do. Obviously somebody's running this place-and it's not the stoops we've seen. The quickest way I know of to get to whoever's in charge is to get in trouble. And once they see us we can explain everything."

It made sense to them. Unfortunately the first restaurant they tried was coin-operated — from the front door on. So were the second to seventh. Ross tried to talk Bernie into slugging a pedestrian so they could all be jugged for disturbing the peace, but failed.

Helena noted at last that the women's wear shops had live attendants who, presumably, would object to trouble. They marched into one of the gaudy places, each took a dress from a rack and methodically tore them to pieces.

A saleslady approached them dithering and asked tremulously: "What for did you do that? Din't you like the dresses?"

"Well yes, very much," Helena began apologetically. "But you see, the fact is — —"

"Shuddup!" Ross told her. He said to the saleslady: "No. We hated them. We hate every dress here. We're going to tear up every dress in the place. Why don't you call the police?"

"Oh," she said vaguely. "All right," and vanished into the rear of the store. She returned after a minute and said, "He wants to know your names."

"Just say 'three desperate strangers,'" Ross told her.

"Oh. Thank you." She vanished again.

The police arrived in five minutes or so. An excited elder man with many stripes on his arms strode up to them excitedly as they stood among the shredded ruins of the dresses. "Where'd they go?" he demanded. "Didja see what they looked like?"

"We're them. We three. We tore these dresses up. You'd better take them along for evidence."

"Oh," the cop said. "Okay. Go on into the wagon. And no funny business, hear me?"

They offered no funny business. In the wagon Ross expounded on his theme that there must be directing intelligences and that they must be at the top. Helena was horribly depressed because she had never been arrested before and Bernie was almost jaunty. Something about him suggested that he felt at home in a patrol wagon.

It stopped and the elderly stripe-wearer opened the door for them. Ross looked on the busy street for anything resembling a station house and found none.

The cop said, "Okay, you people. Get going. An' let's don't have no trouble or I'll run you in."

Ross yelled in outrage, "This is a frame-up! You have no right to turn us loose. We demand to be arrested and tried!"

"Wise guy," sneered the cop, climbed into the wagon and drove off.

They stood forlornly as the crowd eddied and swirled around them. "There was a plate of sandwiches at that party," Helena recalled wistfully. "And a ladies' room." She began to cry. "If only you hadn't acted so darn superior, Ross! I'll bet they would have let us have all the sandwiches we wanted."

Bernie said unexpectedly, "She's right. Watch me."

He buttonholed a pedestrian and said, "Duh."

"Yeah?" asked the pedestrian with kindly interest.

Bernie concentrated and said, "Duh. I yam losted. I yam broke. I losted all my money. Gimme some money, mister, please?"

The pedestrian beamed and said, "That is real tough luck, buddy. If I give you some money will you send it to me when you get some more? Here is my name wrote on a card."

Bernie said, "Sure, mister. I will send the money to you."

"Then," said the pedestrian, "I will give you some money because you will send it back to me. Good luck, buddy."

Bernie, with quiet pride, showed them a piece of paper that bore the interesting legend Twenty Dollars.

"Let's eat," Ross said, awed.

A machine on a restaurant door changed the bill for a surprising heap of coins and they swaggered in, making beelines for the modest twin doors at the rear of the place. Close up the doors were not very modest, but after the initial shock Ross realized that there must be many on this planet who could not read at all. The washroom attendant, for instance, who collected the "dimes" and unlocked the booths. "Dime" seemed to be his total vocabulary.

By comparison the machines in the restaurant proper were intelligent. The three of them ate and ate and ate. Only after coffee did they spare a thought for Dr. Sam Jones, who should about then be awakening with a murderous hangover aboard the starship.

Thinking about him did not mean they could think of anything to do.

"He's in trouble," Bernie said. "*We're* in trouble. First things first."

"What trouble?" asked Helena brightly. "You got twenty dollars by asking for it and I suppose you can get plenty more. And I think we wouldn't have got thrown out of that party if-ah —*we* hadn't gone swaggering around talking as if we knew everything. Maybe these people here aren't very bright — —"

Ross snorted.

Helena went on doggedly, " — —not *very* bright, but they certainly can tell when somebody's brighter than they are. And naturally they don't like it. Would you like it? It's like a really old person talking to a really young person about nothing but age. But here when you're bright you make everybody feel bad every time you open your mouth."

"So," Ross said impatiently, "we can go on begging and drifting. But that's not what we're here for. The answer is supposed to be on Earth. Obviously none of the people we've seen could possibly know anything about genetics. Obviously they can't keep this machine civilization going without guidance. There must be people of normal intelligence around. In the government, is my guess."

"No," said Helena, but she wouldn't say why. She just thought not.

The inconclusive debate ended with them on the street again. Bernie, who seemed to enjoy it, begged a hundred dollars. Ross, who didn't, got eleven dollars in singles and a few threats of violence for acting like a wise guy. Helena got no money and three indecent proposals before Ross indignantly took her out of circulation.

They found a completely automatic hotel at nightfall. Ross tried to inspect Helena's room for comfort and safety, but was turned back at the threshold by a staggering jolt of electricity. "Mechanical house dick," he muttered, picking himself up from the floor. "Well," he said to her sourly, "it's safe. Good night."

And later in the gents' room, to Bernie: "You'd think the damn-fool machine could be adjusted so that a person with perfectly innocent intentions could visit a lady — —"

"Sure," said Bernie soothingly, "sure. Say, Ross, frankly, is this Earth exactly what you expected it to be?"

The attendant moved creakily across the floor and said hopefully, "Dime?"

CHAPTER XIII

Their second day on the bum they accumulated a great deal of change and crowded into a telephone booth. The plan was to try to locate their starship and find out what, if anything, could be done for Sam Jones.

An automatic Central conferred with an automatic Information and decided that they wanted the Captain of the Port, Baltimore Rocket Field.

They got the Port Captain on the wire and Ross asked after the starship. The captain asked, "Who wan'sta know, huh?"

Ross realized he had overdone it and shoved Bernie at the phone. Bernie snorted and guggled and finally got out that he jus' wannit ta know. The captain warmed up immediately and said oh, sure, the funny-lookin' ship, it was still there all right.

"How about the fella that's in it?"

"You mean the funny-lookin' fella? He went someplace."

"He went someplace? What place?"

"Someplace. He went away, like. I din't see him go, mister. I got plenty to do without I should watch out for every dummy that comes along."

"T'anks," said Bernie hopelessly at Ross's signal.

They walked the street, deep in thought. Helena sobbed, "Let's *leave* him here, Ross. I don't like this place."

"No."

Bernie growled, "What's the difference, Ross? He can get a snootful just as easy here as anywhere else — —"

"No! It isn't the Doc, don't you see? But this is the place we're looking for. All the answers we need are here; we've got to get them."

Bernie stepped around two tussling men on the ground, ineffectually thumping each other over a chocolate-covered confection. "Yeah," he said shortly.

* * * * *

Helena said: "Isn't that a silly way to put up a big sign like that?"

Ross looked up. "My God," he said. A gigantic metal sign with the legend, *Buy Smogs — —You Can Smoke Them*, was being hoisted across the street ahead. The street was nominally closed to traffic by cheerfully inattentive men with red flags; a mobile boom hoist was doing the work, and quite obviously doing it wrong. The angle of the boom arm with the vertical was far too great for stability; the block-long sign was tipping the too-light body of the hoisting engine on its treads....

Ross made a flash calculation: when the sign fell, as fall it inevitably would, perhaps two hundred people who had wandered uncaringly past the warning flags would be under it.

There was a sudden aura of blue light around the engine body.

It tipped back to stability. The boom angle decreased, and the engine crawled forward to take up the horizontal difference.

The blue light went out.

Helena choked and coughed and babbled, "But Ross, it *couldn't* have because — —"

Ross said: "It's them!"

"Who?"

Excitedly: "The people behind all this! The people who built the cities and put up the buildings and designed the machines. The people who have the answers! Come on, Bernie. I just seem to antagonize these people —I want you to ask the boom operator what happened."

The boom operator cheerfully explained that nah, it was just somep'n that happened. Nah, nobody did nothin' to make it happen. It was in case if anything went wrong, like. You know?

They retired and regrouped their forces.

"Foolproof machines," Ross said slowly. "And I mean really *fool* proof. Friends, I was wrong, I admit it; I thought that those buildings and cars were something super-special, and they turned out to be just silly gimcracks. But not this blue light thing. That boom *had* to fall."

Bernie shrugged rebelliously. "So what? So they've got some kinds of machines you don't have on Halsey's Planet?"

"A different order of machines, Bernie! Believe me, that blue light was something as far from any safety device I ever heard of as the starships are from oxcarts. When we find the people who designed them — —"

"Suppose they're all dead?"

Ross winced. He said determinedly, "We'll find them." They returned to their begging and were recognized one day by the gray-haired profile of the party. He didn't remember just who they were or where they were from or where he had met them, but he enthusiastically invited them to yet another party. He told them he was Hennery Matson, owner of an airline.

Ross asked about accidents and blue lights. Matson jovially said some o' his pilots talked about them things but he din't bother his head none. Ya get these planes from the field, see, an' they got all kinds of gadgets on them. Come on to the party!

They went, because Hennery promised them another guest-Sanford Eisner, who was a wealthy aircraft manufacturer. But he din't bother his head none either; them rockets was hard to make, you had to feed the patterns, like, into the master jigs just so, and, boy!, if you got 'em in backwards it was a *mess*. Wheredja get the patterns? Look, mister, we *always* had the patterns, an' don't spoil the party, will ya?

The party was a smasher. They all woke with headaches on Matson's deep living room rug.

"You did fine, Ross," Helena softly assured him. "Nobody would have guessed you were any smarter than anybody else here. There wasn't a bit of trouble."

Ross seemed to have a hiatus in his memory.

The importance of the hiatus faded as time passed. There was a general move toward the automatic dispensing bar. It seemed to be regulated by a time clock; no matter what you dialed first thing in the morning, it ruthlessly poured a double rye with Worcestershire and tabasco and plopped a fair imitation of a raw egg into the concoction. It helped!

Along about noon something clicked in the bar's innards. Guests long since surfeited with the prairie oysters joyously dialed martinis and manhattans and the day's serious drinking began.

Ross fuzzily tried to trace the bar's supply. There were nickel pipes that led Heaven knew where. Some vast depot of fermentation tanks and stills? Fed grain and cane by crawling harvest-monsters? Grain and cane planted from seed the harvest-monsters carefully culled from the crop for the plow-and-drag-and-drill-and-fertilize-and-cultivate monsters?

His head was beginning to ache again. A jovial martini-drinker who had something to do with a bank — a *bank!* — roared, "Hey, fellas! I got a idea what we can do! Less go on over to *my* place!"

So they all went, and that disposed of another day.

* * * * *

It blended into a dream of irresponsible childhood. When your clothes grew shabby you helped yourself to something that fit from your host of the moment's wardrobe. When you grew tired of one host you switched to another. They seldom remembered you from day to day, and they never asked questions.

Their sex was uninhibited and most of the women were more or less pregnant most of the time. They fought and sulked and made up and giggled and drank and ate and slept. All of the men had jobs, and all of them, once in a while, would remember and stagger over to a phone and make a call to an automatic receptionist to find out if everything was going all right with their jobs. It always was. They loved their children and tolerated anything from them, except shrewd inquisitiveness which drew a fast bust in the teeth from the most indulgent daddy or adoring mommy. They loved their friends and their guests, as long as they weren't wise guys, and tolerated anything from them-as long as they weren't wise guys.

Did it last a day, a week, a month?

Ross didn't know. The only things that were really bothering Ross were, first, nobody wouldn't tell him nothin' about the blue lights and, second, that Bernie, he was actin' like a wise guy.

There came a morning when it ended as it had begun: on somebody's living room rug with a headache pounding between his eyes. Helena was sobbing softly, and that wise guy, Bernie, was tugging at him.

"Lea' me alone," ordered Captain Ross without opening his eyes. Wouldn't let a man get his rest. What did he have to bring them along for, anyway? Should have left them where he found them, not brought them to this place Earth where they could act like a couple of wise guys and keep getting in his way every time he came close to the blue-light people, the intelligent people, the people with the answers to —— to ——

He lay there, trying to remember what the question was.

" ——have to get him out of here," said Helena's voice with a touch of hysteria.

" ——go back and get that fellow Haarland," said Bernie's voice, equally tense. Ross contemplated the fragments of conversation he had caught, ignoring what the two were saying to him. Haarland, he thought fuzzily, *that* wise guy....

Bernie had him on his feet. "Leggo," ordered Ross, but Bernie was tenacious. He stumbled along and found himself in the men's room of the apartment. The tired-looking attendant appeared from nowhere and Bernie said something to him. The attendant rummaged in his chest and found something that Bernie put into a fizzy drink.

Ross sniffed at it suspiciously. "Wassit?" he asked.

"Please, Ross, drink it. It'll sober you up. We've got to get out of here-we're going nuts, Helena and me. This has been going on for weeks!"

"Nope. Gotta find a blue light," Ross said obstinately, swaying.

"But you aren't finding it, Ross. You aren't doing anything except get drunk and pass out and wake up and get drunk. Come on, drink the drink." Ross impatiently dashed it to the floor. Bernie sighed. "All right, Ross," he said wearily. "Helena can run the ship; we're taking off."

"Go 'head."

"Good-by, Ross. We're going back to Halsey's Planet, where you came from. Maybe Haarland can tell us what to do."

"Go 'head. *That* wise guy!" Ross sneered.

The attendant was watching dubiously as Bernie slammed out and Ross peered at himself in a mirror. "Dime?" the attendant asked in his tired voice. Ross gave him one and went back to the party.

Somehow it was not much fun.

He shuffled back to the bar. The boilermaker didn't taste too good. He set it down and glowered around the room. The party was back in swing already; Helena and Bernie were nowhere in sight. Let them go, then....

He drank, but only when he reminded himself to. This party had become a costume ball; one of the men lurched out of the room and staggered back guffawing. "Looka him!" one of the women shrieked. "He got a woman's hat on! Horace, you get the craziest kinda ideas!"

Ross glowered. He suddenly realized that, while he wasn't exactly sober, he wasn't drunk either. Those soreheads, they had to go and spoil the party....

He began abruptly to get less drunk yet. Back to Halsey's Planet, they said? Ask Haarland what to do, they said? Leave him here ——?

He was cold sober.

He found a telephone. The automatic Central checked the automatic Information and got him the Captain of the Port, Baltimore Rocket Field. The Captain was helpful and sympathetic; caught by the tense note in Ross's voice when he told him who wannit to know, the

Captain said, "Gee, buddy, if I'd of known I woulda stopped them. Stoled your ship, is that what they done? They could get arrested for that. You could call the cops an' maybe they could do something——"

Ross didn't bother to explain. He hung up.

The party was no fun at all. He left it.

Ross walked along the street, hating himself. He couldn't hate Helena and Bernie; they had done the right thing. It had been his fault, all the way down the line. He'd been acting like a silly child; he'd had a job of work to do, and he let himself be sidetracked by a crazy round of drinking and parties.

Of course, he told himself, something had been accomplished. Somebody had built the machines-not the happy morons he had been playing with. Somebody had invented whatever it was that flared with blue light and repaired the idiot errors the morons made. Somebody, somewhere.

Where?

Well, he had some information. All negative. At the parties had been soldiers and politicians and industrialists and clergy and entertainers and, heaven save the mark, scientists. And none of them had had the wit to do more than push the Number Three Button when the Green Light A blinked, by rote. None of them could have given him the answer to the question that threatened to end human domination over the cosmos; none of them would have known what the words meant.

Maybe-Ross made himself face it-maybe there was no answer. Maybe even if he found the intellects that lurked beneath the surface on this ancient planet, they could not or would not tell him what he wanted to know. Maybe the intellects didn't exist.

Maybe he was all wrong in all of his assumptions; maybe he was wasting his time. But, he told himself wryly, he had fixed it for himself that time was all he had left. He might as well waste it. He might as well go right on looking....

A migrant party was staggering down the street toward him, a score of persons going from one host's home to another. He crossed to avoid them. They were singing drunkenly.

Ross looked at them with the distaste of the recently reformed. One of the voices raised in song caught his ear:

"——bobbed his nose and dyed it rose, and kissed his lady fair, And sat her down on a cushion brown in a seven-legged chair. 'By Jones,' he said, 'my shoes are red, and so's my overcoat, And with buttons nine in a zigzag line, I'll——'"

"Doc!" Ross bellowed. "Doc Jones! For God's sake, come over here!"

They got rid of the rest of Doctor Sam Jones's party, and Ross sobered the doctor up in an all-night restaurant. It wasn't hard; the doctor had had plenty of practice.

Ross filled him in, carefully explaining why Bernie and Helena had left him. Doc Jones filled Ross in. He didn't have much to tell. He had come to in the ship, waited around until he got hungry, fallen into a conversation with a rocket pilot on the field-and that was how *his* round of parties had begun.

Like Ross, Doc, in his soberer moments, had come to the conclusion that Earth was run by person or persons unseen. He had learned little that Ross hadn't found out or deduced. The blue lights had bothered him, too; he'd asked the pilot about it, and found out about what Ross had-there appeared to be some sort of built-in safety device which kept the inevitable accidents from becoming unduly fatal. How they worked, he didn't know—

But he had an idea.

"It sounds a little ridiculous, I admit," he said, embarrassed. "But I think it might work. It's a radio program."

"A radio program?"

"I said it sounded ridiculous. They call it, 'What's Biting You,' and one of the fellows was telling me about it. It seems that you can appear before the panel on the program with any sort of problem, any sort at all, and they guarantee to solve it for you. There's some sort of bond posted — I don't know much about the details, but this man assured me that the bond was only a formality; they never failed. Of course," Doc finished, hearing his own proposal with a touch of doubt, "I don't know whether they ever had any problem like this before, but ——"

"Yeah," said Ross. "What have we got to lose?"

They got into the program. It took the techniques of a doubler on an army chow line and a fair amount of brute strength, but they got to the head of the queue at the studio and wedged themselves inside. Doc came close to throttling the man who prowled through the studio audience, selecting the lucky few who would get on stage-but they got on.

The theme music swelled majestically around them, and a chorus crooned, "What's Biting You-Hunh?" It was repeated three times, with crashing cymbals under the "Hunh?"

Ross listened to the beginning of the program and cursed himself for being persuaded into such a harebrained tactic. But, he had to admit, the program offered the only possibility in sight. The central figure was a huge, jovially grinning figure of papier-mâché, smoking a Smog and billowing smoke rings at the audience. An announcer, for some obscure reason in blackface, interviewed the disturbed derelicts who came before Smiley Smog, the papier-mâché figure, and propounded their problems to Smiley in a sort of doggerel. And in doggerel the answers came back.

The first person to go up before Smiley was a woman, clearly in her last month of pregnancy. The announcer introduced her to the audience and begged for a real loud holler of hello for this poor mizzuble li'l girl. "Awright, honey," he said. "You just step right up here an' let ol' Uncle Smiley take care of your troubles for you. Less go, now. What's Bitin' You?"

"Uh," she sobbed, "it's like I'm gonna have a baby."

"Hoddya like that!" the announcer screamed. "She's gonna have a *baby!* Whaddya say to that, folks?" The audience shrieked hysterically. "Awright, honey," the announcer said. "So you're gonna have a baby, so what's bitin' you about that?"

"It's my husband," the woman sniffled. "He don't like kids. We got eight already," she explained. "Jack, he says if we have one more kid he's gonna take off an' marry somebody else."

"He's gonna marry somebody else!" the announcer howled. "Hoddya like that, folks?" There was a tempest of boos. "Awright, now," the announcer said, "you just sit there, honey, while I tell ol' Uncle Smiley about this. Ya ready? Listen:

"What's bitin' this lady is plain to see:
Her husband don't want no more family!"

The huge figure's head rotated on a concealed hinge to look down on the woman. From a squawk-box deep in Smiley's papier-mâché belly, a weary voice declaimed:

"If one more baby is your husband's dread,
Cross him up, lady. Have twins instead!"

The audience roared its approval. The announcer asked anxiously, "Ya get it? When ya get inta the hospital, like, ya jus' tell the nurse ya want to take *two* kids home with you. See?"

The grateful woman staggered away. Ross gave Doc a poisonous look.

"What else is there to do?" the doctor hissed. "All right, perhaps this won't work out-but let's try!" He half rose, and staggered against the man next to him, who was already starting toward the announcer. "Go on, Ross," Doc hissed venomously, blocking off the other man.

Ross went. What else was there to do?

"What's biting me," he said belligerently before the announcer could put him through the preliminaries, "is simply this: L-sub-T equals L-sub-zero e to the minus-T-over-two-N."

Dead silence in the studio. The announcer quavered, "Wh-what was that again, buddy?"

"I said," Ross repeated firmly, "L-sub-T equals L-sub-zero e to the ——"

"Now, wait a minute, buddy," the announcer ordered. "We never had no stuff like that on *this* program before. Whaddya, some kind of a wise guy?"

There might have been violence; the conditions were right for it. But Uncle Smiley Smog saved the day.

The papier-mâché figure puffed a blinding series of smoke rings at Ross. From its molded torso, the weary voice said:

> "If you're looking for counsel sagacious and wise,
> The price is ten cents. It's right under your eyes."

They left the studio in a storm of animosity.

"Maybe we could have collected the forfeit," Doc said hopefully.

"Maybe we could have collected some lumps," Ross growled. "Got any more ideas?"

The doctor sipped his coffee. "No," he admitted. "I wonder-No, I don't suppose that means anything."

"That jingle? Sure it means something, Doc. It means I should have had my head examined for letting you talk me into that performance."

The doctor said rebelliously, "Maybe I'm wrong, Ross, but I don't see that you've had any ideas than panned out much better."

Ross got up. "All right," he admitted. "I'm sorry if I gave you a hard time. It's all this coffee and all the liquor underneath it; I swear, if I ever get back to a civilized planet I'm going on a solid diet for a month."

They headed for the room marked "Gents," Ross sullenly quiet, Doc thoughtfully quiet.

Doc said reflectively, "'The price is ten cents.' Ross, could that mean a paper that we could buy on a newsstand, maybe?"

"Yeah," Ross said in irritation. "Look, Doc, don't give it another thought. There must be some way to straighten this thing out; I'll think of it. Let's just make believe that whole asinine radio program never happened." The attendant materialized and offered Ross a towel.

"Dime?" he said wearily.

Ross fished absently in his pocket. "The thing that bothers me, Doc," he said, "is that I know there are intelligent people somewhere around. I even know what they're doing, I bet. They're doing exactly what I tried to do: acted as stupid as anybody else, or stupider. I'd make a guess," he said, warming up, "that if we could just make a statistical analysis of the whole planet and find the absolute stupidest-seeming people of the lot, we'd — —"

He ran out of breath all at once. His eyes bulged.

He looked at the men's-room attendant, and at the ten-cent piece in his own hand.

"You!" he breathed.

The attendant's face suddenly seemed to come to life. In a voice that was abruptly richer and deeper than before, the man said: "Yes. You had to find us yourself, you know."

CHAPTER XIV.

There was a home base, a gigantic island called Australia, to which they took Ross and Doc Jones in a little car that sprouted no wings and flashed no rockets, but flew.

They lived underground there, invisible to goggling passengers and crewmen aboard the "rockets." (They weren't rockets. They were turbo-jets. But it made the children happy to think that they had rockets, so iron filings were added to the hot jet stream, and they sparkled in magnificent display.)

There they were born, and there they spent strange childhoods, learning such things as psychodynamics and teleportation. By the time they were eight months or so old they thought it amusing to converse of Self and the Meaning of Meaning. By eighteen months a dozen infants would chat in *terza rima*. But by the age of two they had put such toys behind them with a sigh of pleasant regret. They would revert to them only for such purposes as love-making or choral funeral addresses.

They were then of an age to begin their work.

They were born there, and trained there for terrible tasks. And they died there, at whatever risk. For that they would not surrender: their right to die among their own.

But their lives between cradle and grave, those they gave away.

Nursemaids? What else can one call them?

They explained it patiently to Ross and the doctor.

"The pattern emerged clearly in the twentieth century. Swarming slums abrawl with children, children, children everywhere. Walk down a Chicago Southside street, and walk away with the dazed impression that all the world was pregnant. Walk through pretty, pleasant Evanston, and find the impression wrong. Those who lived in Evanston were reasonable people. They waited and thought. Being reasonable, they saved and planned. Being reasonable, they resorted to gadgets or chemicals or continence.

"A woman of the period had some three hundred and ninety opportunities to conceive a child. In the slums and the hills they took advantage of as many of them as they might. But around the universities, in the neighborhoods of the well-educated and the well-to-do, what was the score?

"First, education, until the age of twenty. This left two hundred and ninety-nine opportunities. Then, for perhaps five years, shared work; the car, the mortgage, the furniture, that two salaries would pay off earlier than one. Two hundred and thirty-four opportunities were left. Some of them were seized: a spate of childbearing perhaps would come next. But subtract a good ten years more at the end of the cycle, for the years when a child would be simply too, late-too late for fashion, too late for companionship with the first-born. We started with three hundred and ninety opportunities. We have, perhaps, one hundred and forty-four left.

"Is that the roster complete? No. There is the battle of the budget: No, not right now, not until the summer place is paid for. And more. The visits from the mothers-in-law, the quarterly tax payments, the country-club liaisons and the furtive knives behind the brownstone fronts and what becomes of fertility-they have all been charted. But these are superfluous. The ratio 390:144 points out the inevitable. As three hundred and ninety outweighs one hundred and forty-four, so the genes of the slovenly and heedless outweigh the thoughtful and slow to act.

"We tampered with the inevitable.

"The planet teemed and burst. The starships went forth. The strong, bright, quick ones went out in the ships. Two sorts were left: The strong ones who were not bright, the bright ones who were not strong.

"We are the prisoners of the planet. We cannot leave.

"The children-the witless ones outside-can leave. But who would have them?"

Ross peered into the shifting shadows. "But," he said, "you are the masters of the planet — —"

"*Masters?* We are slaves! Fully alive only here where we are born and die. Abstracted and as witless as they when we are among *them* —well we might be. For each of us, square miles to stand guard over. Our minds roving across the traps we dare not ignore, ready to leap out and straighten these children's toppling walls of blocks, ready to warn the child that sharp things cut and hot things burn. The blue lights-did you think they were machines?" They were *us*!

"You're torturing yourselves!" Ross exploded. "Let them die."

"Let-ten-billion-children-die? We are not such monsters."

Ross was humbled before their tragedy. Diffidently he spoke of Halsey's Planet, Ragansworld, Azor, Jones. He warmed to the task and was growing, he thought, eloquent when their smiles left him standing ashamed.

"I don't understand," he said, almost weeping.

The voice corrected him: "You do. But you do not-yet-know that you do. Consider the facts:

"Your planet. Sterile and slowly dying.

"The planets you have seen. One sterile because it is imprisoned by ancients, one sterile under an in-driven matriarchal custom, one sterile because all traces of divergence have been wiped out.

"Earth. Split into an incurable dichotomy-the sterility of brainless health, the sterility of sick intellect.

"Humanity, then, imprisoned in a thousand sterile tubes, cut off each from the other, dying. We feared war, and so we isolated the members with a wall of time. We have found something worse to fear. What if the walls are cracked?"

"Crack the walls? How? Is it too late?"

Somehow the image of Helena was before him.

"Is it too late?" they gently mocked. "Surely you know. How? Perhaps you will ask her."

The image of Helena was blushing.

Ross's heart leaped. "As simple as that?"

"For you, yes. For others there will be lives spent over the lathes and milling machines, eyes gone blind in calculating and refining trajectories, daring ones lost screaming in the hearts of stars, or gibbering with hunger and pain as the final madness closes down on them, stranded between galaxies. There will be martyrs to undergo the worst martyrdom of all-which is to say, they will never know of it. They will be unhappy traders and stock-chasers, grinding their lives to smooth dull blanks against the wearying routine so that the daring ones may go forth to the stars. But for you-you have seen the answer.

"Old blood runs thin. Thin blood runs cold. Cold blood dies. Let the walls crack."

There was a murmuring in the shadows that Ross could not hear. Then the voice again, saying a sort of good-by.

"We have had a great deal of experience with children, so we know that they must not be told too much. There is nothing more you need be told. You will go back now — —"

Ross dared interrupt. "But our ship-the others have taken it away — —"

Again the soundless laughter. "The ship has not been taken far. Did you think we would leave you stranded here?"

Ross peered hard into the shadows. But only the shadows were there, and then he and Jones were in the shadows no longer.

"Ross!" Helena was hysterical with joy. Even Bernie was stammering and shaking his head incredulously. "Ross, dearest! We thought-And the ship acted all *funny*, and then it landed here and there just wasn't anybody around, and I couldn't make it go again — —"

"It will go now," Ross promised. It did. They sealed ship; he took the controls; and they hung in space, looking back on a blue-green planet with a single moon.

There were questions; but Ross put an end to questions. He said, "We're going back to Halsey's Planet. Haarland wanted an answer. We've found it; we'll bring it to him. The F-T-L families have kept their secret too well. No wars between the planets-but stagnation worse than wars. And Haarland's answer is this: He will be the first of the F-T-L traders. He'll build F-T-L ships, and he'll carelessly let their secrets be stolen. We'll bridge the galaxy with

F-T-L transports; and we'll pack the ships with a galaxy of crews! New genes for old; hybrid vigor for dreary decay!

"Do you see it?" His voice was ringing loud; Helena's eyes on him were adoring. "Mate Jones to Azor, Halsey's Planet to Earth. Smash the smooth, declining curve! Cross the strains, and then breed them back. Let mankind become genetically wild again instead of rabbits isolated in their sterile hutches!"

Exultantly he set up the combinations for Halsey's Planet on the Wesley board.

Helena was beside him, proud and close, as he threw in the drive.

Made in United States
North Haven, CT
25 May 2024

52922286R00076